Miranda's Family

By Anna Jacobs

MIRANDA'S FAMILY SERIES

Miranda's Family

THE LARCH TREE LANE SERIES

Larch Tree Lane • Hawthorn Close • Magnolia Gardens
Lavender Lane

THE PENNY LAKE SERIES

Changing Lara • Finding Cassie • Marrying Simone

THE PEPPERCORN SERIES

Peppercorn Street • Cinnamon Gardens • Saffron Lane
Bay Tree Cottage • Christmas in Peppercorn Street

THE HONEYFIELD SERIES

The Honeyfield Bequest • A Stranger in Honeyfield
Peace Comes to Honeyfield

THE HOPE TRILOGY

A Place of Hope • In Search of Hope • A Time for Hope

THE GREYLADIES SERIES

Heir to Greyladies • Mistress of Greyladies
Legacy of Greyladies

THE WILTSHIRE GIRLS SERIES

Cherry Tree Lane • Elm Tree Road • Yew Tree Gardens

THE WATERFRONT SERIES

Mara's Choice • Sarah's Gift • Paula's Way

∽

Winds of Change • Moving On • Change of Season
Tomorrow's Path • Chestnut Lane • In Focus
The Corrigan Legacy • A Very Special Christmas
Kirsty's Vineyard
The Cotton Lass and Other Stories
The Best Valentine's Day Ever and Other Stories

Miranda's Family

ANNA JACOBS

Allison & Busby Limited
11 Wardour Mews
London W1F 8AN
allisonandbusby.com

First published in Great Britain by Allison & Busby in 2025.

Copyright © 2025 by ANNA JACOBS

The moral right of the author is hereby asserted in accordance with the Copyright, Designs and Patents Act 1988.

*All characters and events in this publication,
other than those clearly in the public domain,
are fictitious and any resemblance to actual persons,
living or dead, is purely coincidental.*

All rights reserved. No part of this publication may be reproduced, stored in a retrieval system, or transmitted, in any form or by any means without the prior written permission of the publisher, nor be otherwise circulated in any form of binding or cover other than that in which it is published and without a similar condition being imposed on the subsequent buyer.

A CIP catalogue record for this book is available from the British Library.

First Edition

ISBN 978-0-7490-3245-6

Typeset in 11/15.5 pt Sabon LT Pro by
Allison & Busby Ltd.

By choosing this product, you help take care of the world's forests.
Learn more: www.fsc.org

Printed and bound in the UK using 100% Renewable Electricity at CPI Group (UK) Ltd, Croydon, CR0 4YY

EU GPSR Authorised Representative
LOGOS EUROPE, 9 rue Nicolas Poussin, 17000, LA ROCHELLE, France
E-mail: Contact@logoseurope.eu

Chapter One

Miranda Westerby walked into her tiny alcove of a kitchen, sighing as she looked at the envelope she'd picked up from the post box in the entrance hall to the block of flats. The letter had a lawyer's name and address printed on the envelope.

She couldn't face opening it yet, just couldn't, so tossed it down on the table. She was always afraid when she got a letter from that law firm that her only close relative would have played another nasty trick to spoil her peaceful life.

Before she did anything, she wanted to sit and relax for a few minutes after ending her working day with another tedious so-called 'team meeting' run by the recently appointed CI (which stood for Chief Idiot, in her opinion, whatever fancy title the senior management might give him). The new man now supervising her working group would win a gold medal in the boring Olympics if such a thing existed.

Unfortunately, Miranda couldn't push the thought of the

unopened envelope out of her mind, so she didn't manage to relax properly. The Westerby family's lawyers had never before contacted her at this time of year and that worried her. What did her great-aunt want?

She picked up the letter and scowled at it. There was a new name given on the back as the actual sender from the lawyers' office. Who was this guy?

It was ridiculous to be so anxious because the main thing these people had contacted her about during the last few years was the annual statement by the auditors, saying that the accounts of the Westerby Family Trust Fund had been found to be correct. She had to approve this formally by letter, not email, each year.

Only, the audit wasn't due for another three months so was there some other problem? Oh please, no! The less she had to do with her only close Westerby relative, the happier she was.

She had unpleasant memories of her great-aunt Phyllis, who had become her guardian when she was orphaned at the age of fourteen. Phyllis had immediately made it clear to Miranda at their first and only meeting that she wanted nothing to do with her young relative and was only doing her family duty by arranging for her to be looked after. She hadn't spoken to her great-aunt in person since then.

Phyllis hadn't sent her another letter until four years later. That one stated that she had done what she considered to be her duty to the family by making arrangements for Miranda's care until she turned eighteen.

Care! No one else would count it 'care' to leave her for four years in a boarding school which lodged and supervised mainly students whose parents were working overseas. There had been no such thing as going home for the school holidays for any of them but at least the others got letters from their families.

When Miranda turned eighteen, she applied to the Trust for help going to university and the lawyers had told her that her great-aunt would agree to the fees and living costs being paid only if she studied accountancy and her marks were good.

At the end of her final term of university, her great-aunt had sent another message saying she felt she had now done her duty to the family and her great-niece could manage her own life in whatever way she chose from then onwards.

There was no offer of money to tide her over till she got her first wage and Miranda was proud of how well she'd coped. She'd got a good degree and worked part-time as a barmaid while she studied, living frugally and saving money so that she'd have something to fall back on.

She was still in touch with some of her university friends but they were now married with children and it wasn't possible to stay close when they moved to other parts of the country.

How pitiful was it now to get anxious about that spiteful old woman simply at the sight of this envelope? 'Get it over with, you fool,' she told herself loudly, so picked up her mug of coffee and went to sit at the small kitchen table.

After another warm, comforting mouthful, she ripped open the envelope and quickly scanned the letter it contained. Gasping in shock, she read it again slowly and carefully.

> Dear Ms Westerby,
>
> I have recently taken over management of your family's account with our company and regret to inform you that your great-aunt Phyllis passed away suddenly two weeks ago.
>
> She did not wish a formal funeral to be held and had made arrangements years ago to be cremated privately when the time came, with only a lawyer in attendance.
>
> This has been done as per her instructions.
>
> I would appreciate it if you could contact our London office and make an appointment to come here as soon as possible to discuss her Will with me.
>
> Since your great-aunt mistrusted modern technology, as you are no doubt aware, the instructions that came with the Will require this to be done in person.
>
> Yours faithfully,
>
> Darren Parker

Miranda's initial reaction was to wonder whether this was some sort of trick. No, her great-aunt must really be dead, but typically she worried that the old witch would still be trying to cause trouble for her great-niece if she could.

Then she snapped her fingers as she guessed that this must be to do with the Westerby Family Trust Fund. There were probably new forms to be signed because, as she'd been informed by the lawyers when she turned twenty-one, the management of the trust would pass from her great-aunt to herself after that lady's death, since Miranda was next in line. Yes, that'd be it.

The trust might have paid for her secondary education after her mother died, but she'd never had to apply to it for financial help since getting her degree. She'd felt deeply ashamed when she found out that her father had incurred debts that had had to be paid off by the trust after his sudden death.

Now that her great-aunt was dead, she would be in charge of managing the trust but there wouldn't be a lot to do, surely, with such a small number of family members involved. This meeting should be quite straightforward, therefore, and would presumably be only to sign relevant documents.

Unfortunately, the lawyers' office was right across the other side of London and it'd take two or three hours out of her working day to get there and back. Her new supervisor wouldn't be happy about that but too bad. It'd be great to get away from him and his fussy ways.

She checked the time and reached for the phone, hoping someone would still be in the lawyers' office but she only got an answering service. Bother! She'd have to wait until the following morning to arrange an appointment.

The letter ruined the peace of her evening, of course. And what a nuisance that this had happened now! She'd booked to go on holiday, starting in three days' time, and had been looking forward to spending a couple of weeks in a luxury hotel in Italy with her friend Libby, who was older than her and had started out as a pleasant new neighbour in their block of flats a couple of years ago, then quickly became a close friend.

Oh well, these things happened. She'd manage. She always did.

* * *

The following morning, Miranda phoned the lawyers' office as soon as it was open to make an appointment to see this Mr Parker.

Whoever picked up the phone told her there were no vacant time slots that day and said it casually, as if it didn't matter.

For once she let her irritation show. 'Then you'll have to make time, won't you? It was your Mr Parker who contacted me to say it was urgent that he speak to me in person and he asked me to make an appointment. However, as I have an overseas holiday booked, either I see him today or he'll have to wait two weeks till after I get back to deal with whatever this is about. Please don't forget to tell him I tried to do as he asked.'

The woman's tone changed. 'Ah. I see. Sorry. Could you please hold on for a moment, Ms Westerby? I'll pass you to our chief clerk, who's just come in.'

Miranda half hoped this man wouldn't be able to arrange an appointment, either. If it was bad news, it could jolly well wait as far as she was concerned. When you didn't particularly enjoy your job, holidays were doubly precious.

However, the chief clerk fitted her in for an appointment just after lunch the next day and said Mr Parker would be very grateful to her for contacting them so promptly.

'Could we not do this online?' she asked.

'I'm afraid not. There is not only the question of passing on management of the trust and signing a contract to that effect, but also your great-aunt's personal Will to deal with.'

'What about her personal Will? That surely won't have anything to do with me.' The old hag had hated her and it wouldn't be likely that she was leaving her great-niece a bequest.

'It's a bit complicated, Ms Westerby. Better if Mr Parker explains in person, then he can answer any questions you may have.'

Miranda worried about that for the rest of the morning. She only hoped she wouldn't have to go to Wiltshire afterwards to deal with the family home, in which her great-aunt had been living for decades and which Miranda could only vaguely remember visiting once as a small child.

She didn't know any details about the place but guessed that at the very least there might be Phyllis's personal possessions to dispose of. Her heart sank at the mere thought of having to go through drawers and cupboards to throw away an old lady's underwear and who knew what else. Ugh.

At just before one o'clock the next day, she walked into the lawyers' rooms and Mr Parker immediately came out to greet her. He was about her own age with a more pleasant manner than the previous elderly man she'd dealt with, which made her immediately feel better about this visit.

'Thank you for coming here so promptly, Ms Westerby. Would you like a cup of tea or coffee?'

'Nothing, thank you.' She just wanted to get everything to do with her great-aunt over and done with and then forget that the woman had ever existed.

He led the way into a luxurious office, gesturing towards a chair. 'Please take a seat.'

She did that and waited. She was so anxious to get this finalised that she spoke more sharply than usual. 'I was surprised that whatever this is about couldn't have been dealt with digitally now that my great-aunt is no longer involved. I know she always refused to deal with things online but surely we can move on from that now?'

'I'm afraid we still have to deal with this in person because of the conditions set by your aunt in her own Will.'

She might have known it'd be that old witch's doing! 'I usually deal with a Mr Lloyd, who understands the situation between my great-aunt and myself, in that she disliked me for some weird reason, so he always used to fill me in on all the details she'd missed out. Isn't he available today?'

'I'm afraid he retired a few months ago. I took over your family's accounts, but it wasn't time for the annual auditing of the trust and Miss Westerby was managing the other things that cropped up as usual, so there was nothing that needed doing until she passed away quite unexpectedly.'

'How did she die?'

'Massive stroke. She was found by her housekeeper, Miss Parnham, who dialled for an ambulance and they took her to hospital, quite rightly informing us. We knew Selma Parnham owned a house in the village so when the hospital informed us that your aunt wasn't likely to recover, we immediately closed up the big house. Your aunt lingered for a week or so but never regained consciousness.'

'I see.'

He got out a folder that appeared to be brand new, with the name *Westerby Family Trust* in big letters on the front label. 'I took the liberty of starting off a new folder because the family records are in rather a mess.'

'My great-aunt hated spending money on administrative matters.'

'That's obvious. Um, did she ever share any information about the contents of her own Will with you?'

'No, never. I've had no contact whatsoever with her in person since I was fourteen.'

He looked at her in surprise. 'Goodness! But I thought you were her closest relative and that she used to be your guardian?'

'Once she'd taken over as my guardian, she did everything through your firm. I never visited her at Fairfield House after that.'

'Ah. I see. Well then, I'm happy to inform you that apart from one other relatively small legacy to a third cousin of yours, a Mr Mitchell Westerby, you're her sole beneficiary.'

'Mr Lloyd informed me when I turned twenty-one that the trust would come under my supervision after my great-aunt died,' she said cautiously, puzzled by how he'd phrased that. Surely he couldn't mean it literally? Phyllis wouldn't leave anything to a niece she hated, surely?

'It's not just a question of you taking over management of your family trust, Ms Westerby. You inherit that task automatically for the rest of your life, then it passes to your next of kin. No, what concerns us more today is that you're also Miss Westerby's main beneficiary and she's left everything she owned personally to you apart from that one small bequest to your cousin.'

Miranda was too surprised to say anything for a few moments, could only gape at him, thinking she must have misheard. In the end she managed to say jerkily, 'There must be some mistake. Why on earth would she do that? She hated me.'

Mr Parker looked startled. 'Surely not!'

'I'm certain of it.' She had been since the age of fourteen.

'But you're her great-niece, her closest relative if I'm not mistaken.'

'I might be related to her but we only ever saw one another a few times and I've not spoken to her in person since I was fourteen. No, there must be some mistake.'

'I can't tell you why she did it but there is definitely no mistake legally. You are her main heir. At least, you will be if you accept the conditions attached to the bequest.'

'Conditions?' Ah. That sounded more like something Phyllis would do, pretend to leave everything to her then make it too awkward for her to accept. 'Go on,' she prompted.

'To inherit you must go to Wiltshire and live in the family home in the village of Fairford Parva for two years.'

'What? Is that sort of condition enforceable legally?'

He shrugged. 'I've made a quick check with my colleagues because it's quite rare for someone to do that these days and I'm not sure of all the ins and outs. You might have to take it to court to find out for certain whether you're obliged to accept the condition, which could waste a lot of your time and inheritance money. One or two senior colleagues whose opinions I respect said that people who inherit substantial amounts which have conditions attached usually do as they've been asked, as long as it's something fairly reasonable – whether it's legally enforceable or not.'

'And does this cousin who also has a bequest have a similar condition attached to his inheritance?'

'That information is confidential.'

When she didn't say anything, he added quietly, 'To return to your bequest. This type of conditional legacy seems to be generally regarded by most inheritors as a moral obligation, especially when they've been left a generous amount of money, as you have been.'

She might as well find out what was involved. 'Oh? How generous?'

'I gather it's enough to live on comfortably for the rest of your life after the two years have ended and that you'd never need to go out to work again.'

She could only stare at him in shock.

He waited then added gently, 'Living in that house as per your aunt's request seems a fairly reasonable thing to ask in view of the amount of money you'd end up with, don't you think, Ms Westerby? It's only for two years after all and there would be no rent to pay, of course.'

Miranda didn't answer at once, was still trying to come to terms with this. There had to be some nasty trick involved if this had been arranged by her great-aunt, she was sure. 'How much has she left me? Will there really be enough to live on and to maintain Fairfield House? And I'd need some regular payments myself during those two years because I'd have to give up my job in London to live there.'

'I don't know the exact financial details, I'm afraid. Your aunt's final Will was drawn up long before I took over your account and there were no copies giving the details left in the office. I therefore only have the summary and the information that the financial details of the trust have been stored in the family home.'

She hesitated, not liking the idea of being beholden to her great-aunt in any way but at the same time unable to get past the fact that it'd free her from working under the Chief Idiot or anyone like him ever again. She stalled for time as she tried to figure out the pros and cons.

'I don't actually know anything much about my great-aunt's finances, except that they include the home that's been in the family for well over a century and is, I gather, entailed so it goes to the Westerby relative who is the next of kin.'

'Nor do we know the details. As I said, all we have here is a summary statement that everything goes to you because of your relationship to her. She kept any other paperwork at the house in Wiltshire for safety, so I'm afraid you'll not find out the full details of the inheritance until you move there.'

Something he'd said puzzled her. 'Why did you say she kept it all there "for safety"?'

'Because most of the older records were lost in a fire at our company's storage unit in London over two decades ago. From then onwards, I gather that your aunt didn't trust us to look after the remaining documents.'

He paused, shaking his head sadly. 'We could actually have retrieved more information from digital sources even then but she said she didn't see the need to waste her time or money on accounts that were long over and done with, and all she needed to carry on was the relevant financial information from her mother's generation onwards.'

'I do wish she'd let you retrieve more of the details. I know hardly anything about my ancestors!' Miranda exclaimed involuntarily. 'You'd think she'd want future generations to understand their family background.'

'Apparently she considered going that far back irrelevant. However, we could still help you to learn more about your family history if you're interested, Ms Westerby. My firm works occasionally with a very good genealogist and I'm sure he'll be happy to see what else he can find out about the earlier records and therefore your ancestors. And we could then add the verified details to your family's account records at no extra cost to you. I'm very much in favour of preserving history.'

'Oh, good.'

'I'm afraid you'd have to bear the extra cost of the research after all these years.'

She knew so little about her family background that she seized this opportunity without hesitation. 'I'd like to do that. I'll check the records at Fairfield House, then get back to you about what I find there, after which you could perhaps arrange a search for any older family records for me by this expert? I wouldn't know how to undertake genealogical research at that level myself.'

'Yes, of course we can arrange that. It's not cheap but the expert we consult from time to time is very skilful. Um, I presume this means you're going to accept the conditions of the inheritance?'

'Yes, I am.' She didn't actually feel she had any choice. She was, after all, the heir and had a duty to the family – well, she considered she did even though the head of that family had neglected her. But she'd love to know more about her family, she had felt so alone in the world.

'I'm delighted to hear that.'

She watched him make a note in the file. She'd regretted for years her lack of knowledge about her mother's side of the family. She had no idea about her father's family either, but had less interest in that. They might be as careless with money as he had apparently been. Did you learn such careless habits or were they engrained in your genes? She was enough of a Westerby to be upset at the idea of him incurring such debts.

She found it hard not to smile at the thought that she would be getting away from her idiot of a boss, and there would be nothing about the reason for her resignation that he could use to blacken her reputation professionally, in case she needed to find another job.

She'd become an accountant because it was the only way Phyllis would agree to finance her university education. She wouldn't miss it as a job, though the skills would probably come in useful for helping her manage her inheritance and the family trust.

Chapter Two

Mr Parker gave Miranda an uncertain look, as if he had something else to tell her. *What next, for heaven's sake?* she wondered. He indicated the brand-new file lying between them. 'This contains copies of our summary documents and when you're at the family home in Wiltshire you'll be able to access the specific financial information of both the trust and your aunt's personal details, which I gather she kept in the safe there.'

He'd already told her that and she wondered why he was repeating it. She frowned down at the file as something else occurred to her abruptly. 'If so much information about the Westerbys has been lost, how do I know someone from another branch of the family won't suddenly appear and claim to be the heir instead of me?'

'I've been calling her your aunt but actually she's your great-aunt, and she still had the relevant records dating from her generation of the family onwards. I followed them up and you can be quite sure that you really are her heir. From what I've heard of her, I doubt Miss Westerby would have made a mistake about something as important to her as that.'

'What about my cousin? How is he involved?'

'Mitchell Westerby is the son of your great-aunt's second cousin, so there isn't the slightest doubt that you take precedence over him as the direct legal heir. And since she'd found out that he was a gambler and not particularly successful at it, she couldn't bear to leave him even the more generous bequest she had originally planned. Since you're accepting her conditions for inheritance, I can now tell you that she's given him the right to live in a small cottage on the estate for his lifetime. You will, presumably, meet him there.'

'Oh. I see.'

'It makes things easier for you that your mother kept the Westerby name when she married and that you did the same, because it was extremely important to your aunt that a female Westerby born and bred inherit the family home.'

Miranda had also been very glad of that when her own brief marriage had broken up. What was wrong with the women of her family, though, that they didn't seem to form happy marriages?

'You also met with your aunt's approval about the way you've managed your own finances since you graduated. That was very important to her.'

'Good heavens! It must be the only thing she ever approved of about me.'

'Well, she always sounded a little surprised about your financial skills, I gathered from my colleague when he was handing over your affairs to me.'

She frowned. 'How did my great-aunt know about that

for sure? As I told you, I've had no actual contact with her since I turned fourteen.'

He hesitated, then said, 'I gather from our records that she hired a private investigator from time to time to check up on you.'

The thought of that annoyed Miranda intensely but done was done, as her friend Libby would say. 'I actually know very little about Phyllis's personal background. She never married, did she?'

'No. She, um, seemed to dislike men, if you don't mind me saying so.'

'I prefer to know the truth about any situation. Did she ever live in a house of her own as well as managing the family home in Wiltshire?'

'No. She didn't have another home when she was younger, either, because she lived with her mother in a cottage in the grounds of the family home, the one that she has now allowed your cousin to live in. So you see, she lived in your family home in Wiltshire all her life, taking charge of it when her own mother died without ever inheriting.'

'So she owned it after the former Westerby died?'

'No, she never actually owned it and you won't either. Fairfield House is owned by the trust and whoever inherits the management of that is entitled to live there rent-free for the rest of their life, as you will be able to do from now on.'

That was a wonderful thought, even if she would have to move away from her friends in London.

'I gather the house is quite old and has belonged to your family trust for nearly two hundred years.'

Why had her mother never told her more about it? That thought made her see another potential problem. 'The house isn't heritage listed, is it?'

'No. Definitely not.'

'Well, thank goodness for that. One of my friends and her husband had a lot of trouble modernising a house she'd inherited because of that. Has this house been modernised at all?'

'I'm afraid I don't know.'

He opened his desk drawer and took out a piece of paper, looking rather embarrassed now. 'There's one other thing I'm required to do. Your great-aunt wrote this a few years ago and when Mr Lloyd retired, she made me promise that I would read it aloud to you after she died. She had apparently insisted he do the same thing. If I hadn't given her my word about that, she would have taken her business away from our law firm, so I can't avoid doing this, I'm afraid. The senior partner reminded me of it only this morning.'

He scowled down at the paper. 'Believe me, these are not my own feelings and if I could avoid doing this, I would.'

Miranda shrugged and waited, feeling quite certain whatever it was would be unpleasant.

He took a deep breath and began to read it in a dull monotone, avoiding her eyes. '"To my great-niece Miranda Westerby when she inherits. There are too few family members nowadays, so it is your bounden duty to get married again as soon as you can find a man willing to have you. Please choose a more decent husband than the last one. It was a relief not to have his genes dumped into our family pool.

'Remember, it's only right that you pay the family back for this generous inheritance by creating a potential heir of your own, preferably more than one daughter to ensure that the Westerby family name and genes survive. Your mother refused my request for her to remarry after your father died, so she only produced one child and that is not secure enough. Phyllis Westerby."'

Miranda's annoyance got the better of her. 'The old bat should have had children herself, then.'

He gave her an uncomfortable glance. 'I was told by the head of our firm when I too queried this aspect that she was unable to bear children because she'd had a bad accident as a youngster and that had precluded it.'

'That's no excuse for her gratuitous insults to me, though.'

He nodded as if he agreed but didn't say anything, only waited for her to gesture to him to continue. He had clearly distanced himself from what he'd had to read, so she didn't hold it against him.

She didn't say anything else about the Will and other documentation. What was the point? Her great-aunt was dead now. But no way was Miranda getting married again merely to provide heirs for the family. 'Once bitten, twice shy' described her feelings about marriage very accurately, because it was too stressful getting unmarried if things didn't go well. She'd only marry if she felt utterly certain someone was decent as well as attractive.

And if her ex ever dared to come near her again, she'd throw something at him on sight and ask questions later. She would never forgive Keith for thumping her, had been taken by surprise at how quickly he'd changed into a bully once they were married. She'd left him after only a few months because he was stronger than her and hadn't kept his promise to seek counselling for his violence.

She realised the lawyer was waiting for her to speak so she asked the first thing that came into her mind to give herself time to calm down again. 'What's Fairfield House like, Mr Parker?'

'Don't you remember?'

'No. I was very young and I only have a vague memory. Isn't there a photo among the records?'

'No. Your aunt said it wasn't appropriate for it to be photographed.'

'Why on earth not?'

'I can't tell you why not. I've only spoken to her a couple of times by telephone since I took over and she was very abrupt both times.'

Had the old woman been losing her marbles? 'Go on then, please.'

She listened carefully as he continued to share the little he did know about the financial side of things. 'Your aunt also bequeathed to you her personal portfolio of shares, her collection of Victorian jewellery and whatever money was left in her bank account when she died. She seems to have been good with finances so I should think the share portfolio will amount to a generous sum.'

'I'm still feeling surprised that she left me any additional bequests after the way she stayed away from me.'

'The senior member of my firm told me when I took over the account that no one ever knew what to expect from Miss Westerby. He said I should just do as she told me and not even bother to try to advise her about better financial alternatives because she would take no notice. She apparently always went her own way in everything she did.'

'I already found that out.'

He gave her what looked like a sympathetic glance then changed the subject slightly. 'Are you at all familiar with the family home?'

'No. I only went there once with my mother just after my father died. I was very young so have only a very vague memory of it. We didn't stay long and my great-aunt didn't offer us any refreshments so I only saw the entrance hall and what was probably a small sitting room.'

'Goodness.'

'My main memory of that visit is of my mother getting angry and shouting at her aunt loudly. I found out later that Phyllis had been very reluctant to provide more generously for us from the trust money.' She shivered at the memories that had brought up of the way her mother had had to scrimp.

'Well, our records show that your aunt helped financially with your education.'

'I can understand now why she kept so close an eye on me. She offered to pay all my expenses only if I studied accounting at university, something I hadn't been interested in.' Still didn't really find it interesting, though it had earned her a steady income for years and she knew that she was a capable accountant.

'That was kind of her.'

'I doubt it was done out of kindness. She still didn't want to see me in person. But I did as she asked and she paid my university fees as promised, which I appreciated.'

When she'd told one of her university friends about it, Rosie had tried to persuade Miranda to refuse to sign the annual trust fund audits unless the lawyers told her more about the family home. She hadn't even considered doing that. She wasn't into quarrelling as a way of solving problems and by then she'd had no desire whatsoever to meet her great-aunt.

She gave him a grim smile. 'I realised even then that she

was doing it to take care of the future of the family, not to help me personally. But I was able to go to university in comfort and not end my course loaded with debts. I enjoyed my years there very much. She not only let me live in a flat she paid for but covered the electricity bills and so on as long as they were reasonable.'

'Yet you still didn't visit Miss Westerby?'

'I was never invited to do that, so I presumed I'd not be welcome and didn't even try. After I graduated, I was given a month's notice to vacate the flat, again through your firm, and told to look after myself from then onwards. You probably know that from your records.'

'Yes. It seemed, um, rather strange, given that you were her heir. I understand the overall situation a little better now and I'm grateful to you for being so frank.'

'I try to live honestly, Mr Parker. My only contact with my great-aunt from then onwards has been your firm's annual statement to confirm that the accounts of the family trust have been certified correct. And to tell the truth, I've always been chary of crossing her.'

She smiled wryly as she saw him shaking his head as if not happy about this either. She was used to her strange and rather hostile family situation and had learnt that it was usually better to keep the details of it to herself in social situations. Mostly she got on with her life in her own way and her only real regret was the failure of her marriage.

She'd been fooled by Keith, who had turned out to be a rat. He'd started thumping her within a few weeks of the wedding, so she'd warned him she wouldn't put up with that. When he didn't stop, she kicked him where it hurt a man most then called for police help to get him and his possessions out of what was, fortunately, her own house.

She'd rushed into a bad choice because she'd been desperate for a family of her own. It was still her duty to marry again and provide an heir, but she was terrified of being fooled by surface charm and making another bad choice. What if she was no good at choosing men? Some women didn't seem to be able to do it well. How could you ever be totally sure of anyone?

'You seem to have managed your own finances much better than your cousin Mitchell has done,' the lawyer said. 'He barely scraped through a similar degree to yours, which Miss Westerby had funded him for as she did you. Then he invested a legacy from his father's side of the family unwisely, tried to remedy things and failed, getting into debt even more deeply. I can't understand why your great-aunt continued to support him.'

'My guess was that she was helping him in order to provide a back-up heir, in case I let her down and one was needed. I don't wish to meet him or have anything to do with him if he's careless with money.'

'You will inevitably meet him because she's still letting him live in that cottage and has arranged for that to continue independently of your management of the estate.'

'So I suppose he'll be staying there.'

'Yes. Does it matter?'

'I suppose not.'

'He's never got into financial trouble since. I guess that your aunt had a soft spot for him personally.'

Given this information, Miranda could feel herself relaxing a little. She'd be able to give up her current job and if she didn't enjoy living in Wiltshire, she could move away after the two years were over. You could put up with nearly anything for two years – except a husband who thumped you.

She'd miss her London friends, though, and would have to try to get to know other congenial people near her new home. Sadly, she didn't think that most of her current friends would be able to come and visit her because nearly all of them were at the having babies and rearing small children stages of life. One baby was relatively easy to take visiting, but a baby plus a couple of toddlers was far too difficult for both sides to cope with, and she had little experience with children, sadly.

She'd miss Libby most of all. Her neighbour had rapidly become a close friend even though she was old enough to be Miranda's mother. The two of them had booked to go on this holiday together but regrettably, she didn't think she should go now, given the conditions attached to the legacy. She'd need to get down to Wiltshire and take a firm hold of the historical family home and everything connected to it. It had been standing empty for weeks and she didn't think it prudent to leave it any longer in such a vulnerable position.

Such a pity. She hoped Libby would forgive her for cancelling the holiday. Perhaps her friend would be able to come down to Wiltshire for a visit soon.

Chapter Three

When Miranda looked across at him again, Mr Parker asked gently, 'Would going to live in Wiltshire interfere with your long-term career plans, Ms Westerby?'

She shook her head. 'I don't have any. I've always seen accounting more as a reasonable way to earn a living rather than as a career I care deeply about. I have no desire whatsoever to climb the so-called corporate ladders in the profession. There's more to life than checking columns of figures and outdoing your colleagues at attracting new clients to the firm you work for, don't you think?'

He smiled. 'I agree absolutely. I'm fortunate that I enjoy my job but I don't think I'd enjoy one that meant dealing with figures day in, day out. It's people I find interesting. Was there nothing else you wanted to study or do for work?'

'Not really. I'd been vaguely considering studying architecture, but my great-aunt refused point blank to pay for me to do that. It was accounting or get into debt for the university fees and spend years paying them off. Only I didn't dare get into debt because I had no other family members to turn to if anything went wrong. So I accepted her offer, got my degree and I presume that's what led to my inheriting and therefore my absolute independence, which is something I shall value highly.'

He was silent, frowning slightly.

'Is something wrong?'

'You won't be independent in some senses while you're living at Fairfield House. Will that upset you?'

She hadn't meant to mention the current situation which had already made her apply for a couple of other jobs, but it slipped out. 'Unfortunately, at the moment we have a new team leader at work and he's going to get a slap across the face if he bumps into me or brushes against certain parts of my body again.'

He gaped at her in shock. 'He's that bad about harassment? In this day and age?'

'Yes.'

'Why haven't you reported him?'

'Because he's very cunning about when and where he harasses me. I think he must have been honing those skills for years. It's been going on for months and there have never been any witnesses nearby or I'd definitely have challenged him publicly. When I warned him privately he just smiled and said that if I accused him of anything he'd sue me because I have no evidence. And CCTV cameras aren't allowed inside our office complex, only at the entrances and exits.'

She couldn't help shuddering. 'He smiles as he eyes my body up and down after each incident. I find him very creepy.'

'I'm sorry to hear that. I had no idea things could still be so bad.'

'Oh, they can, believe me. I only mention this to show why this inheritance is particularly timely. It will give me a good reason to leave my job suddenly and I'll be financially independent afterwards. Please tell me a little more about this family home I'd be living in. I looked up online where the village is situated in Wiltshire but what's the house like?'

'I'm only allowed to tell you that sort of thing after the paperwork has been completed and you've agreed in writing to move in for two years.'

That made her stare. 'My great-aunt wasn't very trusting, was she? Well, all right. If this house has been the family home for nearly two centuries, I would very much like to see it, even without the financial inducements. History is one of my hobbies.'

'Apparently both house and garden are quite large, so it should be a pleasant place to live.'

'Good. Because my flat feels to be growing smaller each year and you can't help acquiring new possessions, especially books, can you? If this house is in pleasant surroundings, I could perhaps set it up as a holiday home after my two-year sentence to live there full time has been completed. I could go there sometimes at weekends on my own or with friends, or even hire it out.'

He shrugged. 'You won't be legally allowed to hire it out, but after you complete your two years there it will be up to you how often you use the house as your home or simply leave it empty. You still won't be able to sell it. And by then you might have become fond of it and want to live there full-time.'

'Who can tell how I'll feel about it afterwards? I've

never had a whole house to live in.'

'She must have been. Though quite frankly, I think only a fool would refuse such a bequest. I'm told that Miss Westerby was good at organising people into doing what she wished.'

'Chivvying them into it might be a better way of describing it.' Miranda was unable to hide her bitterness about her own dealings with her aunt, or lack of dealings unless Phyllis wanted something from her.

He looked at her and added, 'I'll deny that I said this, but from reading my colleague's records, I think you're right. At times it did seem more as if she was tricking people into doing what she wanted.'

She looked at him in surprise and couldn't think what to say so kept quiet and left it to him to continue the conversation.

When she didn't say anything else, he took over again quite quickly as she'd expected. Some people were in more of a hurry than others to fill a conversational silence. 'Well, I've told you everything I was required to but I shall need you to sign a contract agreeing to adhere to your aunt's conditions before we go any further.' He opened the folder and took out a piece of paper.

The contract was very brief and straightforward, though of course no less binding for that. She read it quickly and looked at him. 'Is this the last of the paperwork?'

'Yes.'

'I'll sign it, then.' She reached out for the pen that was lying on the desk.

He put out his hand to stop her. 'Just a minute. I'll have to call in my senior clerk and the receptionist to witness this properly.'

They must have been waiting to be summoned, so the signing was quickly dealt with and once the two witnesses had left, Mr Parker opened a lower drawer in his desk and took out a small padded envelope, pushing it across the table to her.

'These are the keys to your new home and to the safe. They've been changed recently, to keep you more secure there.'

'Good idea. Where in the house shall I find this safe?'

'I have no idea, I'm afraid. The address of the house is written on the envelope and that's all I can tell you about it. A safe shouldn't be hard to find, though. Most of them are too big to be easily hidden and they don't usually look like pieces of furniture. Now, is that all?'

She nodded.

'Then I hope you'll be happy living there. And do get in touch if you find any problems when you arrive, though I doubt there will be. Our clerk was there as soon as we heard about your aunt's death and he took a female colleague with him to pack the housekeeper's things. They made sure that even she couldn't get inside.'

She stared in surprise.

'We didn't know what items should be there so made sure that nothing could be taken away. Our firm has not had good relations with the housekeeper, you see. She has a very sharp tongue and can be very demanding. She got on well with your aunt, though, which is what mattered.'

'Well, thank you for being so careful.' She took the envelope from him and stared down as it, wondering what sort of life this would lead her into.

He asked quietly, 'Do you like living in the country, Ms Westerby? Is it something you're used to?'

'I've never tried it, never even had a whole house to live in. But I'll still have my flat in London to fall back on afterwards if I don't like it in the family home, and I shall be able to live anywhere I wish once the two years are over, shan't I?'

'Yes, indeed.' He took a couple of other folders out of a drawer and clipped his old-fashioned pen back into the breast pocket of his jacket as if making ready for his next client.

She didn't stand up straight away, just ran through mentally what he'd told her in case she had any other questions. She didn't intend to do anything that jeopardised the inheritance, whatever she had to put up with. No way.

This inheritance would make such a wonderful difference to her life. She'd been independent for a few years because she had been determined to own a home of her own since her mother died, absolutely determined. But all she'd been able to afford was a very small flat, on which she had paid off the mortgage the previous year.

And now, here was the opportunity to as good as own a decent-sized house for the next two years and save like mad during that time in case she needed to buy a new home somewhere else afterwards. She wasn't going to waste this opportunity. Independence was something she treasured. Her present flat might be small but it was in an increasingly popular area with good transport links and had gone up nicely in value since she bought it. She would be able to sell it easily after the two years were up and put the money towards whatever she managed to save.

She didn't expect to like a home that had been lived in by her great-aunt, but if she did like it, she'd stay there and rent the flat out. She could feel herself grimacing at her own deep need for independence and security.

She was speaking more to herself than to him when she added, 'I shall enjoy living somewhere more spacious than the flat, I must admit, but I'd prefer it to have been in a leafy London suburb, where I'd still be fairly close to my friends. Is the house in a village or near a town at all?'

'I gather it's at one end of a small village but set a bit apart from the other dwellings on an acre or two of land.'

'I hope it's a pretty village, then.'

He started tidying away the pile of papers dealing with her affairs, then clicked his tongue in annoyance and took the top one from it, holding it out to her. 'Dear me! I nearly forgot to give you this. Will you please let us know officially that you've settled there by signing this and sending it to me a month after you take up residence? You can perhaps get some local council official or a shopkeeper to sign this statement to the effect that you've been living in the house during that time.'

She looked at the piece of paper in surprise. 'My great-aunt never trusted anyone, did she?'

'It doesn't seem like it. And the family trust is still rather old-fashioned, says the money is to be paid quarterly and your ongoing residence in the family home needs to be confirmed each time, which seems a bit excessive. Without that signed witness statement, we can't transfer the payments into your bank account. There are more copies of this form in the folder.'

She didn't say it aloud, but she thought it: trust Phyllis Westerby to make stupid, fiddly conditions, trying to control her from beyond the grave. She took the piece of paper and stuffed it into the file any old how, amused to see him wince at how that crumpled it. 'Very well. I'll do that.'

'And if you find any earlier financial information about the family among the documentation at Fairfield House, I'd appreciate a copy so that I can add it to the family records, which our firm will still be looking after as accurately as we can. I'm afraid you won't be able to change lawyers where this family residence is concerned.'

'I see no need to change and I'll be quite happy to continue dealing with you and your firm, Mr Parker. My great-aunt's penchant for bossing people around during her lifetime, and even after her death, is not your fault and you've handled it all as carefully as you could. Tactfully, too.'

He gave her a genuine smile at that. 'Thank you for your understanding. And by the way, any information you send us will be kept secure, I promise you. Even if our offices were to burn down again, we have now made very careful arrangements to have all our clients' information from previous decades stored digitally as well as on paper. Some of the former senior managers were, I'm afraid, reluctant to move to more modern ways of conducting business but the lady currently in charge of our firm is not old-fashioned, thank goodness.'

She nodded and picked up the folder he'd given her, then realised he was looking at her as if he wanted to speak. 'Is that all or is there something else?'

'There is one other thing I'd like to say to you, Ms Westerby.'

She settled back on the chair and waited, wondering what would be raised next. It wasn't paperwork as he'd put the folders away.

But he seemed a very pleasant chap so she was happy to listen to whatever he had to say.

Chapter Four

Mr Parker hesitated. Unfortunately, he couldn't change how things had been set up or refuse to get involved because his predecessor had arranged all this according to Miss Westerby's requirements and then retired, leaving others in the firm the unpleasant necessity of putting that client's requirements into operation.

However, though their now deceased client would have had a fit at him saying this, his conscience was not easy about what he was being forced to do in his new role. 'This isn't a legal matter and I'd ask that you keep what I'm about to say to yourself. It's a suggestion from me offered as a man only a little older than you and with a sister of about your age.'

She studied his face, then nodded slowly.

Darren took a deep breath and told her his main concern, keeping his voice low. 'Your family home has been standing vacant for nearly two months, ever since the old lady was rushed into hospital after her stroke. That would be known about in the district. And even though the police made sure the house was locked up immediately and our clerk had the locks changed, you can't be sure that no one has got in there, or that it's safe for you to go into it now.'

She nodded again.

'Your aunt remained comatose and although she'd had a live-in housekeeper, the woman was locked out by the police on our senior manager's suggestion and her possessions were packed for her. That is something I didn't agree with and still consider very short-sighted. As a result there was no one to make sure the place remained secure and to check that nothing had been taken.'

That surprised her. 'Didn't your firm keep ongoing checks on the place? There must surely have been a security system of some sort installed already that could have been switched on, even if it was old-fashioned?'

'I'm afraid there has never been any kind of security system. We did contact the police to check what we might be allowed to do, but we've had no authorisation for going inside the house, let alone having a system installed. And in fact no one from our firm had ever been inside it, which rather clinched the matter as far as the police were concerned.'

'Goodness, that sounds very lax.'

'Yes. Your aunt refused more than once to act on our suggestion that she have a modern security system installed. She always claimed that she had a very sensible housekeeper who rarely went out, which was better than any mechanical system. And she said that there were also neighbours she could call on for help if needed. But though we met the housekeeper, the only neighbour we met was your cousin Mitchell, who lives in one of the two nearby cottages. And even then, he occupies the smaller of the two cottages in the grounds of the big house, he goes away quite often.'

'Oh. That sounds very lax.'

'Indeed it is. Your aunt lived a very isolated sort of life, hardly associating with anyone apart from that housekeeper, who is a difficult person to deal with.'

'She was always very secretive about herself in all her interactions with her family, wasn't she? I was her closest relative and yet I only ever met her in person a couple of times, and that was when I was a child.'

'Yes, you're right there. She was always very insistent that we should leave her in peace, as she put it. She dealt with us by post or telephone mainly, never digitally and only once or twice in person. And the family house is rather a long way from our office in London, so it wouldn't have been easy for her to get here, since she didn't drive, or for us to send any of our staff there regularly to check the place because she certainly wouldn't have paid the extra expenses for that.'

He paused and stared at her. 'To be frank, we were always surprised that your family chose to deal with our firm, though pleased to have the Westerbys as clients, of course, some of our firm's earliest clients I gather. So, bearing all that in mind, it was decided that we wouldn't press for access when she was taken ill but just lock the place up.'

'I see.'

'What I'm trying to say is that I'm rather concerned about your safety there, Ms Westerby. I gather that the house is on the edge of a small village called Fairford Parva and the nearest police station is some distance away in

Fairford Magna, which is, as the name suggests, a much bigger village. But the police station isn't staffed at night, so if there's a problem it takes quite a while for an officer to answer a call for help.' He paused and waited for a few moments as if unsure whether to continue or not.

'Do go on.'

'My unofficial advice is that you'd be wise to get some sort of security system installed as soon as you can. Don't ask for permission from my firm, just do it. And perhaps you should get all the locks changed yet again as well. Who knows whether any copies even of the recent new set have been given to others? I must admit that I didn't take to the housekeeper, however highly Miss Westerby thought of her. She was actually a sort of cook-housekeeper. Anyway, this Ms Parnham has been asking about a box of papers which she says she needs to deal with for her former employer, but we have it locked in a cupboard there and since we've no proof that it really is hers, we have refused access. You'll need to check the ownership.'

He paused again as if to let what he'd suggested sink in then went on, 'I also feel it might be wise for you to take someone with you on your first visit, in case the house has been broken into.'

'Aren't there rules about me doing that?' She hoped she hadn't sounded sarcastic, but there were so many rules she would be surprised if there weren't any for this.

'No. I don't think your aunt even considered it a possibility that you'd take anyone with you or she'd have mentioned it. She, um, never seemed to have any friends herself, apparently, unless you count her housekeeper.'

'What did she do about the heavy housework and so on? If it's a large house, she'd need more domestic help than a cook-housekeeper, and perhaps various sorts of personal help as she grew older.'

'I don't really know, I must admit. It was the housekeeper who raised the alarm about her when she had the stroke, remember. She went with her to hospital. And by the time she got home again, the house had been locked up and her personal possessions taken to the cottage in the village that she and her brother had inherited.'

'It sounds to be a very strange set-up.'

'Yes. And things were going downhill rapidly in the grounds, I'm afraid. The gardener moved away from the area last year and wasn't replaced.'

'Where is the housekeeper now?'

'In her own cottage in the village. We terminated her employment when it was clear that your aunt would not recover.'

'These arrangements all seem very chancy.'

'Yes. They are. I presume you can contact the housekeeper and ask her for any further details about the house that you require.' He waited, clearly needing to continue with his day.

'Thank you for your help and your concern about my safety. I'll definitely look at improving security there as soon as possible.' She didn't say it, but she couldn't see a need to take someone with her when she went there. She'd check the exterior of the house for someone breaking in, and that should cover the security side of things.

He stood up. 'Good. I'll show you out, then. You can always get back to me if anything else crops up.'

He had, she thought, satisfied his conscience by telling her about the lack of security in general terms. She'd have to look into that side of things properly when she went to the house. And without delay. But hey, small villages didn't usually harbour criminal gangs, she thought with a smile as she left the building and went back to her car.

She sat for a moment wondering what to do first. She had a lot to think about even before she went down to Wiltshire.

She was sorry not to be going on holiday with Libby now. She didn't like letting her friend down.

Mitchell Westerby walked slowly across to the village shop to pick up his daily newspaper and a loaf. He saw three people standing gossiping near the checkout.

As they didn't see him straight away, he edged to the left just inside the entrance, picking up a few items from nearby shelves and placing them in his wire basket. He did this slowly, pretending to read the labels so that he could listen to what the other customers were saying. It was often the quickest way to find out the latest gossip.

But he could only delay for so long because the couple who owned the shop knew what he usually bought here and he had nothing different in mind today; he couldn't afford anything but necessities. After a while he went to join the others, smiling and saying 'Good morning!' as he waited in line at the checkout.

As usual he received only the faintest of smiles or nods in return. The locals barely tolerated him because they had disliked his mother and not been fond of his great-aunt, either. Well, he had shared their dislike of the old witch, if truth be told, but he hadn't been able to afford to show that because she was the one who'd brought him here and let him stay rent-free in a cottage she owned. Not that he stayed here full time. There was nothing to do in such a benighted spot. When he could afford it, he went to stay with friends.

He'd tried to get on better terms with his neighbours, hoping to join the group of men who met in the pub and sat drinking together there in the evenings. Unfortunately he hadn't succeeded. They did not, it seemed from what he'd heard, wish to associate socially with any connection of his branch of the family.

The old lady had died a few weeks ago, leaving the cottage tenancy to him for fifteen years rent free, then it was to revert to the estate. That had been a big relief because he was going through a bad patch and Lady Luck hadn't been smiling on him. Maybe by that time he'd have his other encumbrance off his hands and be free to spend all his money on himself, not to mention buying a decent flat in London, which was where he'd have preferred to live.

Of course the old hag had wanted him to do something for her in return, but it would fit in easily with his own plans.

When no one spoke to him, he took the initiative. 'You sounded excited. Has something interesting happened?'

They hesitated, then one shrugged and said, 'Don't you know about the new owner of your great-aunt's house coming here to live? It'd be a relative of yours, wouldn't it, surely?'

'I'm from another branch of Westerbys to the ones who own the big house.'

One of the more pleasant villagers said, 'We don't like to gossip but you're bound to find out, or you may even know already that it's a woman who has inherited the big house from your great-aunt. It seems she'll be coming to live here soon.'

'That'll give you a chance to suck up to her as well,' a voice said, not one he recognised or could tie to a face now.

'It's no more than I expected that a woman has inherited. That house has always been passed to the closest female relative.' He managed to say that calmly though the thought of it annoyed him. It was sexism in reverse, that was, aimed against men.

'Do you know who this female is?' someone else asked. 'All we know is she's another Miss Westerby, which doesn't tell us much about her.'

The woman next to him interrupted her friend, 'No, Jean, this one is a Ms Westerby. A person from a younger generation than the last one, probably.'

'That's what I was told,' another man said, giving Mitchell a sneering look. 'There's your chance to find a rich wife, Westerby, then you'll never have to work again.'

'I don't want any sort of wife, thank you very much, rich or not.' Which wasn't a lie. He didn't want another woman to cost him so much money as his one and only wife had done, and then run away with another man and left him with ongoing expenses from the time she'd lived with him. He kept hoping to hear that she'd divorced him, because he didn't want to waste what meagre funds he did have on lawyers or even legal advice. He'd definitely never ever marry again. Well, not unless he found a rich woman who didn't want her husband in attendance all the time.

In the meantime he'd do as the old lady wished and keep an eye on things. Cunning, she'd been, finding out about his weak spot.

He forced a smile as he looked round. 'Well, I don't know all the Westerby family details, but I shall look forward to meeting this distant relative and welcoming her to the village.'

He paid for his purchases, said farewell and left. He heard the conversation strike up in a more lively manner as he left the shop. It always did. They never chatted to him for long.

He strolled back to his cottage, scowling into the distance. The old woman had brought him to the village for a definite purpose, one that was still valid and would bring him in some money if he played his cards right. So he intended to continue doing what she'd paid him to and carry out her wishes if he could.

Did the new owner even know about his existence? He'd better check that the payments were still being made to him as arranged even though the old lady was now dead. He didn't want to waste his time.

Chapter Five

After she came out of the lawyers' rooms, Miranda got into her car but didn't start it straight away. She sat with her hands on the steering wheel, staring blindly into the distance along the street while she attempted to get her thoughts in order.

What a surprise all this was! No, make that huge surprise. Leaving everything to her was the last thing she'd ever have expected her grumpy old recluse of a great-aunt to do. Not just grumpy but nasty and manipulative, as Miranda had found out in several painful ways over the years. Phyllis had always seemed to hate her great-niece, though what the reason for that was had been a mystery.

She started to relax a little. Unlike her great-aunt, she'd want to have the place protected by a good electronic security system, so she'd need to get one installed as soon as possible if she was to feel safe living there.

Actually, she couldn't imagine what it would feel like to be the sole occupant of a large house, because her life had been spent mainly in small flats. She couldn't bear to think that an intruder might have broken in and damaged or stolen things, hated even more the thought that someone might break in and attack her after she took up residence unless she made some changes.

Someone had once tried to mug her on a quiet street that was usually safe and it still upset her sometimes to remember how she'd felt as she struggled to fight him off in the darkness and yelled for help. She was worrying about being raped when a passer-by heard her yells for help and came to her aid.

'Note to self,' she muttered, 'fit a bolt to the inside of the bedroom door straight away if possible.' She'd stop and buy one on the way there and take her household tools with her, minimal as they were. She would probably be able to fit it herself, even if it wasn't a neat job. She had a screwdriver and a small gadget for drilling holes, because she hadn't wanted to pay the high prices tradies could charge for doing even a small job.

Naturally, she didn't go back to work after that shock news. She drove home and chose a time to phone the office when she was fairly certain that her new team leader would be at one of those regular meetings he seemed to love so much. She left a vague message about having to go out of town to deal with a family bereavement and added that she wouldn't be able to come in tomorrow or the next day either.

'Lucky you. You'll be off on your holiday after that,' the young guy who'd answered her call commented enviously.

No, she wouldn't, she thought sadly as she ended the call. Only in the sense of not working for that employer would she be having any sort of holiday for quite a while now. In fact, she'd probably be even busier than usual sorting out her unexpected inheritance. The bequest sounded complicated, what with a rental cottage in the grounds whose tenant, Mitchell something or other, was apparently a distant relative and wouldn't be paying her any money for a good many years yet. There was another cottage whose tenant was called Ryan and would be paying rent. In other words, there would be all sorts of details to organise. There were also stocks, shares and bank deposits to check from Phyllis's personal estate.

Sighing, she left Libby a voice message, because her friend worked part-time in a job where she couldn't be spoken to on the phone during the day. Libby probably wouldn't be able to pick this message up until she took her lunch break.

Miranda left a brief message explaining what had happened with the answering service and said she'd appreciate it if Libby could cancel her holiday booking straight away. She'd have done it herself but her friend was the one who had made the arrangements for it with someone she knew.

The double inheritances had surprised her and she didn't feel ready to talk about this inheritance to anyone else yet, except for Libby. She'd be telling her friend the details later. Actually, she was still coming to terms with the idea of having to move to the country and change her life so completely. It'd be worth it, surely, but it'd be hard to do in some ways.

She wouldn't miss living in a small flat, nor would she be unhappy to leave her job, but she would miss having Libby living in the same block of flats, miss her greatly after the move.

Her neighbour had quickly become her closest friend, possibly the closest friend she'd ever made. Surely they'd find a way to stay in touch and make occasional visits, even if they could only interact online most of the time?

Since she was determined to do everything sensibly, Miranda had a quick snack after she got home and jotted down what to do and in what order as she sipped a mug of drinking chocolate. It would be wise to go prepared to stay overnight at the Wiltshire house, no doubt about that.

Her one and only suitcase was lying open in the second bedroom, already containing some items she'd have needed when holidaying in a warm country, such as her swimming costume. She pulled everything she'd dumped into it out again, then simplified the toiletries first, sighing regretfully as she put away the sun block lotion.

The small pile of items that was left looked forlorn in the bottom of the large suitcase. She put a nightie back with them, smiling as she did so. Most women seemed to wear pyjamas these days, but she infinitely preferred nighties, and if that made her old-fashioned, too bad. She added a couple of changes of underwear and after a few moments' thought, a more formal outfit as well. She might need to look reasonably smart to deal with the local council. Who knew? She'd never owned a big property before, only struggled her way financially into taking out a mortgage on her small flat.

Then she stared at the suitcase again. Hmm. What if it took longer than a day or two to sort out taking over ownership of the house and moving in? Better safe than sorry. She put in a few more items of clothing and her smartest business clothes. It never hurt to be well-dressed in formal work situations and this might be similar. Who knew?

She smiled, suddenly remembering a landlady who had always talked about 'business typhoons'. Was this inheritance going to turn her into one of those?

This was going to be new territory for her in several ways. Well, life sometimes took you by the throat and gave you a good shaking up, didn't it? This was probably going to be the biggest set of changes she'd ever had to face and cope with since her mother died when she was a teenager and she'd been left alone in the world emotionally.

She'd coped with that and she'd cope with this more easily, she was sure.

Given the strangeness of her great-aunt keeping all the financial details at this family house, she needed to be prepared for anything – well, as much as you ever could be when dealing with matters set in place by someone not famed for being kind to anyone except herself. She'd heard that Phyllis had got very fat in her old age, thanks to a passion for eating sweets and chocolate more often than real food.

Miranda would, of course, take along her laptop and some letter-writing materials as well, in case she had to send hard copy responses to anyone, because not everyone liked using emails or other digital communication systems. Though stationery ought to be available in Fairfield House, she had never been able to be sure of anything with her great-aunt.

After more consideration, she sorted out the fresh food that wouldn't freeze well but would go off even in the fridge if she had to stay away for a few days. She didn't like wasting anything, never ever, not anything. She'd had to be too careful with money all her adult life. She'd give this lot to Libby.

Then someone rang her doorbell and she hurried across the living area of the flat to check the spy hole. When she saw who it was, she flung the door wide open.

'Libby! Did you get my message?'

'Yes. I've cancelled your holiday. I'm afraid you get only a fifty per cent refund with it being so close to the departure date and the whole fare already paid, and you wouldn't have got that if Pam hadn't been an old friend of mine. I came to see if there was anything I could do to help you.'

'You could come in and have a glass of wine with me.'

'Excellent idea.'

They sat down and toasted lost holidays, then Libby asked gently, 'Was the person who died someone you cared about? You rarely mention your family, except for saying you haven't got any close relatives left.'

'I definitely didn't care about this woman! On the contrary. It was the old great-aunt, the one who was my guardian for several years after my mother died.'

'The one who never wanted to see you in person? You mentioned her vaguely but never gave me any details about her.'

'I didn't see the point. I never knew much about her as a person anyway and I thought my dealings with her were long over and done with.'

'That was a cruel way to treat a grieving girl.'

'Yes. She wasn't a nice person.'

'Is that why you don't talk about your family?'

She could only shrug. 'I don't have any family left to talk about now, except for a distant cousin, and I've never met him, only know about him from the family records.

But I make up for that by having some very good friends, especially you, Libby.'

She gave Miranda a quick hug. 'Thank you for that delightful compliment. I feel the same way about you.' She looked round at the signs of packing. 'Are you going down to Wiltshire tomorrow?'

'Yes. I'll have to. I'm the sole heir to two legacies, it turns out, one in the form of a family trust, the other personal from the old aunt. How weird is that? I wouldn't have expected her to leave me anything voluntarily.'

Libby listened to the account of the bequests and said only, 'Bizarre. But I hope you can use the proceeds of the trust to make a more pleasant life for yourself eventually.'

'I'll suspend judgement on that because heaven knows what I'll find there. I've never been further inside the big house than the entrance hall and the room off it, and that was as a small child. I'm not at all looking forward to going inside what I remember as a big house on my own.'

They had poured a glass of white wine each but when Miranda hardly touched hers, and kept losing track of what she was saying, Libby smiled, leant forward to pat her hand and then stood up. 'I can see that you're a bit on edge, so I'll leave you to it. I'll drink the rest of my wine at home because it's too nice to waste and I'll bring the glass back another time.'

'All right. Enjoy! And don't forget that bag of food.'

Libby pretended to tug a forelock in humble gratitude and they both chuckled.

As she stood in the open doorway, Libby said, 'It's very useful living on the ground floor here. I'll come out and wave goodbye to you tomorrow and if you think of anything you want me to take care of here while you're away, you've only to ask. What's the point of having each other's keys if we don't use them in helpful ways?'

'You could collect my post, if you don't mind. Those letter boxes in the entrance hall are far too small and any bigger envelopes stick out. Talk about skimping on details when they built this place!'

'Collecting the post is easy to do. Are you sure that's all you need doing?'

'Fairly certain. I can tell you tomorrow if I think of anything else.'

When Libby had gone, Miranda finished her packing, then tried to watch one of her favourite programmes on TV. But she couldn't settle even to that so poured her remaining wine down the sink, washed up the final few pieces of crockery, then went to read in bed.

That didn't help much, either. Even though she'd been looking forward to this new story, which was the latest book in a gripping series by her favourite author, she couldn't relax into it as she usually did.

She closed the book and put it down next to the bed, lying there staring into space till sleep overtook her. She was sure there would be unpleasant surprises waiting for her at the old family home. Phyllis would never have lost an opportunity to hurt her.

Chapter Six

When Jim Tucker's wife was diagnosed with breast cancer, they were both in shock for the first few days. Then Gracie began the course of treatment recommended by her specialist and Jim arranged to take the few months' unspent annual leave his employer had been nagging him about using up.

He had to be with his darling wife through it all. They'd fight this horrible affliction together and win, he was sure they would. They had to. He couldn't even begin to imagine life without her.

Until this happened he'd never bothered much with taking leave formally from his job as head gardener, because he loved what he did. But now he used up every single day he was entitled to. And he and Gracie certainly fought hard. They tried anything and everything, which meant a couple of stays in hospital for her.

But in spite of their best efforts, joint efforts in every way possible, she began to lose the battle. He could tell, tried not to show it, but knew she too realised she was dying. Sadly, as her condition grew rapidly worse, they had to convert their dining room into a miniature hospital.

Just as things were getting really bad, her great-nephew from Australia turned up to see her. Jim and Gracie had visited Ellery's parents in Australia once but the Deans hadn't made old bones and were both dead now.

He hadn't expected to see anyone from her side of the family, but Ellery turned out to be one of the nicest, kindest guys you could ever hope to meet and of course they invited him to stay with them, even in these circumstances. Well, apart from anything else, it distracted Gracie and she enjoyed her great-nephew's company and tales of what his parents had done down under. In addition, he was able to help Jim with the house and garden in several practical ways.

Then things went rapidly downhill and Gracie became so ill her doctor tried to persuade Jim to put her in a hospice. But she begged him not to do that, wanted to be with him as much as he wanted to be with her for every second they had left together.

With the wonderful gift of her nephew's full-time help, and some visiting palliative care nurses, Jim managed to look after her at home. He knew he'd always be glad he'd been with her till the end and she'd whispered her thanks for that many times.

Then they got to the final stage and Gracie accepted that more quickly than Jim did. It was she who tried to help him through it now. She had always been a brave lass, coping with life's problems better than he did.

It took it out of you when you were seventy, working hard to look after someone who was so very ill but with Ellery's help, and that of other kind friends, he'd managed to cope . . . somehow.

She'd whispered her thanks for that every single day and died with her hand in his and her face turned towards him with love shining out of it. He didn't know how he'd managed to smile fondly back but somehow he had, and he knew he'd always be glad he'd been with her till the very end.

The arrangements for the funeral kept him busy for a while, then the fuss ended and the empty days began.

Losing her broke his heart. People used that phrase so carelessly but it was exactly how it felt, broken into tiny pieces. He'd been so determined to save her, would have given his own life in exchange for hers willingly. But he'd failed to prevent it all happening.

Ellery comforted Jim as much as anyone could and to his relief Gracie's great-nephew stayed on a little longer.

Jim was so numb with the shock, he could hardly put two words together, so he knew he was poor company but Ellery seemed happy to sit quietly with him in the evenings without saying anything.

After a few days, however, Ellery apologised but said it was time he set off on his travels again because he didn't want to miss a cruise round Norway's coast that he was booked on.

'I'd have stayed if Gracie had still been alive and you'd needed my help,' he said apologetically.

'I'm grateful for all you've done, Ellery lad. I hope you have a wonderful time. You've more than earned that cruise.'

When he began living totally alone, Jim tried to pull himself together, to cope with the empty house, the need to cook and wash his clothes and other daily tasks. As if he cared about details like that now. But he knew Gracie would be upset if he didn't keep going to the best of his ability, so he sort of managed for a while.

He returned to his job as head gardener at Buswell House, but felt as though he was walking through mists most of the time and if it hadn't been for his two assistants helping out and covering up his lacks, the gardens would have suffered and his employer would probably have had to sack him.

But just as he was starting to settle down and do his work properly, things once more went from bad to worse. Buswell House and its extensive grounds were sold to a building company. For a while, no one seemed to know what Pearmarsh Potter, the new owners, intended to do with it.

And it wasn't only Jim who was worried now. Everyone he worked with was.

Several weeks after the funeral, when he'd been back working full-time for nearly a month, Jim was handed a letter by a uniformed courier who was waiting for him when he arrived at his office-cum-workshop in the morning. It was from the new owners, Pearmarsh Potter, and he had to sign for it.

He took the letter out to the rose garden to open it, unable to face whatever news it was the fancy envelope brought inside the office, where he always spent as little time as possible. He was an outdoor man, whatever the weather, always had been. Gracie had understood that and arranged their life accordingly.

He'd lived and worked at Buswell House for almost fifty years and knew every tree and bush there, so went to sit on his own special bench near his favourite rose bush to do this. He stared down at the envelope with its fancy letterhead in one corner, but still couldn't force himself to open it.

He knew somehow it'd be bad news – just knew it.

He hadn't paid much attention to the takeover gossip when he'd been on leave and dealing day and night with Gracie's problems. Even Mr Buswell's illness had seemed unimportant after losing her. Now, a nephew had inherited the estate and Jim had supposed things would tick along as usual with small changes.

He couldn't arouse much interest in anything except his plants as he tried to cope with life without Gracie. Were these people going to appoint one of their own gardeners to take charge now? Well, if they were, so be it. He'd done what he had to for his darling, that was what counted, not whether the gardens were thriving.

He stared across this part of the grounds. Surely these people would let him continue working here as an ordinary gardener? He was relying on his beloved plants to see him through the sadness of life without her. If anything could help him recover, it was this place. As much as you could recover from the death of your soulmate of half a century.

He frowned at the envelope again. 'Just open it,' he muttered to himself, but worries about what it contained twisted round inside his head and he didn't dare do it. What would he find? Why were these people at head office writing to him so formally now? He'd made it clear that he'd be coming back to work again this week.

What he needed now was recovery time, needed to start doing that here, in his garden, because he was still so torn apart by his great loss.

He took a deep breath and tore open the envelope suddenly, pulling out a two-page letter on paper as fancy as its covering. 'Here goes,' he muttered.

After he'd read it, he had to read it again, and even so it took a few moments for the information it contained to sink in fully. He'd been made redundant – redundant! – and they hadn't even told him that in person, just sent some bits of paper through the post.

Was he not a human being to them?

He stared down at the second part of the letter, because he didn't want to believe this could be true on top of the other news. In three brief sentences it said he had to vacate the house as well because it was a tied dwelling, one that went with the job. That shocked him even more. Didn't these new owners know this was his home?

In fact, he felt shocked rigid. He'd always thought that phrase was just a way of expressing in words your feelings at something unexpected and unpleasant but he now found it applied very accurately to how you were affected. He couldn't move for a good few minutes, was quite literally rigid with the shock of it all.

How could he ever leave this house? It was not just a home but the place where he and Gracie had lived for decades, all he had left of her now.

He studied the second page of the letter again. He had to leave the gardens as well, his gardens, so that these new owners could destroy them. It seemed that they were going to sub-divide the land into building plots and therefore wouldn't need any more work doing on the grounds as all the trees and plants needed to be removed and the area levelled before it was built on.

They were going to destroy his beautiful gardens as well as his home!

He moaned aloud and screwed the letter up, throwing

it away from him onto the ground. After a few moments he picked it up and smoothed it out, starting to read it yet again. Repetition seemed the only way to make the details of how this was to happen sink in.

They thanked him for his years of service and in view of his recent personal problems, they would give him a few weeks before he would be required to move out of his house. He would be the last person to leave and they suggested he do that at the end of this quarter, in two months' time. His redundancy money would be paid once he had cleared and vacated his cottage.

The big house and small workers' cottages like his would all have to be demolished to make way for a new arrangement of dwellings and small gardens, so as a bonus for his years of sterling service, he could take anything he wanted at no cost, including the house fittings and any plants from his own or nearby gardens.

Even the beautiful big house was to be destroyed, he read, betrayed into a few sad sobs as this further horror sank in. Why had it not been heritage listed? Then he remembered the nephew who had now inherited persuading his uncle not to do that. The fellow must have been planning this destruction for years.

The news upset Jim so much, he wept himself to sleep that night, not as bitterly as when he'd lost Gracie but getting on that way. His wife had made their home so pleasant and comfortable that being here after her death had comforted him more than anything else ever could.

He still had her ornaments on the mantelpiece, dusted them every day. Indeed, the home felt as if it was keeping the two of them together still.

Now, the three main pillars of his life were all being

taken away from him in what seemed like the blink of an eye and he wished fate had swept him away with them as well. Why had he been left behind like this? He was no use to anyone now.

To make matters worse, he had completely run out of energy and was feeling his age fully for the first time ever. It hurt him to the depths of his soul that he couldn't even stay in his home and he lay in bed for the whole of one morning, just lay there, couldn't find the strength to get up.

The original owner had once promised that Jim would be allowed to stay on there even after he retired, but Mr Buswell clearly hadn't put that in writing as Jim had assumed he would do after their chat.

Once Mr Buswell's money-hungry nephew had come to live with him and help, everything had begun to change for the worse. He'd nibbled off a bit of land here and sold it to a stranger to build a big ugly house on. Nibbled off another bit there and then sold that as well, all with council agreement to the changes.

And once Mr Buswell died, they'd started to plan total destruction of what was left. Previously the council had refused to approve such changes to land use. What had made them change their minds? Who knew?

Two days later, Jim pulled himself together and went to the nearest job exchange. This was not because he wanted or even needed to go on 'the dole' as he still thought of it, because he had enough money to 'see him out' as people often put it. Well, he'd hardly ever spent much, only when Gracie decided she wanted something, and his work had provided plenty of home-grown fruit and vegetables so living had been relatively cheap.

What he intended to do now was ask for these people's help in finding a similar job. It was his only hope.

He needed another garden to care for if he was going to lose this one, needed it quite desperately. The only place he felt he could manage to go on living without his lass or their long-time home was in another garden. He'd care for the plants skilfully because he knew his job. And he'd find a way to put in the sort of flowers she'd loved most and let them comfort him as much as anything could.

Gardens did that. He simply couldn't live without one. Just – could – not. Surely that wasn't too selfish, too much to ask? Surely the modern world still needed gardeners?

The woman at the job exchange sat him in front of a computer and asked him to answer some questions showing on the screen. He stared at them in bewilderment. Not only did the questions it was asking have no connection with what he needed from these people, but he didn't know how to use a computer. Gracie had always seen to that sort of thing and he'd given hers away to one of his friends after she died.

When he confessed to that lack of knowledge, the woman sighed loudly and an uppity young chap was called out of the back part of the building to help. This fellow took him into a cubicle to ask him questions, fiddling with the computer after each of the first two, then stopping to stare at Jim, looking surprised.

'I'm sorry, Mr Tucker, but you've turned seventy. That's too old to be found work by us, especially the hard physical work you're asking for. You're far too old to cope with that anyway.'

'I'm not! I've not been coping with it, I've been enjoying it all my life! I still am! I was working in a garden digging out a new flower bed only yesterday.' He'd sneaked one in at the side, near the hedge, hoping they'd keep it after he'd gone.

'Good for you. But why do you want another job when you can retire, collect the state pension, or your private superannuation if you've got some, and take things more easily from now on?'

'I need another job, need it very much. I don't like sitting around doing nothing.' Jim explained about losing his wife and home.

'Ah. I see. Well, we'll find a place for you in an old folks' home since your house is going to be demolished. You'll be able to make new friends there and the management will put on entertainments and little hobby classes for you to attend. They may even allow you to potter about in their garden if you can show them you know what you're doing.'

He glared at the arrogant young sod, speaking more sharply than usual. 'I've earned my living gardening for more than fifty years and ended up as head gardener on a large estate, Buswell House in fact. Do you think they would have employed me for over fifty years, or I'd have ended up managing the grounds and two workers for them if I hadn't known what I was doing?'

The man blinked, didn't even try to answer that, then shrugged and ignored what he'd said. 'Please calm down, sir, and listen carefully. You're coming into a new phase of life now where you won't have to work so hard. And anyway, work is changing for us all these days, isn't it?'

He didn't say it but he couldn't help thinking that plants didn't know that, not unless humans fiddled around with them anyway. He tried to concentrate on what this chap was rabbiting on about, as Gracie would have said, but had difficulty concentrating.

'We'll give you priority for a place to live and in the meantime we'll put you in some emergency accommodation until somewhere suitable becomes vacant.'

'What do you mean by emergency accommodation?'

'A temporary lodging house for people to stay in till we can find them somewhere suitable to live. There's a bit of a shortage of permanent accommodation round here for people your age at the moment, I'm afraid, but we do make sure these temporary places are clean and you'll have people your own age to chat to there, at least. You'll only be sharing a bedroom with one other person at most and there will be a common room to sit in during the daytime, if you're not out for walks or off to visit the library. Most people get bedrooms of their own later on in their stay, even before they move on to a permanent placing.'

It was hard not to show his indignation. He would never willingly share a bedroom with a stranger and after only a few seconds of reflection, he immediately vowed mentally to refuse point blank to do that. 'I'd rather get a job and support myself, thank you. I enjoy my work and I've always been an active sort of chap, so I'm very fit for my age.'

'I can't help you to find the sort of work you're used to, I'm afraid. It's dealt with by another section of the department, one which finds jobs for the younger folk with families to support. They take priority. Oldies like you usually want to retire.' He stared at Jim indignantly.

'I'm perfectly capable of working and supporting myself, and I'd much prefer to go on doing that, thank you very much. Surely the government will want to save the money it'd have to spend paying me a pension for doing nothing?'

But the young fellow didn't seem to be listening and began fiddling with the keyboard again.

What were these officials intending to do with the information they'd taken down about him? Jim wondered. Where did that computer send it to? He had no idea what those damned machines did with what you told them, only that they could apparently communicate with one another across long distances. All he knew was that they absolutely baffled him and he had better things to do than spend his days fiddling around on those tiny keys and ruining his eyesight by squinting at a screen only a few inches from his nose.

The young man pushed his chair back and stood up. 'Thank you, sir. That'll do for a start. This way, please.'

He showed Jim into another stuffy little room where there was some food sitting on a shelf at the back and two small plastic tables, each with garish matching green plastic chairs to sit on while you ate the anonymous sandwiches and the tiny greyish-beige cakes with their uneven dabs of bright pink icing sugar on top. Ugh! The sight of them took away his appetite. Gracie would never have made him something as nasty in appearance as that. The cakes looked as if they were made of plastic as well as the chairs and table.

'It'll be an hour or two at least before I can find you somewhere to stay tonight, so just help yourself to food if you're hungry,' the young fellow said with another of those glassy-eyed smiles that meant nothing. 'The toilets are next door and you can switch on that TV and watch it if you like while you're waiting.'

As if he ever sat and watched TV when the sun was shining outside, Jim thought scornfully. He tried to tell the young chap that he didn't have to leave his home for a week or two but the idiot hurried out without listening. A lot of youngsters were like that when dealing with older folk. It felt sometimes as if they spoke a different language or had lost their hearing when you did manage to get a word in edgeways about what they'd asked you without them repeating it wrongly.

A minute later, the young chap popped through the doorway again and tossed an envelope on the small table. It landed next to Jim's hand. Couldn't he even be bothered to pass it, or was he afraid of touching a client?

'I nearly forgot to give you this emergency pension book, Mr Tucker. You can take it to any post office once a week on a Thursday and they'll pay you that week's pension. Once you're living somewhere permanent again we can get you a bank account proper payment system sorted out for paying your old age pension. But you might have to move lodgings once or twice before you're settled so we'll leave that till later.'

Once again, he spoke to Jim as if he was a half-witted child, not a mature adult, adding slowly in words of one syllable, 'You paid in for this. You should have been claiming it for years.'

Jim breathed deeply but didn't let his temper loose, or waste his breath telling this young idiot again that he'd much rather work for a living, thank you very much. What was the point? There were none so deaf as those who closed their eyes and ears to other folk, as his dear Gracie used to say.

He blinked, determined not to let these strangers see how upset the thought of her always made him feel.

The man mistook why he was upset, of course he did, not bothering to ask what was wrong. 'No hurry for you to do anything from now on, Mr Tucker. I'll sort everything out for you.'

'But I don't need to—'

The youngster didn't even try to listen, had already turned his back and was walking out.

Jim tossed the worst curses he could think of after him, speaking them aloud, something he normally only did out in the garden when pests got at his seedlings. Or he might whisper them soundlessly inside his mind when someone particularly annoyed him as this chappie had.

After that he got himself organised to escape as quickly as he could.

He was not, repeat not, moving into an old folks' home and ending his life shut away indoors. Never, ever. He'd feel as if he were suffocating.

Chapter Seven

As part of preparing for his escape, Jim gobbled down one of the bland-looking sandwiches, pulling a face at its lack of taste. He couldn't identify what sort of meat was in this floppy lump and the bread was not only distinctly stale but pure white in colour. It was utterly tasteless after Gracie's lovely wholemeal bread and they'd taken all the goodness out of it by removing the husk.

But nonetheless it was free and would fill him for a while, so he ate another couple of the sandwiches anyway because these officials had kept him waiting a long time for this so-called interview and he was actually hungry now. He'd always had a hearty appetite – well, he had done till Gracie died, anyway.

He moved towards the door, thinking to leave, then turned back and packed a few more of the sandwiches and some of the little cakes into a couple of the polythene bags he always kept in his knapsack because you never knew when they'd come in useful for putting plants or cuttings in. And they were useful for other unexpected needs too, like today's debacle.

Afterwards he put the bags of food gently back into the top of his backpack for a later meal because he didn't have much food left at home – or much appetite for it either, a lot of the time. It was probably the anger that had made him hungry today. But things were going downhill so rapidly he felt it was best to be prepared now in case he had to run away to avoid being forcibly removed from his house and locked up inside an old folks' home.

He remembered a song Gracie had loved and had always sung so beautifully along with the record. 'Fly Me to the Moon', it was called, well, he thought it was. He wished he could do that now, fly far away. With her beside him, of course.

He kept glancing at his watch. He needed to hurry because he wanted to get away from here before the young chap returned. Besides, this was such an airless place it made him feel as if he were suffocating and he desperately needed some fresh air to breathe real life into his mind and body. Being outside would allow him to think more clearly about his current problems, he hoped. It usually did anyway.

He visited the conveniences, then investigated where all the other doors in the hallway led and found one that opened straight into the outside. He studied a yard which had a line of dustbins set neatly next to a gate. He breathed a deep sigh of relief as he was able to leave through that gate without being seen by that other young fusspot at the front desk.

Taking a few deep breaths of fresh air – well, as fresh as you got near the centre of a town – he walked quietly along the alley behind this big square monster of a building, which had lots of small, square windows in it. He'd bet that inside the place was full of small square offices like those on the floor he'd had to get out of the airless lift at. Ugh! Imagine spending your life shut up in a place like that.

He came out of the alley at a nearby street and turned away from the town centre instinctively. He'd never liked going into busy town centres, though of course you couldn't always avoid it. The streets always stank of traffic fumes and inside most shops you got the reek of stale bodies and of sickly air fresheners, which were nothing like natural flower scents, whatever the labels on them said.

When a taxi slowed right down as it drove past him with the driver bending his head to look sideways at him as if asking whether he needed a ride, he nodded and asked to be taken home. He knew it was extravagant not waiting for the bus, but he needed to sort out a few things then escape from this part of the world before they could try to shut him in a shared bedroom inside another stuffy building.

It was going to hurt to leave the only home he'd known for so many years, hurt so very badly, but he wanted to get as far away as possible in case they used his home address to trace him and come after him. He wasn't quite sure who was running the world in this way, but he didn't intend whoever it was to catch up with him and stuff him inside a building for the rest of his life.

At home, he shoved some basic necessities into his knapsack, underclothes and packets of nuts and biscuits. He had some left so shook open a bin liner and put them in that. Thank goodness for his years of being a Scout, and then a Scout Leader. You learnt a lot of useful practical stuff in the Scouts. He could pack bags with the best of them, and do it quickly and efficiently too.

Next he phoned an old friend who lived in a nearby village and asked Brook to come over early the following morning and pick up a few boxes then store them in his second shed until Jim could come and retrieve them. He knew Brook would say yes when he heard about them taking away the car. He and his wife had been good friends of Jim and Gracie for many years.

A rather fancy box contained the family photos, though he took one small photo of Gracie and another of their wedding out of it to carry with him for comfort, then was tempted into taking a few more. How young and full of hope he and Gracie had looked at their wedding! They'd felt it too, young and optimistic, with a happy life stretching in front of them.

Where had all their years together gone? Disappeared without leaving a real trace in the world, he thought sadly. If only they'd been able to have children, he might not be on his own now. You liked to think your family would carry on when you were gone. He didn't even know where any relatives were these days. They'd scattered all round the world, the Tuckers had, and so had Gracie's lot, the Westerbys.

He stared bleakly round the rest of the house, which looked an utter mess now. Eh, his wife would throw a fit if she saw it. He could do better than leaving it like this for people to view scornfully, so he phoned the local charity shop and asked them if they'd like to come round the following afternoon and clear out the rest of the things in the house he was leaving because it was going to be demolished and he was going to live in another part of the country.

'You want everything clearing out?' the voice at the other end asked, sounding cautious.

'Every single thing, including the cooker and washing machine if they're any use. They're in good working order and I was told by the owners that if I don't want to take them they'll be going to the tip.'

'Who said that?'

'It's written on a piece of paper, by someone at the council, I suppose.' He shook his head sadly. The wasteful fools took all sorts of half-used things to the tip these days. It made him so angry at times, when these could have been reused or repurposed as folk seemed to call it nowadays.

'We'll do that happily, sir, as long as you leave us the paper authorising this.'

'I'll leave it on the mantelpiece in the living room.'

'That'll be fine, sir. Tomorrow afternoon, you said. Thank you for thinking of us.'

They couldn't see him shrug. Well, he didn't think he'd ever need a house full of furniture again so why not give it to someone with the sense to get more use out of it. When he settled down somewhere once more, he supposed it'd be in accommodation supplied with a job. Surely he'd find a job again, working in some place in the country with a decent garden. He just couldn't abide to living in a town. And you didn't need much furniture for just one person.

If he didn't find a live-in job, maybe he'd buy a little caravan for himself and find a permanent place to park it, deep in the country, somewhere with allotments nearby where he could still grow things. He went to bed intending to think about that, but was so tired he slept quite well for the first time since he'd lost Gracie.

* * *

The following morning, Brook arrived soon after dawn and took away the boxes of things Jim wanted to keep and when invited to take any of the furniture he could use, he selected a couple of small pieces, Gracie's sewing box for one.

'Where are you going, Jim lad? Do you have a phone number for it or for a mobile?'

'I don't know where so I don't have one, and you know I don't use one of those fiddly little phones. But you have my email address, don't you, Brook lad? Gracie got one for me on that damned computer of hers and I can always get someone to help me check it. I hardly ever use it, mind, so don't expect a quick response, but she said it'd work wherever I went.'

'Yes, I do have it. And I can keep your things here in my old shed for as long as you need, with or without you contacting me. What's more, if you're ever short of somewhere to stay in an emergency, you can come to us for a while. Just turn up. You know that, don't you?'

'Yes. And it's a great comfort. Thanks. I've got cousins I can go to as well. For the moment, I just want to get away from here because I don't want to watch these developers knock my home down and flatten my lovely trees and shrubs.'

'I'd feel the same. Don't you need a car of your own to get away in, though, now they've taken that company car away from you? There's a place that sells second-hand vehicles just down the road on the way into town, you know. They're well thought of locally.'

He wasn't doing that and giving anyone a chance to trace him wherever he went. 'I feel like a good long walk first. You know how I love going for walks. It'll clear my head to tramp across the countryside and make me feel younger again, I hope. I can get a B&B somewhere when it grows dark, and I'll buy a car in a day or two, when I tire of walking.'

'Well, as long as you've got enough money to do that, I'll say goodbye and let you get on with your preparations. Take care of yourself, lad. And don't forget that we're here if you need us.' Brook gave him one of those abrupt manly hugs that always embarrassed Jim, then got into his car and drove off.

Now, there was a good friend, he thought. Only, he needed to be on his own for a while now to find himself again. It was over fifty years since he'd lived on his own. It was going to be hard getting used to it. He went back to his preparations, turning a couple of times to ask Gracie something, then remembering that she was dead and losing a few more tears.

It was very early the following morning that Jim walked away from his home. He didn't look back. Tears trickled down his cheeks and he let himself weep. He had a lot to weep for, couldn't hold them in sometimes and didn't care who saw him crying now. But he didn't meet anyone out so early, let alone anyone he knew, which was a bit of a relief in one way because it took him a while to stop crying.

He wished he still had what he thought of as his own car. He'd had the inside of it organised to suit his needs and had always carried a few small emergency items. Those damned developers had refused to sell it to him whatever he said or did. Heartless, they were.

When he persisted with his nagging, they told him they no longer owned the car. They'd done a mass deal for all the company cars and couldn't make any exceptions and would he please stop being such a nuisance? He was to hand it over at the end of the week, as they'd already told him, because this batch of vehicles was due to be taken away next Monday and it'd need a good clean.

No, it wouldn't! he thought indignantly. He always prided himself on keeping it immaculate. You weren't an individual these days, just a number, and your own needs couldn't be catered for. These big companies seemed only to serve the great god Money – and their senior executives' needs. Oh, yes. They didn't go short!

He wiped his last few tears away and walked slowly on towards the main road where he started trying to hitch a lift. And for the first time in ages his luck was in, which he hoped was a sign that he was doing the right thing.

A kindly lorry driver stopped almost at once and took him right out of town, away from the stinking fumes and the heartless folk who pulled your life to pieces and couldn't make any exceptions.

Eh, he was still upset about that, upset about losing everything he'd once valued. In fact, his head was a blurry jumble of anguish but he thought he managed to answer the driver's questions, more or less anyway. He hoped he had, because it wasn't this chap's fault. He seemed a nice young fellow.

Only Jim couldn't be sure he'd been as polite with him as he usually was with strangers. He told the chap he was heading to the same part of the country as the sign on the side of the lorry and got a quick smile in response.

'I'll be able to take you most of the way there, then, Grandad.' His voice softened. 'Will you be all right after that? You seem a bit upset.'

'I've just lost, um, a good friend.'

'Oh, sorry to hear that. My commiserations. My grandad's friends keep dying and he gets upset too. Well, you would, wouldn't you?'

After a minute or two he realised the driver was waiting for him to speak, so he said, 'Thank you for picking me up.'

'My pleasure. Will you be all right after I drop you?'

'Yes. It's just that I, um, only heard yesterday, haven't got used to it yet.'

'I'm sorry about that. It can be hard. I lost my mother last year. I still remember things she used to say and it makes me feel sad. Eh, I loved her strong Lancashire accent. Funny thing to miss, isn't it? I've never met anyone who spoke quite like her. She didn't lose the accent even after she married Dad and moved south.'

Jim nodded and made a sound in his throat. As he'd hoped, the man took it as a sign to carry on, doing most of the talking from then on, thank goodness.

They seemed to get to Bristol more quickly than Jim had expected and he asked the young guy to pull up in a layby on the outskirts of the city.

'Will you be all right from here, Grandad?'

'Yes, thank you, lad. I'll get another lift quickly, I'm sure. Folk are usually very kind. I need to turn off the main road now. I'm really grateful for your help today.'

'I enjoyed your company. Good luck!'

Jim stood watching him go, smiling till his face ached as the man insisted on giving him a can of some bright red fizzy drink he'd never touch and a piece of his wife's homemade cake, which did look good.

He let the smile fade as he watched the vehicle move

away. What this kind chap had enjoyed most had been having a tame listener. And it had been a small payment to give him in return for the lift. Besides, the mindless chat had saved Jim the trouble of forcing out words very often.

He set off walking, a slow, steady tramp along the side of the road, looking for a turn-off into the countryside. He needed some fresh air now, not these car fumes. He was grateful that it was late spring and quite mild today. It made walking a pleasure. He decided to stick to small villages as much as he could, so avoided following any signposts that directed travellers to bigger towns and turning towards villages instead.

During the next few days he found places to sleep in old and sometimes half-ruined barns and sheds. He was more or less comfortable because he slept more soundly after a day's walking than in a bed with no Gracie beside him. And he was no longer shut up in rooms he considered airless, with windows that only opened a little.

He forgot about providing food for himself the second day. He'd been so lost in thought and memories that darkness caught him unawares. There were no shops nearby, just a few houses in a small group. He was so hungry he was reduced to scrabbling in the dustbins of a nearby house whose occupants must have gone away recently. Luckily, he found some unspoilt food.

Eh, Gracie would have been disgusted about him eating that. But he needed something to eat badly by then, because the walking had made him ravenously hungry.

He dreamt of his wife, which was lovely till he woke up to bleak reality again.

Chapter Eight

Miranda was ready to leave at twenty to eight the following morning so decided not to hang about in the flat but to set off straight away and risk meeting busier rush hour traffic at the start of her journey. She took her case and insulated bag of food with some containers of leftovers in it out to her car.

When she'd closed them in the boot she turned to see Libby standing nearby and sadness welled up. She was going to miss this particular neighbour so much and knew Libby would miss her just as badly.

'I thought I'd come and wave you off.' Her friend tried to smile but didn't manage to do it properly and still looked sad. 'I had a bet with myself that you'd be ready to leave well before eight, and you are.'

'I didn't sleep very well.'

'Why am I not surprised about that?'

She came across and gave the younger woman a long, rocking hug. 'Drive double carefully, love, and come back safely to visit me whenever you can. And at least email me regularly or I'll worry.'

Then she stepped back, looking even more sad now as she murmured, 'I'll miss you so much.'

But when Miranda settled herself in the car and turned on the engine, all she got from the motor was a sick-sounding cough then silence. She tried several more times to start the car, but to no avail.

Libby walked across the car park in her slippers and signalled to her to raise the bonnet, then fiddled with some of the connections, looking as if she knew what she was doing, and she did know a lot more about cars than Miranda. Most people did.

But even Libby's efforts were in vain. The only sound that could be persuaded from the motor now was the faint click of the key turning.

Miranda abandoned the attempts to start the car and got out, scowling at it. 'I suppose I'll have to call a breakdown service and if they can't get it started, I'll see if I can hire a car for a few days.'

'You certainly shouldn't try to go anywhere in this one even if someone can get it going for you. What if it broke down again in the middle of nowhere? When's the last time you had it serviced, my dear girl? Your engine could do with a good clean and who knows what else?'

Miranda shrugged. 'I don't use the car all that often, as you know, because I can walk to the Underground station and I've been working only two streets away from one of the stops on that line. So I only get my car serviced about once a year, if that.'

She held up one hand as Libby looked as if she was going to scold her. 'I'm not utterly stupid. I did check the water and petrol yesterday afternoon as I was getting ready, and they were fine.'

'It's a very old car, you know, and this model never was well thought of. Yours probably died of fright at the mere idea of making such a long journey. You really should trade it in – though you might not get anyone to offer you more than twenty pence for it in that condition.'

Miranda managed a faint smile at the feeble joke – well, she hoped it had been a joke. Only, with public transport being so good round here and easier to get to work on, she went for very few drives apart from to and from the shops when she needed a big buy-in of basics and heavier items. She'd not seen any point in upgrading to a more modern vehicle.

She turned to her friend, saw Libby hesitate and asked, 'Is there something else you need to tell me about it?'

'Not tell you, but I was wondering—' She broke off.

'Go on. Wondering what?'

'Whether you'd like me to drive you there in my car. It's not only far more modern than yours, but far more comfortable too.'

'That's a lovely, kind offer but I can't ask you to do that. You're going on holiday in another couple of days.'

'You didn't ask; I volunteered. And actually I've got two weeks' leave and nothing much to do with it now.' She gave her a rueful smile. 'I cancelled for both of us yesterday, you see, not just you. I didn't fancy going abroad on my own. I was looking forward to your company as much as to seeing Italy again. And if you've stayed in one luxury hotel – and I've stayed in quite a few in my time – you won't find much difference in what the next one can offer you once you've looked at the nearby scenery.'

Miranda could only gape and wasn't at first sure what to say. Then she saw the utter kindness in her friend's expression, and also the diffidence and look of someone fearing a rebuff, so said, 'Do you really mean that? You'd drive me there?'

'Of course I mean it. I'd not have offered otherwise. I enjoy driving, actually.'

'Then I accept gratefully but you must let me pay for the petrol and any other incidental expenses. We may even need to stay overnight somewhere if the house is in too much of a mess, and if so, that'll be on me as well.'

'Well, my petrol tank is full at the moment but you can pay to refill it when we get back or while we're away, whenever it's needed. And we surely ought to be able to sleep in your new home if we have to stay in Wiltshire overnight. I shan't care if the place is rather run-down and dusty. Don't forget, that house is yours now to do what you want with so we can clear things up as we choose and sleep on the living-room furniture if necessary.' She cocked her head at Miranda. 'There won't be anyone there to tell you it's not allowed. You're sole owner of the place now.'

'I keep having to remind myself of that.' She shook her head. 'Maybe it'll feel like it's mine once I've seen it. I don't even have a clear idea of what it looks like, you know, inside or out, let alone whether it's fit to be slept in.'

'I'm happy to take the risk. We can always find a bed and breakfast place if it's too bad. Just don't forget to take the front door key that the lawyer gave you.'

'It's safe in my shoulder bag.' Miranda still hesitated. 'You're sure about this?'

'Of course I'm sure and it's good that we'll be going on a trip together as far as I'm concerned. It's what we were planning to do anyway when we booked a joint holiday in Italy.'

Miranda flung her arms round her. 'You're wonderful. The more time I spend with you, Libby, the more I enjoy and appreciate your company. It's what I've always imagine having an aunt would be like, if you don't mind me saying that. I've never really had any relatives, just that horrible great-aunt and I didn't want to be related to her. So it's you I think of when people at work talk about aunts.'

'That's a lovely thing to say.'

'I meant it totally. And it'll be a relief to have someone with me, I must admit. I've been a bit worried about what I'll find there because the house has been unoccupied for several weeks and the lawyer said it'd be wiser not to go on my own.'

'Did he really? Then that's what we'd better do, go together.'

'I won't even know what things ought to be like, inside or out, because I've only visited it once, and that was when I was about four. My mother and I didn't get past a small sitting room at the front and I have only a hazy memory of the main entrance, which I think had double doors.'

She added softly, as if thinking aloud, 'Mostly I remember Mum and another lady, who turned out to be the old aunt, shouting and arguing really loudly, and that frightened me.' She felt sadness wrap round her as it often did when she thought about her mother, who had died young, thanks to a drunken lorry driver slamming into her car and shunting it into a tree.

When she looked up again she saw her friend looking at her sympathetically. 'Sorry. That reminded me of my mother. I still remember her so clearly and miss her hugs.'

'Of course you do. That's natural when you've loved someone, so take your time. I must say, though, that you and I have bonded very quickly and I too feel like a sort of aunt. I often want to hug you, especially when I see you with that lost, closed expression on your face, trying to hide your loneliness from the world.'

Trust Libby to notice that about her, Miranda thought. She was a very caring sort of person and extremely perceptive.

Her friend hesitated, then began speaking again. 'There's something I've been wondering about . . .'

But she frowned and stopped so Miranda said, 'Go on. Tell me. Surely we know one another well enough by now to share what we really feel.'

'I don't have any close relatives left in England, haven't had for a good while. The family members I loved most when I was young emigrated to Canada many years ago. They asked me to go with them, but I didn't want to leave England. It's not only my country but my heart's home, somehow.'

She took a deep breath then added slowly, 'My oldies are all dead now and I'm getting older myself, so how about you adopt me as an honorary aunt? I'd love to return the favour and adopt you as a niece.'

Miranda stared at her visitor, so touched by this offer that tears welled suddenly in her eyes and her voice came out as a scratchy whisper. 'It really does feel sometimes as if you and I are related and you're how I imagine a proper aunt would be, not like that horrible old hag was.'

'You only sometimes feel as though I'm an aunt?' she teased.

'All the time, actually, now I've got to know you better. I

don't understand why, but it's as if you and I are linked, as if I could turn to you with any problem and ask your help in solving it, and share my joys with you, too.'

She'd never had anyone else close enough to share her innermost feelings with since her mother's death. Phyllis Westerby had been the nastiest person she'd ever met and she'd quickly learnt not to betray any weaknesses to her.

Those guarded ways had mostly stayed up against the rest of the world too. But somehow, this woman was different, somehow she was utterly certain she could say anything to Libby, trust her with any secrets or thoughts.

'You can ask for my help any time you like and I'll be happy to give it, Miranda. But you don't have to agree to treat me as an aunt unless you're absolutely sure about it.'

'I've never had a loving aunt, so don't really know what I can say or do with one, but I always feel comfortable with you so maybe that's a good start.'

She shook her head in disgust and added, 'I certainly don't count my great-aunt as a genuine relative, because I haven't spoken to her in person since I was a teenager. I remember her eyes so clearly still. They had no warmth in them, let alone love or kindness, none whatsoever. Even as a small child I noticed that and was afraid of even standing too close to her. Luckily for me, she didn't want me to.'

She paused for a moment, staring blindly into the distance again. 'Now that she's dead, I'm the last remaining Westerby in this branch of the family and I only know of one other distant connection from another branch. So an adopted aunt would be absolutely wonderful.'

'That must make you feel very lonely. Tell me about the other remaining Westerby.'

'It's some male cousin but I don't even want to meet

him. He's about my age and I've heard that he's already been made bankrupt once because of his spendthrift ways and gambling.'

'Who did you hear it from?'

She froze and stared at her companion. 'My great-aunt.'

'Then you'd be better waiting to meet him before you pass judgement, don't you think?'

She nodded slowly. 'Why did that not occur to me?'

Libby's voice grew softer. 'Because financial security is very important to you, isn't it, love? That great-aunt knew exactly which buttons to press to keep you two apart.'

'Money is all I've had to rely on for most of my life. If you treat it carefully it doesn't let you down. Relatives are more chancy.'

'Well, I grew up with lots of them and even so the younger ones scattered across the world and never came back to the UK to live. None of them bother to keep in touch these days, even at Christmas, so I might as well not have any relatives at all. The oldies were better at keeping in touch, but most of them have passed away now.'

She smiled rather sadly. 'They were always full of fascinating stories about family members from previous generations and I loved to listen to them. But as the years passed, the people ebbed and flowed like human tides and all the ones still alive have been washed away and presumably made landfall permanently on distant shores now.'

'I made some good friends at university,' Miranda said softly, 'but you don't stay as close once you all graduate and scatter across the country. And when they get married and start building their own families and having kids, relationships with far-away friends inevitably seem to become less important to them. Unfortunately, my one and only attempt at marriage was a disaster.'

'Your life isn't over yet. There's still time to do better about that.'

Miranda felt tears welling in her eyes again and fumbled for a tissue, muttering, 'Sorry!'

Libby pressed a tissue into her hand, gave her fingers a quick squeeze around it then sat staring out of the window as her companion dabbed at her eyes. When she looked across again she smiled gently, waiting, not seeming at all impatient to carry on the conversation till her companion was ready.

Miranda looked back at her and then, feeling solemn, as if this was an important moment in her life, she asked, 'What made you offer to be my honorary aunt, Libby?'

'I've grown fond of you. And also – well, this may sound silly but I had my fortune told once when I was in my late teens and the clairvoyant was very impressive. She told me things about myself she couldn't have found out from public sources, shouldn't have known at all, and they were all true or have come true since. She ended up saying I'd have to find new relatives as I grew older because my own family would have scattered around the world by then. And she said one person in particular would need and care about my friendship as much as I'd need and value hers.'

Tears were trickling down her cheeks now. 'I remembered that clairvoyant as I started getting to know you, and I began to wonder if I should think about trying to adopt some relatives. If so you'll be the first one I've found, though I hope not the last.'

'I hope we can find others together,' Miranda said quietly. 'Form a family of our own.'

'So I'm going to start by gaining a niece to love?'

'Yes please.' Miranda gulped audibly. 'Do you want to be Auntie Libby or Aunt Libby?'

'Use whichever term comes into your mind at the time. Either would be great.' She pulled the younger woman into another hug, then smoothed her hair back from her forehead in a motherly gesture and said, 'Stop worrying about unimportant details. The main thing was that this hug felt right and was the first of many, I hope. Never hesitate to hug me.'

'You've always been a touchy-feely person. Even with near strangers, I watch you sometimes pat their hands or their shoulders casually. I think that's a lovely trait.'

'Good. You can hug me as often as you please, and can call on me for help or company or whatever else you may need at any time.'

'And you must do the same with me.'

As they stepped back from one another, Libby raised an imaginary glass and said, 'We'll drink to that properly tomorrow in Wiltshire and get an early night tonight. We'd better take some wine with us in case your great-aunt didn't indulge, yes and fizzy wine too, which always makes things seem more special. I shall enjoy sharing a glass or two of bubbly with my new niece in her new home.'

More imaginary glasses were raised and they both took invisible sips from them then chuckled at the same time.

'You need to share a similar sense of humour, too, to get really close to people,' Miranda said thoughtfully.

'I agree. Anyway, how about getting on with planning the other thing I offered to do for you? How quickly do you want to set off for Wiltshire tomorrow?'

'As soon as we can so that we get as much daylight as

possible to look round the house and gardens at the other end. The lawyer said the services like electricity have been left on, but you see things so much more clearly in daylight, don't you? No nasty surprises can lurk in dark corners if there are no patches of darkness.'

'Good thinking.'

Miranda beamed at her. 'I always enjoy your company, apart from needing your help now. Are you sure you can spare the time this week?'

'Utterly certain. I'd better phone my boss and let him know I won't be able to go into work tomorrow as I've been called away. I'll do the same as you and say I've had a family bereavement, because it's sort of true. As it's just before my annual holiday he'll tell me to stay away till I get back, then to let him know once whatever needs doing is all sorted out, and we can set up a new work schedule then. He's such a kind man.'

'Won't he mind you taking over two weeks off?'

'No. I inherited some money from an old cousin years ago, so if I'm careful I don't need to go out to work. I go in part time because I enjoy the company there but he's got plenty of other part-timers he can call on for help. It's not skilled work serving the sort of elderly customers you get in shops in that part of town but I really enjoy looking after their needs. They often come in for a bit of company as well as to buy food.'

'Old age can be lonely. I saw a TV programme about it only a week or two ago.'

'Yes, it can. Middle age isn't always wonderful, either.'

She didn't elaborate on that, which made Miranda wonder if she'd been lonely as well.

Libby waved one hand. 'Anyway let's get back to

tomorrow's arrangements. I'll pack tonight and we can set off as soon as it's daylight. I think we should take one or two changes of clothes just in case we need to stay for a few days.'

'Yes. Good idea. You're a brilliant organiser. I've noticed that before. Will you be all right driving all the way? I'm not all that good at coping with strange cars because I don't actually do a lot of driving. And do you know Wiltshire at all?'

'I don't know it very well. I've only driven through it on my way to Devon but not stayed there or explored the countryside.'

'I don't know much about that part of the world either, so we can explore it together if we decide to stay in the house for a while.'

'I'd enjoy that. And to answer your original question, yes, I shall not only be fine about driving there but extremely happy to do it, with the help of my trusty satnav. I don't get enough long-distance outings because it's no fun going anywhere on your own.'

'Thank goodness for you.'

'We'll set off tomorrow at dawn, then, shall we?'

'Yes.'

'And we could pool our leftovers for tea tonight.'

'Great thought.'

Miranda walked back up to her own flat, feeling distinctly happier about the coming changes to her life. She packed a few additional items of clothing, one set of what she called business clothes in case she had to deal with officials, and another outfit that was casually smart, suitable for going into a pub for a drink or two with a friend. Only this time it'd be with a relative. She was going to consider Libby a real relative, she decided, and dabbed her eyes at the mere thought of that, it felt so wonderful.

Strange that she hadn't hesitated to accept Libby's offer when she was normally so cautious about getting pushed into new situations that might cause difficulties. Only, it had felt right as they made plans, more than right, absolutely perfect in every respect.

She'd been alone for so long. How wonderful to have someone once again whom she trusted. She had certainly never trusted her great-aunt, on the contrary, and even though she hadn't dealt with the old witch in person, there had been quite a few times when things had gone wrong unexpectedly and she'd wondered if the woman was trying to hurt her or stop her doing something she'd planned.

That evening, she and Libby enjoyed a strange mixture of leftover foods for tea, then separated to get an early night.

Miranda was smiling as she got into bed, looking forward to going with someone. She hoped she would get a good night's sleep for once. She wanted to be very alert when she got to her new home, just in case there were any nasty surprises waiting for her there. She'd have to warn Libby about her great-aunt but hadn't wanted to spoil an enjoyable evening.

She snuggled down, murmuring, 'Auntie Libby'. And for once she did sleep well.

Chapter Nine

Ryan Sinclair was now waiting for the finalisation of the purchase of the country cottage. At last he would own a home of his own, fully own it with no mortgage owing.

He raised a clenched fist in a gesture of triumph at that thought, then finished packing his final bag of odds and ends early, and grinned as he caught sight of his face in the mirror. He knew he wouldn't be able to stop smiling like a happy idiot all day once he'd left here.

He glanced round with a scowl now replacing the smile. He'd been longing to leave this cheapie rented flat for months, cheap partly because it was small but mainly because it was on the edge of a busy and very noisy industrial area of the town. He'd vowed when he came to live here, so that he could save more money, that his next home would be in the country, somewhere quiet and pleasant.

He didn't anticipate having any regrets about moving away from London, whatever people told him, and he beamed at the smoky morning suburb as he put the final box of household possessions into the back of the four-wheel drive. Not long to put up with this now, only a few minutes hopefully.

He patted the vehicle as he closed the boot. He'd traded in his ancient little runabout and bought this vehicle second-hand a few months ago because it seemed a better bargain to buy a two-year-old car with low mileage than a brand-new one which would instantly have lost a huge chunk of its value once he put it on the road. This one had had very low mileage, which had made it even more of a good buy.

All he needed now was a phone call to say that the settlement to pay for his new home had gone through this morning as expected. He wasn't moving out until that was done and dusted. They'd promised to do it early in the day, so he was waiting impatiently for confirmation and then he'd set off.

When his phone rang, he answered at the second ring and the woman who spoke to him was curt and to the point, ending the call as soon as she'd told him that the sale had now been completed in every detail and thanking him in a formulaic way for his custom.

'I'll be out of here within ten minutes,' he said aloud as he ended the call. It was actually only seven minutes, he noted in amusement as he got into his car. He blew a farewell derisive raspberry noise in the direction of the four-storey, old-fashioned block of flats and set off, not even turning his head to look back as he went round the corner.

He drove out of London in a leisurely way, heading towards the tiny village of Fairford Parva in beautiful Wiltshire and occasionally singing along with the radio. He could just about hold a tune, but knew he didn't have a particularly sonorous voice. But who was there to hear him?

'Farewell, rat race and bustle!' he yelled as he drove between hedges and fields for the first time.

'Hey, world, take note! I need only take on jobs that suit me from now on,' he yelled a little later. He laughed at himself but as the words echoed in his mind as well as in the car, he liked what they were proclaiming so much that he shouted them aloud once more.

He had been longing to get away from urban life for a few years and he was doing it at last. He had dreamt of moving into the peace and quiet of a cottage in a small village. It didn't matter where it was in England as long as it was a small place and surrounded by attractive countryside, not traffic and harassed-looking people. He'd wanted his new forever home to look out over the natural world and it did.

After the break-up of his one and only attempt at a permanent relationship, he'd worked extra hard and lived super frugally for over four years to give himself a secure financial basis for making this move. There would be no mortgage or rent to pay from now on, nor ever again if he could help it. He'd live sensibly and carefully, making sure he never did anything that brought him into debt and jeopardised his hard-won freedom. He'd take on a few job contracts here and there to make a living and the rest of the time he'd do what he wanted, which was paint pictures of rural scenes and wildlife.

For the past few months he'd kept an eye on the property sales websites online, especially those featuring homes with a little land attached in parts of the country where the house prices were generally lower. His vigilance had paid off big time and he'd managed to snap up a small cottage cheaply because it was rather dilapidated, without needing to take out a mortgage. And he'd done it a few months earlier than he'd expected. He had actually danced round his tiny flat when he heard that his offer on it had been accepted.

This cottage had the additional benefit not only of a large garden at the rear but a strip of arable land beyond it available for a modest extra sum. Its narrowness and lack of a view had apparently put buyers off, but he hadn't hesitated to buy it because it had been neglected for years and the ground wasn't loaded with pesticide residue. He would be able to grow a lot of his own food from now on without using dangerous chemicals.

In his opinion, organic food tasted nicer as well as being better for you, though many people told him it didn't taste any different. He didn't bother to argue about that.

He intended to live in this cottage, grow as much of his own food as possible organically and continue running a small IT consultancy online. You could do so much online these days and he wouldn't have to live in the city to show himself as available for enough smaller jobs to provide the money he needed to live on.

He was particularly skilled at sorting out smaller problems for people without good technical skills and creating inexpensive little websites quickly for them from a portfolio of simple templates he'd built up over the past few years. He also did all sorts of smaller IT repair jobs on request and did them well, if he said so himself.

Two of the things he thoroughly enjoyed about his new way of working were firstly, the interest of doing a variety of tasks and secondly, actually meeting in person the people who needed his help. He didn't intend to work for a narrowly focused high-tech company ever again, especially one that was extremely competitive and wanted to own you body and soul, twenty-four-seven, as well as using your know-how to make a lot more money that they didn't share with you, however good the innovations you'd produced for them might be.

When he'd left a company like that as the first step towards making his dream come true, he'd found he could earn more than he'd expected in the niche he'd sussed out and had therefore been able to make this lifestyle change even earlier than his original plans had suggested. How wonderful was that?

He'd have time for his art from now on, perhaps even manage to sell more of his paintings of the small creatures and delicate plants most people didn't even notice as they walked past them in the countryside. He hoped to find some interesting scenes to paint.

Then he arrived at Fairford Parva and forgot everything else as he turned into the village from the main road and drew up in front of his new home. The sun was shining brightly and every window seemed to twinkle a welcome at him, even though these windows needed a good clean.

'Hello, Daisy Cottage,' he said softly, switching off the car engine and smiling at the attractive little building set in narrow gardens at the front, with most of its land behind it. OK, so the house needed the front door painting and various small renovations on other parts, but it was still basically attractive. He sat for a few more moments with the car door open, finding it wonderful how quiet it was round here at this time of day.

Then he wondered why was he sitting here for so long instead of going inside his new home and got out of the car, striding along the path that cut the front garden neatly in two. At the old-fashioned door he stopped to pull the key out of his pocket, unlocking his new home slowly and reverently, but not going inside yet. Instead he stood staring in at the living room into which the front door opened. No fancy hallway here but he had plans to build a small entrance porch himself. Oh, he had all sorts of plans!

It felt to him as if the cottage was telling him how lovely it was to see him moving in here at last. And wasn't he an idiot to think like that? He stayed in the doorway, wanting to take in every tiny detail, inside and out, and make this place his own emotionally from now on.

At last he walked slowly into the living room, remembering the phrase 'take seisin of', which he'd found in a historical novel and never forgotten. He loved collecting unusual words and phrases. That was one of his minor passions, as well as taking photos of the small world of insects and tiny animals that most people moved past without noticing or caring about the smaller creatures humans shared their world with.

Today those three words echoed in his mind, sounding exactly like what he was about to do: take seisin of Daisy Cottage and its gardens. He'd invest love and toil into it to make it look and feel well-cared-for again.

He didn't wish to spend his whole life working on a computer, though he enjoyed doing it part of the time, especially when he was truly helping people solve problems that were messing up their lives. He intended to create a new and more varied way of living for himself here in the country, partly painting, partly working on digital stuff.

As he walked back outside, he waved his clenched right fist in the air in a gesture of happy triumph, then looked round guiltily, not wanting to seem an idiot to his new neighbours. But there was no one else around at this end of the village street.

He stared inside, smiling slightly. He'd bought the contents of the cottage for a bargain price from the family of the old lady who'd lived here – well, all except for the two sagging single beds with stained mattresses, which he'd asked the vendors to remove. The double bed in the largest upstairs room, the one at the front, had been immaculate, thank goodness, and something told him that this particular room and its bed hadn't been used by her much, if at all.

Perhaps the old lady had preferred the view from the rear windows from bedrooms too small to comfortably house a double bed. It certainly had a very attractive outlook from them.

There was only one bathroom at the moment but then, there would only be him using it, so who cared?

He'd paid a local business to do a thorough clean and then shampoo all the carpets and upholstery. The cottage now felt and smelt fresh even if it still looked shabby.

He intended to put an en suite bathroom in the attic, doing most of the work himself, and to use that area as the master bedroom eventually. It already had dormer windows, one looking out onto the village street at the front and the two rear ones looking over the grounds of the larger house next door at the rear.

He was fairly handy with tools, thanks to his uncle, and would be able to do a lot of the modernisation and repair work himself. He'd enjoy that, take his time, do it slowly and carefully.

At the rear, his kitchen also looked out at the nearby 'big house', as locals called it. This stood well back from the rest of the houses, hidden away on a couple of acres or so of land. But as Ryan's extra strip of land ran along one side of its couple of acres, he had an excellent view of the place from there as well as from the sitting room as well. He didn't know who owned it but it was a very pretty house, a 'gentleman's residence' rather than a manor house. It seemed to be hiding away from the world, though. Was that just an illusion or had it been positioned and built with that purpose?

From one of the smaller bedroom windows he also had a view of a small patch of woodland at his side of the grounds. The real estate agent had told him it was a carpet of bluebells in spring. He'd just missed seeing it this year unfortunately but was looking forward to seeing it next year and hoping to get some good photos out of it to translate into paintings later on. The two he'd done of bluebells had sold easily.

So this cottage might be small but it was well situated for what he wanted from his life. The only thing that marred the view was a shabby cottage at the rear of the land belonging to the big house. It was situated at the same side of the grounds as his own home.

It wouldn't have taken much to put a lick of paint on the peeling front door or to tidy up the garden but no one seemed to have made the slightest attempt to do anything to it.

He'd been told by an older woman he'd got chatting to at the village shop that the other cottage had been rented out for years to a guy who didn't join in anything that was going on in the village, and who even did most of his food shopping elsewhere – when he was at home, which was only about half the time. The chap's car received a lot of loving care, though, as Ryan had already seen for himself, and he apparently went away in it quite often for a few days at a time. He also made a lot of unnecessary noise at intrusive hours of the day or night with his comings and goings.

When showing Ryan round, the real estate agent had shown similar signs of disapproval, gesturing towards the run-down cottage and grimacing, then saying in tones of distinct disapproval, 'The guy who's renting that doesn't seem to associate with any of the locals, so you'd probably be wasting your time trying to get to know him. And I'm told he goes away a lot.'

Since his move here, Ryan had seen other people grimace at one another when the guy came into the shop and to his astonishment shoved his way to the front of the queue. He'd never seen anyone actually do that before but when he commented people just said it was a good thing, because it got rid of 'that oik' more quickly. And anyway he hardly ever did any shopping there.

And why was he thinking of such a nasty oik on this lovely sunny day? He smiled. He'd never heard anyone except his grandfather use that old-fashioned insult but it was now how he thought of the fellow.

Ryan returned the wave of a woman three doors away as he carried another bundle inside. He'd found the other people in the village easy to chat to, not pushing to find out about his life but letting time reveal one part of it or another when a relevant subject cropped up. And they mentioning things about themselves or the village occasionally too, gradually teaching him about his surroundings.

He went out to his four-wheel drive for another box and took a moment or two to look along the road. The village was hardly more than a small hamlet and consisted mainly of this single higgledy-piggledy street of houses dating from several eras, which was perhaps the reason they weren't all positioned in the usual straight line.

Apart from the village shop there was a pub called The Jolly Monk, and both of them were set back a little way from the main street with car-parking space in front of them. The place was perfect as far as he was concerned! He could walk to the pub for a pint occasionally, or to the shop if he didn't intend to buy anything too heavy, for which he would use his car because he wasn't going to risk damaging his back by lumping heavy stuff around.

Ryan went indoors again and moved slowly through the cottage, pausing now and then to study some detail. Everything showed very clearly that the house had previously belonged to an old person because the furniture he'd bought with it was not only old-fashioned but well-used and the seats were higher than those of modern furniture.

He didn't mind the latter because he was tall enough to prefer higher seats, so he would manage with these pieces for a while. Anyway, his happiness wasn't dependent on fancy furnishings or inviting people round for fine dining at dinner parties, and as for wearing suits and ties again, forget it! What he craved were peaceful surroundings, a peaceful life and the visual beauties of nature. Though he hoped to make a few friends here, if he was lucky.

But as to the modernisation of his new home, it'd have to wait. Not only did he want to avoid further depleting his savings but he wasn't sure yet exactly what he wanted to do to his new home long term – except repaint the front door. That he'd do quite soon because its shabbiness annoyed him.

He sat down in the big armchair, rocking it gently to and fro and finding it extremely comfortable once he got rid of the lumpy, mostly threadbare cushions that been piled on it any old how. The chair was upholstered in a plain dark maroon material that nearly matched the nearby elderly sofa. The chair must have been reupholstered recently because it wasn't showing any signs of wear and tear like the other items. Perhaps it had been her favourite seat.

He would allow himself to spend a little money on a colourful new cushion or two at the local market or wherever he could find them to brighten up the chair and the old sofa, but he didn't intend to spend a fortune on new furniture.

No need to be efficient with his time now. He could sit here all day if he wanted. He let out a long, happy sigh as he stared round the living room and contemplated his future. He would set up his office next door in what was supposed to be the dining room. He could push the small but solid mahogany Victorian dining table to one side and use it as a second desk, leaving enough room for his own modern office equipment, which would clash visually with the old furniture but too bad.

He would set up his painting things in the old-fashioned sunroom at the back of the house for the time being. It wasn't overshadowed by trees so was light and bright, which was the main thing he needed. Someone had removed all the furniture from it quite a while ago judging by how dusty the floor had been, but that suited him because that left just enough room for his own art equipment.

He would be able to fit his easel, the stand that held all his small pieces of equipment and his big storage cupboard in there but nothing much else. The room was smaller than he'd like but he could make do with that because it was still a lot bigger than the flat had been.

Nodding approval of how everything was feeling so far, he went back into the kitchen and began opening and closing cupboards and drawers. The appliances were very old-fashioned and he would definitely need to buy some new cooking equipment as well as a big modern fridge-freezer. But the ugly little green plastic dining table and four matching chairs standing in the space near some French doors that led out to the rear would do just fine till he got round to updating this whole area and putting in a new and much larger conservatory at the other side of the rear to use as his studio.

It wasn't as if he was going to be giving dinner parties or even inviting people round for drinks. He'd been there and done that with his one try at having a live-in partner. He wished Sadie well, but the two of them had proved quite quickly that they were not meant to live together, fond as they were of one another. She couldn't understand why he wanted quiet weekends and time with his painting. He didn't want to go out drinking till late and lie in bed till late. He was an early to bed, early to rise sort of guy, and his body fell asleep on him if he tried to keep going till late.

After only a few months the two of them had agreed to separate. They'd shared out their few joint goods and chattels amicably enough, then gone their own different ways.

Sadie was working somewhere in France now, he'd heard, but wasn't sure where. He had her emergency email address but he doubted he'd ever use it. He didn't think she'd contact him again, either, because she too was getting on with her own style of life and someone had told him she was shacked up with a new guy. Good luck to them.

* * *

After he'd carried the remaining boxes and miscellaneous bits and pieces from his car into the cottage, he locked the place up again and drove to the village shop, where he introduced himself to the owners as a new and, he hoped, regular customer.

He knew food items would cost him more if he shopped here but he'd save part of that extra cost by using less petrol and getting things done more quickly if he didn't have to drive several miles to the nearest big supermarket.

Not that he'd have to be quite as careful with money and time in the same way once he'd moved into the cottage he'd bought. But after seeing a friend drop dead at the age of thirty-five, he didn't intend to waste a minute of his life. It had taken him a few years to get over the shock of losing Guy so suddenly and it had seemed unfair for him to die so young, especially when he'd been a keep-fit freak.

Anyway, the local shop would do fine most of the time and those big supermarkets could manage without his contribution to their profits while this smaller business would genuinely benefit from his regular custom, he was sure. Sadly, these days small shops often had rather a struggle to stay viable, especially those in places as remote as Fairford Parva.

He nodded to the shopkeeper and walked round studying the contents of the shelves and displays. He was delighted to find that they sold frozen ready meals which the owners made themselves. He picked up one of the slim boxes and studied its contents, pleased that it looked to be adequate in serving size. Then he read the list of other ingredients, even more pleased that unlike some commercially mass-produced ready meals, it didn't contain any of the mock flavourings he regarded as being bad for human bodies.

After that he got chatting to the male half of the husband-and-wife owners, who told him he'd been a cook in Bristol before he got married and settled here after his wife inherited the shop. He promised Ryan that their own food was as free as was possible from artificial flavourings without having to charge a fortune for it. They had several regular customers for whom they made meals to order in batches ready for freezing, and any of the others who bought them would be happy to vouch for the taste and food quality.

'I'm confident enough of our product to give you one as a free sample,' he ended. 'Just choose the meal you fancy most and it's yours.'

'And I'll put our menu in the box with your other purchases,' the female half of the owner duo added cheerfully.

'I'll definitely be interested in that,' Ryan told her. 'I enjoy cooking sometimes but don't want to do it every single day.'

They were also happy to order in one or two other items especially for him. He loved curries and spicy food, and enjoyed making his own, but needed some proper spices not to mention packets of dried poppadums, of which he was very fond. He explained to the proprietors that boxes of ready-cooked poppadums like the ones on display went a bit stale by the time he'd eaten all those in one packet, but he'd got cooking the dried poppadums as he needed them down to a fine art using his microwave.

The male proprietor immediately asked for the exact method and time it took to cook them, and gave him a free packet of poppadums in return for the tip of a way he hadn't tried before.

Ryan enjoyed this bargaining and sharing session, which

you didn't get in big stores, where it was hard enough to gain the attention of an assistant who often looked bored, let alone to find the items you really wanted among so many. Some of the old-fashioned approaches were actually more efficient and productive for individual customers than the modern approaches to selling, he reckoned.

By the time he left the shop, Ryan had bought a pile of basic foods, ordered other things he'd need regularly to be brought in for him as special orders and made an excellent start on getting on good terms with the owners. He was pleased to leave them both beaming after 'call me Greg' had helped him carry several boxes of purchases out to his vehicle.

If their homemade food was good, he'd order some regularly once he got a new freezer because work often came in sudden hectic spurts when you were the sole operator of a small consultancy. And anyway, even though he was not so helpless that he couldn't feed himself decently enough when needed, he simply didn't want to cook every single day.

He smiled as he always did when thinking of that sort of thing, remembering his mother. He wasn't one of those fools who called themselves adults but couldn't look after their own basic needs. Well, she hadn't allowed him to grow up without what she called 'the necessary life skills' like cooking and washing the clothes you'd dirtied.

But he also preferred to be independent for his own self-respect. His girlfriend hadn't been nearly as good a cook as he was and had wanted to eat out all the time, which wasn't a good way to save money to buy a house.

He stood in the front doorway of his cottage once he'd put all the food away, breathing with immense pleasure air that really was fresh. He took the time to stare along the village street, first one way then the other, assimilating more details. It was as pretty as he remembered. And the pub was only about a hundred yards along from his cottage with a sign outside saying The Jolly Monk. It was a lovely old building, black-and-white-timbered in the upper half. The car park had two or three vehicles in it, early as it was.

After that Ryan went inside again and began to move some of the pieces of furniture around into what felt like more comfortable living patterns for himself. That was one of the things he and Sadie had disagreed strongly about, how to arrange the contents of their joint living space. Strange how much the other partner's ways about that sort of thing had annoyed them both.

Then he forgot about her and the past, smiling as a small bird landed on the outer windowsill, a perky little thing. 'You're welcome here any time, little sparrow,' he told it and listened with delight as it sang a little chirruping song for him. There was a bird table near the house at the back and he guessed the old lady had enjoyed feeding the birds and watching their antics.

He'd make a bigger bird table and photograph its small visitors sneakily, which would probably give him ideas for a few paintings. They might be good sellers too if he managed to catch the perkiness and charm of his first little visitor, which was what his mother had always called 'a tiggy little bird'. He was getting better not just at painting but at selecting a scene or creature that would appeal to people likely to buy original paintings.

He had seen two little groups of people further along the street standing gossiping and had watched them for a few moments. He loved watching people at any time. The ones in each group looked to be on very good terms with one another, smiling and gesticulating as they chatted. A quartet had gathered at one corner of the pub car park and three others were standing outside the open door of one of a group of a few small terraced two-up, two-down cottages, laughing heartily at something.

He hoped he'd make a few genuine friends here, not just mere acquaintances. He wasn't into boozing and partying but he did enjoy the occasional glass of beer or cider at a pub and cosy little chats with neighbours like the ones going on here down the road.

He gave another happy sigh. Yes, Fairford Parva looked as if it might satisfy his lifestyle needs very nicely.

Then he went back to sorting out more details of how his new home could be re-organised, and dumping two ugly ornaments that had been lurking in a corner into a bag he was planning to fill with similar items and take to the nearest charity shop. He wasn't into mass-produced cute pottery children, let alone allowing them to stand on his mantelpiece, and absolutely loathed the way their unrealistic rosebud lips were pursed into tiny unconvincing mouths.

He didn't know exactly what he'd be into from now on. Life, the universe and giving new experiences a try, perhaps – as well as having more interactions with the small animals and birds he loved to paint.

Chapter Ten

When Miranda joined Libby outside the following morning just as dawn was filling the sky with vivid colour, her friend smiled at her so warmly she felt instantly happier. What a difference that lovely woman had already made to how she felt about the world!

She hadn't the slightest doubt that this new and closer relationship the two of them had created would last. She just knew it, somehow. How wonderful was that?

They didn't hang around but got on the road and listened to the early morning news, which for once was mostly good news. After that Libby switched the wireless off and they chatted now and then but mostly enjoyed the scenery.

As they got closer to their destination, Libby pulled into a petrol station to fill the car so that they didn't arrive with a nearly empty tank. She didn't even try to protest when Miranda gave her a determined look and went to pay for that.

They grabbed a quick mug of coffee from a self-service

machine near the pay desk then sat at a small table outside to drink it and get a little sun on their faces.

As they sipped the coffee and ate the biscuits that came with it, Miranda decided that it was only fair to warn Libby about the possible pitfalls of the situation they were getting into.

'Look, I need to tell you something about, well, the background to this inheritance.'

Libby looked at her in surprise. 'Oh? You sound as if it's not something good.'

'I'm afraid it isn't or at least it might not be. I know it sounds as if we're living in a glorious fantasy story about a poor young woman suddenly inheriting a big house and a lot of money but with my great-aunt involved, this may turn out to be a horror story instead, with the potential for traps being set for me around every corner.'

Libby looked at her in puzzlement. 'But she's dead now! How can she set any more traps for you?'

'She may have already done that. I feel the words to use are "has probably set up some nasty surprises". She's made conditions about me going to live there, hasn't she? I'd be mad to refuse to adhere to them and lose the property and financial benefits I'm inheriting but I'm all too well aware that I'll need to tread carefully once I get there. She's made sure I have to stay there for two years to inherit, for a start. That's a long time to have to watch your back for sneaky tricks.'

'Well, no one with half an ounce of sense in their skull would refuse to agree to her terms with such a large sum of money at stake.'

'Precisely. And I didn't refuse, did I? Who knows what she's got planned to happen during those two years, though.

I can't help wondering what I'll be facing, so although it won't be aimed at you, you might suffer collateral damage, so you should keep your eyes open, too.'

'Can I ask why has she has always behaved so badly to you that you're afraid of her even after she's dead? Have you any idea?'

'My guess is it's because she hated my father and therefore doesn't want his daughter to have an easy life – nor did she like the idea of me taking control of the cosy little world she had created for herself and the money she loved to manage and accumulate. I may be wrong and I hope I am, but I'm preparing myself mentally for all sorts of nasty tricks, which is why I felt I had to warn you to be careful too.'

'And you're utterly certain she'll try to hurt you?'

'Fairly certain. Who knows what she'll do, Libby? I never knew her well enough.' She frowned and stared into space for a few moments, then shook her head. 'No, I don't think she'll wish me dead, because she wants the family line to continue and I'm the sole female descendant of the right age in this generation, so I have the right genes for providing an heir. And of course at my age I'm still likely to be fertile. I'm not nearly up to my last chances of motherhood yet.'

Her friend gave her a wry look. 'Healthy women usually are fertile but there are never any guarantees.'

'Yes, I know. Which is why she's kept an eye on the only close male heir as well. In fact, she sent me a message to say I was to marry and produce more than one heir as soon as possible because she doesn't approve of him. She did leave him a long free tenancy in a cottage on the estate, though, presumably to keep him available.'

'That sounds ominous.'

'Who knows? She seems not to care a jot about my

happiness or even who I might marry, as long as he's physically healthy, comes from a decent background and is willing and able to produce several heirs. My father didn't want more than one, which I think is one of the reasons why she disliked him so much, and he got into debt that the trust had to pay off for my mother's sake, which made her furious.'

She chuckled suddenly. 'I reckon she put up with me mainly because she regarded me as a sort of human brood mare, for lack of there being anyone else suitable.'

'You always sound very negative when you talk about marriage.'

'I can't help it. I already have a bad track record for finding a suitable man. I chose a nasty guy, thinking we were truly in love, and his tenderness didn't last long, did it? He'd thumped me within a couple of months of us starting to live together. I wondered why he thought he'd get away with it, but my best guess is that he thought I was meek enough to stay with him because I usually try to avoid quarrelling and hassles, as you know.'

'That wasn't you to blame for being bad at choosing a partner. If he was abusive, it was his choice to act like that and therefore his fault. What's more, I reckon you did the right thing to leave him quickly before he could really hurt you. Some people, both males and females, seem to be born nasty and it doesn't necessarily show in their faces. I've met one or two shockers in my time.' She scowled, probably at some unpleasant memory of her own, but didn't share any details.

'Well, my horrible old great-aunt may have arranged for me to be forced into spending two years living at Fairfield House, but she didn't say anything about me not being allowed a companion to come and live there with me, did she, Auntie Libby?'

'No, she didn't, my dear niece. Are you inviting me to stay?'

'Yes, I am. And for the whole time I'm there. We already know how well we get on, after all, and it's apparently a big house so we won't be under each other's feet all the time.'

'We do get on well, don't we? So I accept happily. We'll stick together, Miranda, and I'll stay there with you for as long as you need me. Having people on your side can make a big difference to just about any awkward situation in this life, I've found, whether they're family born and bred, adopted family or just good friends. But I'll heed your warning and make sure I tread very carefully into our life together at your new home, keeping my eyes open for traps. And we are neither of us stupid. In fact, quite the opposite, I believe. So we'll each keep an eye on each other as well.'

Miranda smiled at her new 'aunt' and nodded. 'The nice lawyer who took over the Westerby account when the old one retired was as shrewd as they come and he advised me to take someone with me when I went there the first time, and now fate in the shape of my old car has brought you and me together to do it, which fits in very nicely.'

She paused again for thought then added, 'I think he'll be pleased about it and I suspect he'll be keeping an eye on what's happening officially as well as unofficially because there are legal aspects to the situation. He certainly didn't like what my great-aunt had made him promise to say to me and he didn't try to hide his worries about my safety.'

'Tell me about what your other aunt made him say.' She drew inverted commas in the air as she said 'other aunt', which brought a brief smile to her younger companion's face.

'Not worth repeating. It was petty, spiteful stuff and I

was used to that from her so I ignored it. I reckon her mind must have been failing towards the end because what she did and said seemed to get steadily worse, and more openly weird too.'

'She sounds to me to have always been nasty towards you, so I don't think much of her mindset at any time.'

Miranda shrugged. 'She's gone now. Even she can't come back from the dead.'

They drove along the motorway in silence for a while, then Libby said thoughtfully, 'This home and inheritance all come from your mother's family, don't they, the maternal side of her lot?'

'Yes. But I know virtually nothing about the relatives on her paternal side, just the Westerby bunch. And nothing about my father's side of the family either. If I tried to talk or ask about it, Mum just said that we would never be going back to Fairfield House and told me to forget about the existence of all the rest of the family, both sides. It was why we moved to live on the other side of London, to make a fresh start.'

'Except she didn't change your surname, did she? None of the females in your family seem to have done that, even if they got married.'

'Well, why should they? Men don't change their surnames when they marry.'

'Some of them sound to have done that when they married one of the Westerby heirs.'

'That's all water under the bridge now. Sadly, Mum's efforts at keeping me away from Phyllis were in vain because when she was killed in the traffic accident, I fell totally into my great-aunt's power again. I didn't go to live with her, though. She sent me away to boarding school immediately, and I even stayed there during the school holidays.'

'Did you not make any long-term friends there?'

'Sort of. By the time I got there, however, most of the others had been in that boarding school for years, often since primary school, and they'd already formed some very close friendships. They weren't unpleasant to me but I didn't get as close to any of them as they already had done to one another.'

Libby's voice was gentle. 'You've been very much alone since you lost your mother, haven't you? Did she never tell you anything about the Westerby side of her family?'

'Not much. And that was deliberate. Her main advice was that I should ignore them completely, as she had done. She even once suggested I emigrate once I'd finished my studies.'

'Did you consider doing that?'

'No. I feel too English. And now Fate's tossed me into the Westerby family at the deep end and here I am about to start running the family trust. I had no choice about being the one to inherit, did I? What's more, I'll be moving into the long-time family home, as arranged by the wicked great-aunt my mother mistrusted. Ironic, isn't it? It's the old saying: Man proposes, God disposes. Or in this case, old aunt disposes.'

Libby cocked her head to one side, frowning in thought. 'Who said that originally? And was it in the fifteenth or sixteenth century? I know it was one or the other.'

'Does that matter?'

'It does to me. I hate not remembering things accurately.'

'I think it was Thomas à Kempis. Hmm. Was it in the sixteenth, no, definitely the fifteenth century. I collect useless information like that too. I don't set out to do it, the facts simply stick in my brain and usually it only takes a couple of quick nudges to bring them back out of storage again.'

'Well, I'm glad to get that detail sorted out. It'd have irritated me till I'd remembered, otherwise. I would have remembered eventually, mind you. I always do.'

'We're a bit like one another in that way, aren't we?'

They nodded and exchanged smiles.

'So let's change the subject to something more positive, shall we, Miranda? We're out of the busy traffic from here onwards and I'll drive the rest of the way at a steady pace, not surrounded by people in a hurry. I like driving along country roads slowly enough to enjoy the scenery, don't you?'

'I haven't had much chance to do that.'

'Well, seize the moment from now on. Wiltshire has some really pretty countryside if I remember correctly, and there's nothing in your contract that prevents me from taking you out for little drives to explore it after we're settled there. I'm sure we'll both enjoy doing that. We'll be able to visit Stonehenge and Avebury, for a start.'

'Ooh, yes.' Miranda gave her a sudden beaming smile. 'It really cheers me up how confident you are about what we're doing.'

'Not confident that it'll turn out perfectly, but confident that we'll give it our best shot. That's all you can do sometimes, then at least you don't have to blame yourself for a disappointing outcome.'

'I like that way of thinking about life. I wish I'd had someone like you to bring me up after Mum died.'

'*Merci du compliment.*'

After that they were mostly silent and Miranda found it soothing to sit peacefully in the front passenger seat, marvelling as how confidently her companion was driving and how pretty this part of England was, and also, how interesting her life had become lately.

'I'm so glad I shan't need to work for that fool of a boss, or for any other fool for a long time.'

'Did you mean to say that out loud?'

Miranda chuckled. 'No. But the money I've inherited is a good thing for that reason as well, as far as I'm concerned. If I never see that horrible boss or the so-called team leader again, it'll be too soon.'

A short time later she said thoughtfully, 'I shan't know how much my great-aunt has left me till we get there, but I'm hoping there will be enough left in my kitty if I live frugally to buy a little house for myself after the two years are over. My biggest ambition is to own a proper house of my own, one nobody can take away from me.'

'You may enjoy living in the family home. That would solve that problem for you in one fell swoop.'

'And pigs may fly!'

'They definitely don't do that! But strange things do happen sometimes in people's lives, unexpected things.'

'I can do without anything else unexpected. I'm still trying to get used to the idea of this family house.'

'Let's hope we find the house untouched by intruders, then. That'd make a good start to your new life. After all, that lawyer had the external locks changed straight away, didn't he? And he said he hadn't given a key to anyone except you.'

Miranda nodded slowly. 'And surely someone in the village would have noticed if Fairfield House had been broken into?'

'Who knows?' Libby paused then said thoughtfully, 'I

keep coming back to the idea that your whole situation is strange financially for another reason. Why leave all the paperwork in a safe in an empty house? That's asking for trouble.'

'Why do that, indeed? I hope the safe is a big, clunky old thing because I haven't even been told where it's located in the house, let alone what it looks like. It may be hidden behind something like a painting or a secret panel.'

'Let's hope not. But there are two of us to search for it. We must be getting quite close to Fairfield now, so we'll probably find out more about your legacy quite soon. The scenery has been lovely since we left the motorway, hasn't it?'

'Yes. The country round here has been really pretty so far. I shall enjoy exploring it.'

After a couple more miles, Miranda suddenly let out an involuntary 'Ugh!'

'What's the matter?'

'I had a sudden stupid thought. You know how you do sometimes? Stupid details drop into your mind. I realised that when I move into the house, one of my earliest jobs will probably be to clear out my great-aunt's clothing and personal possessions, and some of it might include her dirty washing.'

'You're not Mrs Cheerful today, are you? But I must agree with your "Ugh" moment. Dealing with someone else's dirty washing wouldn't be my idea of a pleasant job, either.'

'Let's hope my aunt wasn't a hoarder. And that she'd mainly left clean underwear. It'll be bad enough clearing out her drawers and cupboards.'

Libby chuckled suddenly. 'What a silly thing to focus on!

There are such things as rubber gloves, remember!'

Miranda laughed at herself too. 'You're right. My brain is hopping about like a flea in a tar pit today, to quote the author Georgette Heyer.'

'What a lovely image! Not.'

The satnav interrupted just then to tell them to turn left here and Libby slowed down because they were now on a rather narrow road, not much more than a lane.

'Here we go,' she said quietly. 'We must be getting close now.'

Miranda's smile faded and a tense expression replaced it.

But then the road grew wider for a while as it led them into a pretty village instead of the grounds of the large country residence they'd been expecting.

'Let's stop and grab a quick snack and comfort break while we can,' Libby said quietly.

'Good idea.'

Libby braked hard and pulled up in front of the village shop, which was clearly a mixture of shop and café. It looked to be thriving, even in such a small village, with a couple of cars parked outside and a few shopping trolleys lined up next to the entrance.

They both got out and stretched.

'This may be your local shop once you settle in,' Libby said.

'Our local shop. It looks to have a good variety of stock. But what I want now is a mug of strong coffee, not a basket of groceries. And ooh, I'll have one of those pieces of chocolate cake. They look so delicious it makes you feel hungry.'

'I'll second that.'

Chapter Eleven

Jim woke with a start. Where was he? Then it all came flooding back to shock him, as it did most mornings. Tears welled in his eyes. No avoiding the facts: his beloved wife was dead and without Gracie he not only felt like a lost soul, he was lost.

He'd had a disturbed night's sleep as was usual since he'd been on the tramp and he still felt tired, deep down weary as well as sad. And he didn't feel well today, nothing specific, just felt feverish, couldn't seem to think straight and had a bad headache. Flu, perhaps.

He stood up, trying to tidy his clothes as best he could. When he looked round, he wasn't even sure where he was. He must have been trudging round the countryside for a week or two now, moving blindly, not knowing where to settle or what to do with himself without Gracie.

As he walked, he began to worry. Oh dear, he definitely was feeling worse physically today! And it was suddenly all too clear to him that he was too old to cope with this sort of life for long.

He was desperate to find somewhere he could stop for a while, longed for some undisturbed peace and quiet mostly outdoors, surrounded by trees and shrubs and plants, especially now when so many of them were in bloom. Their blossoms made him feel better; they always did, just to see their beauty.

The trouble was where to settle. He'd just about given up hope of finding somewhere. There seemed to be people and houses crammed in everywhere he turned. How could he ever find a quiet path through life for himself again crammed in with others like sardines in a can? Perhaps he should have bought a car. He could have slept in it. But he'd be shut in and the weather had been kind to him, sunny with only a day or two when there were showers.

He shook his head sadly. He still hadn't the faintest idea what to do with himself, couldn't seem to work anything out. He'd seen a few new places, some of them very pleasant, but few open spaces. There were people everywhere. He'd looked in the windows of a couple of estate agents' and found that he didn't have enough money to buy himself anything except a tiny flat and they didn't have gardens at all. Even a small home in the country would cost more than he could afford. And he wanted, no, needed a decent-sized garden to spend his time in.

He wanted to earn a living, not go on the pension. You needed to do something you could be proud of. And for him that meant something to do with gardening. He loved tending plants and was still perfectly capable of doing that, given half a chance.

The social worker he'd spoken to after Gracie died had wanted to take over his life and re-organise it for him. People like that young fellow meant well but Jim didn't think they really understood what he wanted because it didn't fit in with how they usually looked after oldies.

They'd insisted he'd get used to an old folks' home, would quickly make new friends and settle down but he'd never been able to make friends easily, had never had a lot of them or needed them either. Gracie and his plants, and one or two people who also loved gardens had been enough. Even on rainy days he'd worked in his shed with the doors open. There were always lots of small jobs that needed doing, except in winter, and then he'd done wood carving at one end of his shed, and sold some of his pieces too.

He had never liked living in groups or even walking along crowded streets, and he never would. He belonged outdoors, had done even as a child. Gracie had known that before they married and had let him spend his days as he chose. And she'd been so very special and so good with house plants that he'd enjoyed her company during their quiet evenings together. Eh, there had been greenery on nearly every surface in their house.

He sighed and even his thoughts seemed to pause for a moment in tribute to her. He'd been lucky in his wife, very lucky indeed.

Then, just as he felt he couldn't manage another day's tramping, he found a garden shed behind a house which had a big *FOR SALE* sign at the front. The family must have moved out already because when he peeped in through a downstairs window where the curtains weren't properly drawn, he saw that there was no furniture at all inside.

Whoever had owned the house had left a couple of folded and rather tatty tarpaulins in the garden shed and those softened the ground for him to sleep on more comfortably that night as well as preventing the damp from creeping up on him. That made it one of the better sleeping spots he'd found. This place would do him for a few days – well, it would if no one found him and kicked him out.

That evening he went to bed early. He still thought about it as 'going to bed', even though there was no actual bed these days. He enjoyed the peace and quiet, especially with the door of the shed left open to a calm, still night so that he could watch a beautiful sunset and then see the stars twinkling down on the world.

That respite and the pleasure of surroundings like these only made him more determined that he'd find another garden to tend. He'd do whatever it took to stay away from those old folks' homes.

His poor friend had had no choice and ended up in one of them because he wasn't well. Jim had gone to see Stan there regularly till the cancer killed him. Only for such a good mate would he have gone back again after the first visit. It left him shuddering at the memory of the cramped conditions and the shuffling old people in the corridors, many leaning on those walking frames.

He pushed the sad memories away and let himself enjoy this place with its big, comfy shed. Over the next three days, the neighbours who lived near the empty house noticed him, of course they did. But they could see that he wasn't doing any harm so they didn't try to chase him away.

They were nice folk, these, always polite to him. Some even stopped to pass the time of day and one of them offered him some food leftovers, which he accepted gladly.

That saved him moving on, because there were no shops

within walking distance. He began to relax and felt he was starting to recover a little from losing his wife – as much as you ever could anyway.

He was still managing to get money out of Post Offices with that temporary pension book, so he hadn't needed to touch what he thought of as his own money, which was sitting waiting for him to find a use for it. If only there had been enough to buy a cottage with some land.

He wasn't spending a lot of the temporary pension money because he didn't seem to get all that hungry these days. Since he'd learnt better ways to manage this tramping life, he'd not been reduced to grubbing in dustbins again. Eh, he'd been so hungry that day he'd have eaten an old shoe if you'd fried it, as an uncle of his used to joke.

Jim smiled at that memory. He was starting to feel a bit better and was hoping he could stay in this nice little shed for a few more days.

Then an estate agent turned up to show people round the house. He thought he'd got away quickly enough to avoid being seen, but when he saw the big luxury car drive away and went back, he found that the shed now had a sturdy padlock on its door and his possessions were neatly piled at the side hidden from the street.

At least the woman doing the selling hadn't thrown his things away. But he'd cried at having to move on again, couldn't help it. He was still feeling exhausted underneath and the thought of tramping further that day almost overwhelmed him.

When he'd stopped weeping like a child and pulled himself together a bit, he muttered, 'Looks like we're off on our travels again, Gracie lass.' It was comforting to chat to her sometimes, and he always knew what she would have said in reply. 'Chin up,' she'd have said today and 'Just get on with it.'

He looked down at his walking stick, taking comfort from it too, as always, because she'd bought it for him their last Christmas together when he was recovering from a bad sprain of his right ankle. He might not know the exact calendar date these days, hadn't even known which day of the week it was in the beginning. He kept an eye on that better now, though not as many shops closed on Sundays as they had in the old days so he could usually find somewhere open to buy food.

However, he knew exactly how many days had passed since he'd lost Gracie because he marked each one on her stick at teatime, doing it every day just before he ate his tea. He didn't think he'd missed a single one.

On that thought, he took the stick and made a neat little scratch in the row down one side. There! Another one added to it, so many days without her. That was the hardest part of his new way of life, turning to say something to her and then remembering.

He was too old to live like this for much longer, though, and certainly wouldn't be able to do it when the weather got colder; even late autumn would be too much of a problem at night. He admitted that to himself now. But at least he was trying to find a new way to go, looking more carefully at the places he found himself in.

Only, none of them appealed to him and he couldn't seem to work out what to do beyond moving further on the next day to wherever his current road took him.

He needed to find a place where he could bear to stay. And he would do that one day, surely? There was no rush at the moment. The weather was still warm and he could wash himself all over in streams or ponds, wash his clothes too sometimes.

He didn't want to see any of their old friends, or for them to see him in this sad state. His redundancy payment would be waiting for him in the bank together with the savings that now belonged only to him, but he was managing without any of those and it was good to know they were mounting up. The temporary pension was more than enough for the time being.

Strange, that. Even though he had never been a money-hungry sort of chap, he hadn't fully realised how very unimportant money was compared to the people you'd loved and lost, and the home you'd lost too.

Since he and Gracie had never been blessed with children, in spite of their efforts and the doctor's help, there wasn't anyone who would have reason to worry about where he was, so he could do what he wanted, whatever he seemed to need. He knew that Gracie had had a child once, a daughter, when she was quite young, but her parents had forced her to have it adopted and though she'd told him about it, they'd decided to leave the situation be and not upset somebody's life. It was a pity he had no one to turn to now if he met trouble suddenly. That worried him sometimes.

His feeling of being lost in a bewildering, empty world sometimes threatened to overwhelm him completely, though not as badly as it had at the beginning.

He supposed he was getting used to the emptiness of his personal world but he hadn't realised men could cry as often and as bitterly as women.

A few weeks had passed and his desire to stop tramping around had grown stronger, but he still didn't know where to settle to make this new life.

He kept thinking he'd carry on for just another day or two. It was a lovely summer, with very few rainy days. He passed through some beautiful places 'in England's green and pleasant land'.

Now who had written that? He racked his brain but didn't remember till he woke up the next morning and said it aloud again. William Blake, of course. If he couldn't find his own book of poetry among his things that his friend was keeping for him once he settled down again, he'd buy another one.

One of the few things he was still quite sure of, however, was that he wasn't going to live in an old folks' home, definitely not. Once they got you inside, they locked the doors and kept you there, perhaps because they needed to lock in the ones who were losing their wits, poor things. They sat you in rows, made you all do the same sort of thing, childish things too, like sing-songs using music from World War Two, which had taken place well before the younger days of his own generation. Why did they think every old person had sung those particular war songs?

No, Jim had spent most of his life out of doors and that was where he hoped to end his days. Whatever it took, he'd find a place he liked.

Chapter Twelve

A week or two later, it began to rain as Jim walked into a small Wiltshire village he'd never seen before. He found a huge leafy tree to shelter under for a while, but to his dismay the rain didn't ease. Indeed, after a while it began to beat down on the world even more strongly, big fat drops of moisture finding their way through the leaves and pounding away at him and the tree both.

When he looked up at the sky, he groaned at how dark the clouds had become. He hadn't been paying enough attention to the weather today, that was certain, had been lost in memories and longings.

The wet weather had clearly set in for the day and water was dripping onto his face and shoulders. He couldn't stay here or he'd be soaked to the skin and probably catch pneumonia. Gracie wouldn't want him to do that. He'd have to look for proper shelter.

He pulled out a big black bin liner from his backpack. He'd already poked holes in the end to put his head and arms through, so he slipped it quickly over his clothes to keep them more or less dry, then plonked a child's sou'wester on his head. Who cared what he looked like? He'd found it lying in the grass next to a minor road one day and it had obviously been there a while, so he'd taken it with him and cleaned it up. It had come in useful a few times since.

It matched his clothes in one way, though, a way he didn't like. In fact, he felt ashamed of how ragged and dirty he must be looking now. He had a poor sense of smell these days, too, another gift of old age, and he didn't dare think what the clothes must smell like. Or his body, either, though he did try to find ways to wash himself on warmer days. Little streams could be a godsend for that. He'd had a few rough baths that way.

Gracie would be furious at him for letting things get to this stage. He hadn't cared at first, but now he did, which showed he was making progress.

Didn't it?

He turned off the main road and set off walking along a narrow country road which led him into a village. It wasn't a large place and had only one shop, so it only took a few minutes to walk all the way through it.

He stopped in surprise when he came to the last in the untidy row of mismatched houses and realised he'd reached the far end already. He'd have to turn back if he was to buy himself a nice warm mug of tea and maybe a packet of chocolate biscuits or small cakes from that shop. He'd be able to shelter from the rain there for a while as he sat eating them slowly, because there were several café-style tables inside, crammed into one corner, as well as the ones the rain was drumming on outside.

He'd just take a quick look at where this little turn-off led before he went back to the café. Sometimes you could find a place to stop for a few days if you went down the narrower, less-used lanes like this one – well, if you were lucky. Over the centuries, some farmers had plonked little sheds in stray corners of fields as well as near their houses.

Some of the old sheds were no longer in use and in a rather ramshackle condition, but they could be nice, peaceful places to sleep. Others were nearly in ruins, inhabited by little creatures, whose company he didn't mind at all as long as the roof kept off the rain.

Was he going to be lucky today? He trudged slowly on, walking as closely as he could to the rhythm of the rain on the plastic liner. Thank goodness for it today because the rain seemed to be settling in. He dreaded to think what he must look like wearing it, though.

The turn-off led to some beautiful wrought-iron gates that barred the way to what looked like the drive of a large house. He couldn't see a building from here, if there still was one, but drives like this didn't usually lead to cottages, did they? There were no recent tyre marks on it so perhaps no one was in residence or else the house had fallen into ruins.

He couldn't resist finding out. He pushed down the twirly iron handle of one gate, expecting it to be locked, but it wasn't. It moved easily and the gate swung back so he carried on through it, closing it carefully again behind him, of course, as you always should. Then he walked slowly along the curved drive, picking his way carefully between the potholes that were starting to fill with water as the rain continued to beat down steadily.

When a house came into view – not a stately home, just a

largish house sitting squarely at the end of the drive with more land and trees behind and to one side of it – he stopped to study the whole scene before continuing. What an attractive building! It had two storeys with dormer attics in the roof forming a third one. There was a balanced eighteenth-century look to it. He loved the architecture of that era and nodded approval of its style.

He'd not try to get inside a place like that but would see if he could find somewhere to sleep in the grounds. If he went into the house, someone might call the police and accuse him of breaking and entering. He might walk round the outside of it the next day and have a look inside through the windows, but not today. He needed to find somewhere dry to stay the night. He did hope the rain would let up soon. He was wet enough, didn't want to get even wetter. No, his first priority had to be to find shelter and then he'd go back into the village to get some food.

As he skirted the house, he could see that all the curtains were firmly closed and it had a neglected air to it. It looked as if it was sad for lack of occupants whose company it could enjoy. The gardens had been let go to seed too and looked equally sad. He'd love to sort them out.

He rolled his eyes at his own silliness in acting as though houses had feelings. Even if they did, how would he know about them? They'd have their own language, wouldn't they? He had a quiet chuckle at himself. He was getting daft in his old age to think that way, but who would know? Or care?

When he went round to the rear of the house, he saw what looked like a former stable and several small sheds nearby. Outbuildings, they'd be called. One smaller shed stood on its own further from the house than the rest. It had what looked like an open-sided patio area attached to one end of it with a long rough bench along the wall it abutted. Perhaps the building had been a potting shed. It could have been. He'd had one similar to it. This one looked completely unused at the moment, though. What a waste when the garden needed so much attention!

There was even a rough track along the side hedge nearest the village that started near that particular shed. This way into the grounds looked to him as though it was meant for a gardener to bring in a vehicle carrying plants and other items without disturbing the people in the big house. Well, that's how he'd have used it anyway.

He moved across towards the shed. Was it possible that he might be able to get into it? Could he be that lucky? He'd really like to stay here for a while because in spite of the rather sad air of neglect, there was a pleasant feel to the whole place.

He'd love to get his hands on the poor neglected grounds. These would repay you generously for some loving care, he was sure, because the soil looked fertile. He bent to rub a little of the damp earth between his fingertip and thumb, nodding approval. Yes, basically good soil, this, or would be with a bit of care.

He tried the shed door and to his delight it opened gently, not making even the faintest squeaking noise. A squeaking door always sounded like a protest to him and during his walk that noise had a couple of times been so sharp it had put him off entering.

The interior of this shed was nice and neat, too, with broad shelves along one side. The bench at the far end was underneath a dirty window which looked out onto the matching outside bench, and yes, it opened out onto it as well when the window was unlocked. Definitely a potting area.

He turned slowly round on the spot, staring. It felt as if someone had tidied the shed up just for him, so that he'd feel almost as comfortable here mentally as he had in his own garden when his lass was in charge of their home. Gracie had certainly known how to make a place feel cosy after a satisfying day's work outside.

He stood for a minute or two in the doorway, taking it all in, then patted the door frame and murmured, 'I'd like to stay for a few days here if you don't mind.'

He felt a distinct sense of welcome after he said that, he really did, so he added, 'I won't make a mess, I promise.' And if saying that was daft, who would ever know? It made him feel better about staying here and that was worth a lot these days.

There was enough space to spread out a couple of plastic bin liners on the floor and then he'd see if there was anything softer to lie on, so he peeped into the nearest of the scruffy-looking canvas bags standing on the top metal shelf. He let out an involuntary exclamation of delight when he found these contained shabby and in some cases tattered old curtains and blankets. Presumably these had been set aside for use as rags or for pet animals to lie on. They'd make him a much more comfortable bed than he'd enjoyed for a week or two.

'Do you mind if I use a few of these covers?' he asked aloud and one of the blankets fell out of the bag he'd just put back on the shelf and landed at his feet. He swallowed hard at that. Was there a ghost here? He didn't believe in ghosts, not really, but there was something about this whole place that was . . . different. It was fey. That was a word Gracie had used in a couple of similar situations, so he said it aloud now.

The shed still felt welcoming, though, so he murmured another thank you, then set down his bin-liner bag of oddments in one corner and left it there. He went out again, closing the shed door carefully behind him because he needed to buy some food if he was to stay here. He was feeling quite hungry, for once.

He was taking a risk leaving his things, he knew, but if they were still here when he got back, he'd feel it was a sign that he was meant to linger here for a few days. He certainly wanted to. It had been a long day and he was feeling more tired than usual.

The rain had almost stopped now so he went out through the side entrance to the grounds and strolled down the rough track towards the road. He'd get to the village more quickly this way. It was quite a shortcut.

He stopped as he got close to the main road and saw how some overgrown bushes hid where the side track started. He hadn't noticed it when he'd walked past it. He took care not to crush the leaves or longer clumps of grass, holding the branches to one side and edging past so that anything he trampled in passing was hidden by the lower branches of the trees and bushes.

He trudged back along the road to the little shop, taking off his improvised raincoat and hat before going inside so that he didn't look quite so scruffy. Well, he hoped he didn't.

He was greeted with a smile, so ordered a simple meal of egg and chips, washed down by a pot of good strong tea. As it was still raining and he seemed to have more appetite today, he also ordered some of their lovely fluffy scones with what was advertised as homemade strawberry jam.

The scones tasted nearly as good as his wife's had done, nearly but not quite because they weren't served up with a loving smile, just a cool friendly stranger's smile. And the jam was indeed homemade. You could usually tell.

When it was time to leave, he was delighted to see that it had completely stopped raining and thank goodness for that.

He went into the shop part of the building and bought a packet of the same scones, a loaf, a bag of apples and a couple of tins of food. You couldn't carry much when you were on the tramp – well, he couldn't. He was losing some of his strength as he grew older, no doubt about it, though he wasn't doing badly for a seventy-year-old. This time, however, he felt he dared buy enough food for a few meals. There was no sign of anyone living at that nice house, after all.

He found a two-day-old newspaper sticking out of the external rubbish bin of the shop and it had been sheltered from the rain by a rough roof of corrugated iron sheltering it. And since no one else was around to see him, he took the newspaper out of the bin and to his delight found it still clean all the way through, if a bit crumpled in places. He'd even have some reading material tonight till it grew dark and after he'd finished reading this, he'd have useful pieces of paper left to wrap things in.

He'd open a tin of baked beans for tea, he decided. They were nearly as nice cold as hot. Well, they were if you were a hungry man who'd walked for most of the day. They were very good for you too, people said. And you didn't need butter to enjoy a slice of crusty bread, though he sometimes carried a jar of jam because that didn't get squashed and make a mess like cartons of food did. He had some blackberry jam left at the moment. Wonderful! He'd spread some on a slice of bread for afters and tonight's meal would feel like a feast. He'd eat the scones and an apple for breakfast.

He went back to the shed and studied its surroundings more carefully. There were two cottages nearby. The one further away from the road looked rather neglected and there was no sign of anyone living in it. He'd keep an eye on them, though, just in case people lived there.

He studied the area round his shed and found to his further delight that on the far side of it was what must have once been part of a kitchen garden. There were even some small self-set plants starting to show. Without taking any conscious decision, he bent down and pulled up some intrusive weeds to give three pale embryonic lettuces some time in the sun, then he found some other little plants that needed help too and liberated them from weeds.

He enjoyed a bit more general weeding. And why not? No one would object to him doing some free gardening for them and he'd greatly missed cherishing all sorts of plants and banishing useless weeds from food-producing areas. He cleared up a bigger area than he'd intended, the size he'd use if he wanted to put in a few runner beans and peas for himself. That made him feel sad. He so wished he could stay here and plant some things that would really be for himself. Oh, he did wish he was free to do that!

He knew suddenly that he'd had enough of tramping through the countryside. Did he dare settle somewhere near here? Who knew? He'd check out the area more carefully in the next day or two if he was able to stay.

He sat on an upturned old bucket with his back against the shed wall and read a few articles in the newspaper, catching up with the world a bit.

Then it was sunset so he went to lie down on his makeshift bed with the door open to the moon and stars. He slept better that night than he had for a long time. When he woke, he didn't feel exactly happy but a bit more like a civilised person at least.

In the middle of the next day, he even managed a rapid all-over wash in a little stream he found at one side of the grounds. Gracie would have approved of him taking the trouble to do that, but it left him feeling a bit shivery and unfortunately, he couldn't seem to get properly warm again.

How long would he be able to stay here? Several days, he hoped. Oh please, let it be more than one more night!

He had enough food to start his day, so he could do what he'd set his heart on, some proper gardening. He'd liberate some more of these self-set plants from weeds and grass. Maybe by the time they bore their little crops, someone would be here to eat them, even though he'd probably have had to move on long before then. If no one came here, there would be no harm done by his gardening and the birds might benefit, but it'd be a pity because this was definitely good soil.

Time passed quickly and he got quite a bit done, then realised that the sun was high in the sky and he'd better save some energy for walking into the village and buying more provisions. He'd stay there for a while to enjoy another flat white. He did love his coffees. But he didn't have much appetite today. He'd probably done too much gardening.

He sat down for a rest but it didn't do much good. He

was still feeling rather weary and a bit sneezy. He prayed he wasn't starting a cold. It would be hard to cope with one when you were living rough. He'd better buy another box of tissues, just in case.

He might treat himself to a hot meal at the café tonight. That'd do him good and banish the cold symptoms, he was sure. Or at least reduce them. Yes, another hot meal would be a lovely treat. There wasn't always a café as close as this one to give him that pleasure.

After he'd eaten he'd come back and have another sound sleep. He really felt he had a chance of staying here, perhaps even a few days of it.

He looked up towards the sky, blue now and gently sunny, and offered up a little plea. Oh, please! Whatever fate was pushing him along, let it not force him to move on from here yet. He so needed a rest. Needed it quite desperately.

Chapter Thirteen

After a stop for a quick snack, Libby and Miranda set off again, following the continuing instructions cooed at them by the posh female voice of the satnav. They passed an old woman walking slowly and wearily along by the side of the road, carrying a shopping bag and looking tired.

'When I see someone struggling along like that, I never know whether to stop and try to help them or not,' Libby said. 'I'm probably rich compared to her.'

Miranda had turned to watch her but then shrugged. 'Sadly, you can't help everyone. And we'd better not keep stopping. We need to carry on and catch all the daylight we can to explore the house I've inherited.'

They forgot about the old woman as they followed instructions, turning off the road and entering what they had thought was the beginning of another of those narrow lanes bordered by patches of wildflowers that they'd met before. However, they had to stop abruptly a short distance along it because where it started to curve quite sharply to the right, a pair of tall wrought-iron gates closed off what seemed to be the grounds of a house.

'This isn't a public road at all; it's the end of someone's drive,' Miranda said in a low voice, as if afraid of being overheard.

At that moment, the satnav voice spoke again: 'You have reached your destination.'

They both stared at the gates in surprise, then Miranda turned to her friend. 'It said "your destination". Can this really be the entrance to Fairfield House?'

'Must be. I don't think a satnav program will have made that serious an error, do you? It seems to have stopped guiding us at the gate, not at a house, so perhaps the land we can see is the grounds of a house.'

'It'd have to be a big house.'

'Yes. And these are rather elegant gates, too.'

Miranda shot her a worried glance. 'What if this isn't my great-aunt's house?'

'Then whoever it does belong to will no doubt tell us to leave and we'll have to ask better directions at that shop we just passed. Now, stop worrying. No one's going to shoot us if we've made a mistake.'

'I'll get out and open the gates for you to drive through, shall I – unless they're locked, of course?'

But they weren't locked and to her relief they swung back easily after she'd unlatched them. She paused for a minute to stare down at some marks on the soft earth that had been made quite recently, she'd guess. She wondered how recently. Those were undoubtedly footprints to one side as well, so someone had definitely got out of their vehicle to open the gates. There were no tyre marks from other vehicles, however. Strange.

She waited for Libby to drive through, so she could close them again.

'We might as well leave them open!' Libby called out through the open driver's window as she drove the car slowly up the shallow slope and through the entrance. 'We'll need to come back this way, after all, to buy some food in the village.'

Miranda got into the car again, still feeling worried. 'This definitely looks like a piece of private land, though.'

'It does, doesn't it? Wouldn't it be nice if it all belonged to you?'

She rolled her eyes at the mere idea. 'I doubt that would be possible, even in my wildest dreams. My family isn't rich that I know of. My mother and I always had trouble making ends meet.'

'What about the old aunt? She must have been comfortable enough financially if she could send you to a private boarding school.'

'I think the family trust paid for those, though Phyllis certainly seemed to have more money than we did. I doubt she was comfortable enough to have left me a big fortune and a country estate. This is more likely to be a modern gated housing development and if the house I've inherited really is here, it'll be just one of several. They sometimes build groups of better-class homes in places like this for security reasons.'

'It's a good idea these days, especially out in the country, and you'll probably get to know your neighbours quite easily if you live in a place like that.'

'You always seem to find something positive to say about every situation, my dearest Auntie Libby. I wish I were more like you. I can't help worrying about things I have to deal with, especially at the moment, when there are so many uncertainties about what exactly I'm facing.'

'I think you've had a sadder and far more difficult life than I have, and that's left you expecting things to go wrong. But you've still got plenty of time for the world to brighten up for you and things to start going right, especially now you're more in charge of your own life and will have a comfortable amount of money behind you.'

Miranda's tone was wistful. 'Yes, that will be a big improvement. Mum used to worry about that old aunt and what she would do next, and I was the same after Mum died, feeling vaguely threatened all the time after great-aunt Phyllis took control of my life. She was the most cunning person I've ever met, or even heard of, which is why I can't help worrying even now about what nasty surprises she might have left for me. But I don't worry nearly as much as I did when she was alive, I promise you.'

'I'll be very careful but she couldn't have known you'd bring someone here with you, so I don't think I'm in any great danger.'

'No, of course not. I'm being foolish, but believe me it's based on experience, not imagination.'

'Well, I'll do my best to make sure some good things happen to you from now on and we'll do our best to wipe out some of your worries. But in the meantime we'd better get back in the car and move on. Because of the way the drive curves round and the trees at this end of it, we can't see most of the plot of land from here, so who knows what we'll find? Something exciting, I hope. A big house, perhaps.'

Miranda suddenly reached out and gave her a hug. 'You make me feel better just by being with me. You're worth a whole street of big houses.'

Her friend and new auntie went a bit pink. 'I'm glad you

feel that. Now, let's get going. There could be a big house standing on its own or a group of houses ahead of us, or everything could have been knocked down and flattened ready for building on, for all we know. Onwards and upwards, whatever it is.'

'Wait!' Libby was still standing looking down at the ground their vehicle was standing on. 'Look at that! This track is only bare earth, but it's rock hard. Wouldn't they have put down a tarmac surface if it was the new entrance to a modern housing development? And if the drive had only just been made, it wouldn't have had time to become so compressed.'

Miranda opened her door and studied the ground next to the car at her side. 'Yes, I think you're right. This drive looks old to me, as if so many wheels have run over the ground that they've made it into a permanent roadway. There are no weeds growing in it along this edge, either, not till further away. Are there any close by on your side?'

'No, none.'

Libby made no attempt to move the car along and thought aloud. 'If it were a gated development, it could have been built on the site of a former big house, I suppose. That'd account for the firmness of the drive. But I still think they'd have resurfaced this.'

'Hmm. Well, we'll see. I know you like working things out, but I'm dying to see for myself what's inside this fenced area, not just make guesses.'

'Oops! Sorry.'

'Could you drive quite slowly from now on, please? These are such beautiful old trees that it's a pleasure to drive through the patterns of light and shade. It feels to me as if this grove is standing sentinel at the entrance to the property.' Miranda hesitated, then shook her head slightly.

'You looked as if you were about to say something else. Go on.'

'It'll sound stupid.'

'So? Who cares? Say it anyway. You may as well tell me the rest now that you've caught my attention.'

'All right, then. I feel as if – well, as if the place is welcoming me.'

She saw Libby give her a surprised look but that was truly how it felt and Miranda wasn't going to take back what she'd said and replace it with something more negative in tone. She really did feel positive about this place.

The drive curled gently round to the right, the ground further back from it at both sides of it covered by a variety of weeds and grassy plants, one taller patch rippling in the sunlight as a light breeze stirred it.

'The grass can't have been mowed for a while to have grown so tall,' Libby murmured. 'Oh! Good heavens!'

Libby braked instinctively as they got further round the bend and a large house came into sight about a hundred yards ahead of them.

They exchanged surprised glances. There were no other houses to be seen, only this one. It wasn't anything like the size of a stately home but it was larger than most of today's so-called luxury detached residences nonetheless. They could just see part of an outbuilding at the rear of it and there were a couple of smaller, freestanding sheds further back still, the most distant one close to the side fence.

'Let's edge forward a little then stop for a few moments and take a good look at it because we ought to be able to see the whole of it quite clearly once we get past this big tree,' Miranda suggested.

Libby nodded and edged forward a little then switched off the engine, wriggling her shoulders to ease the stiffness with a satisfied murmur.

Both women got out of the vehicle again, not saying anything but standing where they were, one on either side of it, each with the hand closest to it resting lightly on the car roof as they studied the large building, now clearly visible.

'It's beautiful,' Miranda murmured after a while. 'Old-fashioned and utterly charming. But a house like that can't be mine, surely?'

'Why not? Wouldn't you want it if it were?'

'Of course I would! Who wouldn't? But how could my horrible old great-aunt have left such a gorgeous house to me?' She frowned. 'There's a saying: "I fear the Greeks, even when bearing gifts." It certainly fits this situation. Now, where does that quote come from?'

'I'm not sure but it could be one of Virgil's pieces of distilled wisdom, perhaps? And if so, from the *Aeneid*, probably. His quotes often do come from it. But that's not important at the moment. We're a pair of idiots even to stop to consider a quote. Let's get back to considering your great-aunt's legacy.'

'Well, this house would certainly make a wonderful gift. And yet, to echo the quotation, I do fear what she was plotting by leaving it to me. So that quote fits this situation very well and is worth bearing in mind. She hated me. I could feel it and was quite certain of that even as a small child. Later on it even showed in the messages she sent to me. And I never knew why.' She shrugged, then her expression softened as she continued to stare at the house. 'Isn't it an elegant building?'

'Beautiful. So balanced in design, everything fitting well

together rather than one part of the house dominating another.'

It was built of creamy golden stone, big oblong chunks of it, each about as wide as two outstretched hands and one hand deep from top to bottom. The stones were slightly worn and marked by age and weathering but somehow they suited the house like that, helped give it some gravitas.

It definitely seemed like a home, though, not a show-off mansion, and Miranda felt as if it was not only welcoming these two visitors but inviting them to go inside. 'I don't think the modern homes erected by builders to tempt the more affluent customers usually hold a candle to this one,' she murmured. 'I can't wait to see the interior.'

The lawyer had told her that the house was old and it was clear from the styles of architecture that the main part must have been built nearly a couple of centuries ago, with some small additional rooms and various decorative changes made later at the rear of one end in a similar style, giving it an L shape, but still not upsetting its balanced appearance.

After studying it for a few more moments, Miranda said quietly, 'The additions are similar in style both physically and artistically, don't you think? I bet they were to add some more modern amenities.'

'Whatever they're for, I agree. It's been very nicely done,' Libby said. 'In fact, I think this house has been built with a lot of love, if that doesn't sound too fanciful. It's the sort of house you could very easily love.'

'Only the recent owner doesn't seem to have loved it or even kept it in good repair. There are a couple of tiles missing from the roof over there and the paintwork is peeling in some parts.' She pointed, then shook her head sadly. 'I wonder what the inside will be like. Not good, I'd guess. I doubt my aunt ever truly loved anyone or anything.'

'Except herself and money. Maybe she kept the inside nice for her own pleasure and comfort.'

'Well, from what I've heard, what she really loved was making money. Perhaps she saved all her affection for doing that.'

They didn't hurry to start moving again, simply continued to take in the details of the building, occasionally murmuring a comment or pointing out some detail.

'It can't have been heritage listed,' Libby said slowly. 'I'm sure the lawyer would have told you if it had. I wonder why not? It's beautiful enough, surely? Or it could be.'

'I was just wondering about that too. Houses like this one should be preserved for future generations of the nation, don't you think?'

'Yes, I do. It's the prettiest house I've ever seen. But it's survived, even without that formal labelling and heritage protection, hasn't it? And presumably you'll be able to do what's needed to bring everything up to scratch again, after which you can enjoy taking care of it properly.'

'If it really is mine.'

'Of course it is.'

There was silence for a few moments then Miranda said, 'Well, if it is mine, I'm glad the old witch has left it to me but another reason is more important to me than its monetary value. It makes me feel that I'm a genuine part of the Westerby family.'

Libby gave her a quick sideways glance, knowing how unhappy her friend felt, much as she tried to hide it, at that lack of belonging to a family since her mother's death. 'It doesn't change your great-aunt's nastiness towards you, or the fact that you'll still need to stay on your guard against hidden traps,' she warned quietly.

'I know and I won't forget that.' Miranda tried to smile but couldn't because emotion was welling up inside her in great waves. Nothing had prepared her for falling in love with her new home on sight and she felt like weeping for joy to think that she'd inherited this, could stay here for the rest of her life. Surely it wouldn't be too much to ask that she could meet a nice guy one day and create a new branch of the Westerby family?

Strangely, she didn't need a lawyer to confirm that this house was indeed hers because the longer she stood here, the more certain she felt of that.

The silence went on for a while but Libby didn't break it, only stood quietly to one side of her companion, giving her time to look her fill.

'It's utterly beautiful,' Miranda said at last. 'Why don't I remember anything about it? I did come here once, after all.'

'Because you were far too young. The exterior is very shabby at present when you study it in detail, isn't it? It looks pretty at a distance but from close by you can see that some parts are looking distinctly run-down. Why didn't she take better care of it?'

'I didn't notice the wear and tear at first but yes, I'm starting to see how much needs doing. Why did she let it deteriorate so much? The lawyer said there was probably a decent amount of money savings included in the legacy. Some things are easy to fix, like those broken tiles at that right-hand end. And I bet that stain on the house wall below them comes from the gutters leaking whenever it rains. Another easy thing to fix.'

She turned slowly round on the spot, looking at the gardens now. 'If those straggling hedges mark the boundaries, there's more land comes with it than I'd expected.'

'A couple of acres, perhaps a bit less, at a guess.'

'I'll have to take your word for how much. I'm not very good at judging that because I grew up in towns and was locked away in boarding school for most of the time after my mother died until I went to university. I concentrated more on passing exams and saving money than physical activities and sports. I used to enjoy going on the supervised walks with school groups at weekends, though, and I regretted having to go back into the building after all the fresh air and sunshine.'

'I love going for long walks.'

'We'll do some together once we've settled in, then. Ooh, look!' Miranda pointed to one side. 'That bigger shed, the one furthest away from the house, is just next to a side entrance and there's a definite track leading from it down the side to the road. Could that be a back entrance to the grounds, do you think?'

'Could be. A gardener's entrance, maybe. You couldn't manage to care for a piece of land this big on your own.'

'I suppose so. It's wonderful that there are so many huge old trees dotted around the grounds, isn't it? They look gorgeous.'

'Larch trees outside the gates and horse chestnuts further in. We had one of those in our street when I was finishing primary school. The boys used their nuts to play conkers with.'

Miranda smiled across the car roof at her friend. 'You could fit half a dozen flats like ours into a house that size, couldn't you?'

'Yes. We won't have any trouble finding bedrooms for ourselves, will we?'

'No trouble at all.' She still didn't move. Everything was quiet except for a few faint and intermittent natural sounds: birds, insects and the gentle soughing of tree branches as the light breeze made them swish to and fro. There wasn't even a distant hum of traffic to be heard from here.

And yet . . . she frowned and stared sharply round. At first sight she'd seen only the beauty of the house, and that was still there, of course. But now she'd also sensed that even though she'd felt happy to be here, the house didn't look happy because its upkeep had been neglected in a lot of small ways. What was the problem?

This was her mother's side of the family coming out in another way. She'd tried very hard to train herself to suppress premonitions about the future but they still sometimes came to her. Her mother had said that in every generation one or two members of the Westerby family seemed to have psychic gifts and had told Miranda that when she reached puberty she would be one of them and not to let Phyllis know about that. She'd get used to sometimes sensing future events or problems as she grew older, but it was usually better not to tell people about that.

She hadn't even talked about these premonitions to Libby and had tried to tell herself that she didn't believe in all that woo-woo stuff, only she hadn't been able to persuade herself that they were merely flights of her imagination. Well, how could she when they came true, if not always in the way she'd expected?

This side of her stayed quiet most of the time, but it wouldn't always behave. And right now it had come surging up with a strength that she couldn't deny. Even though the house felt to have welcomed her, at the same time it was as if something unpleasant had touched the place and was still lingering and threatening her, as if she needed to take care.

Could that feeling have been caused by her nasty old great-aunt living there? Only if so, why was it lingering now that the old woman was dead? And why did she feel as if it was still guarding itself against someone of ill intent?

As the new owner, she intended to care for it again, had fallen in love with it on sight. She got angry at herself now because she'd get nothing done by standing here giving in to her tendency to daydream. That's all it was, daydreaming, merely speculating a little about the future.

She straightened up abruptly. 'Shall we move on now, Libby?'

'I was waiting for you. You've been standing here staring at the house for several minutes, not seeming to be aware of anything or anyone else.'

'That long? Oh. I'm sorry. It's not every day you inherit a big old house, though, is it? I'm ready to carry on exploring now. I'm dying to go inside my future home.'

They got back into the car and set off again, bumping slowly along the rest of the drive towards the front door and parking a few yards to one side of it.

'I'm stopping here because I don't want to spoil our view of the entrance,' Libby explained. 'The way those double doors are set back under the porch is very attractive, don't you think? And surely those are stained-glass windows at either side of them? I bet panels like that light up the hall beautifully when the sun shines on them.'

'Oh, yes. One of the few things I remember about my childhood visit is walking through different colours slanting across the hall. I wanted to stay there and play in them, but Mum pulled me along. Anyway, come on!' She got out of the car and waited for her friend to join her. 'Isn't this exciting?'

Chapter Fourteen

Miranda took out the clunky old house key and was about to unlock the door of her new home and go straight inside when she remembered what the lawyer had suggested, and he'd said it very emphatically too.

She stopped and put the key back in her pocket. Reluctant as she was to delay seeing the interior, she knew he'd been right to warn her to check the outside of the building before going into it. He'd been concerned for her personal safety but if someone really had broken in, the police wouldn't want anything touched until they got the chance to examine it carefully.

The world seemed to be getting more dangerous for ordinary people by the decade, sadly. And she'd better take care about how she dealt with an inheritance from a wicked old woman.

She grasped Libby's arm to stop her friend moving towards the front door. 'The lawyer suggested that before I go into the house I walk round the outside and check it for signs of someone having broken in.'

'Oh. Right. I suppose that would be a sensible thing to do, given how isolated it is.'

'And he also said I shouldn't come here on my own the first time. I agreed with him on both counts, though reluctantly on this one at the moment, because I'm absolutely dying to see the inside. You stay here and I'll do a quick circuit of the exterior.'

Libby frowned at that. 'Wouldn't it be safer for us to walk round it together?'

Miranda shook her head. 'I don't think so. You should stay here and keep an eye on the front of the house to make sure no one comes creeping round the side to get away from me as I walk round. It won't take me long. And believe me, I'll run straight back to you if there's any trouble, screaming loudly all the way.' She grinned at her companion as she added, 'I'm a very loud screamer when I want to be, and a fast runner too.'

Libby didn't smile back. 'Well, if you're sure you're OK doing that, it would be a sensible way to do it, I suppose.'

'There's no perfect way with only two of us, but this seems the best way to handle it for now.' She turned to stare to the right to check something. 'It looks as though there's a rough gravel path leading round that corner of building so I'll start there.'

'Take care. If I hear you screaming, I'll come running. In fact, I'll lock my car straight away so that I can come rushing instantly to your aid at top speed if necessary.'

'Who's looking on the negative side now?' Miranda teased. 'Still, I suppose it's better to be overcareful than sorry when you're exploring new territory.'

She reached into her shoulder bag and got out the set

of new house keys the lawyer had given her, which were threaded on a large key ring. After fitting them between the fingers of her right hand with the pointed ends sticking out upwards in case she needed to defend herself, she held that hand out to show her friend and pulled a wry face at it. 'Look. Am I being silly? Is it worth bothering to set up this old-fashioned way of defending myself?'

But Libby didn't share her amusement. 'I don't think you're being silly at all. In fact the keys are a good idea. I'll do the same thing with mine.' She took out her own pair of keys and placed them at the ready then brandished them, though they were smaller modern ones and didn't look nearly as impressive as some of the large older keys Miranda was holding.

'I've always wondered whether this really works when I read about heroines doing it in novels. I doubt I'll find out today, though. As if anyone is going to attack us in such a peaceful place! I can't see that happening.'

'It's a very pretty setting but there aren't any people close enough to come to our aid if we needed help, so better safe than sorry, eh?'

'Have you got the front door key handy?'

Miranda pulled a single key out of her jacket pocket and waved it at her.

Libby stared round again. 'It doesn't look at all like a potential crime scene to me, I must admit.'

'Nor to me, but here goes.'

She set off walking along the front of the house, glancing down and smiling at the keys sticking out of her hand. Then she felt her smile fade. She might be dying to see what the house was like inside, but if a sensible lawyer had felt he needed to warn her about checking the place first then she would heed him. That meant walking along slowly enough to study every window she passed and the ground beneath them.

She paused to wave farewell to Libby just before she turned the first corner and as they lost sight of one another, she felt herself go on the alert to a much greater extent, especially when she got to the rear corner and realised there were no other houses or people to come to her aid if she shouted from this part of the house. The two cottages could only be seen properly from the front of the building, and from here she could see the roof of a cottage in the street.

This was a very isolated house and she'd only have herself to rely on if she met any problems on her way round today. And Libby, of course, if her friend could hear a shout for help from the front. It'd definitely be wise to get a security system installed as soon as possible, and a good one too with her phone linked to it.

As she got to the far end of the rear part, she thought she heard something, so stopped to check that there was no sign of anyone nearby. Just as she was about to move on, she looked at the taller grasses and weeds at the edge of the back garden and frowned. Something or someone had flattened those plants near the shed at the edge of the garden. Who could have done that?

That particular shed was the furthest away from the house and it really did look as if someone had been walking around that area recently. She didn't move on straight away at the next corner, but studied the shed and its surroundings again, suddenly realising that the patch of cleared ground with tidy rows of greenery in the dark earth could only have been caused by someone weeding a group of young plants and watering them. In fact, it looked like the early stages of a vegetable garden.

That puzzled her. Who would have done that to the garden of a deserted property? Had there been an intruder and if so, was the person still hanging around?

She studied the ground between the big house and that shed but none of the grass between them had been flattened. They hadn't thought to study the grass near the entrance drive all that carefully, so she stood for a little longer, listening intently. But once again she could hear nothing except the sounds of nature and couldn't see any other suspicious signs.

Perhaps a youngster from the village had been making a garden. Children did that sort of thing, made little dens and hiding places for themselves away from the adults if possible. When she was a child, she must have read the children's book *The Secret Garden* at least a dozen times and had wished she had a place like that to escape to.

Phyllis had thrown away all her childhood books when she sent Miranda to boarding school, telling her scornfully that they were far too young for someone of her age and therefore a total waste of space.

She'd cried about that, though not till she was alone in bed. By then she knew not to show any reaction when her great-aunt did something hurtful. Those books had felt like old friends. Well, as near as she got to having any old friends.

She clicked her tongue in annoyance at herself. She had to stop thinking about the past and concentrate on the present and the better life this inheritance seemed to promise for the future.

She took a final look round then continued round the corner of the house and down the other side of the building.

There were no signs of footprints in the softer earth of the flowerbeds on this side either. Once she got back to the front of the house, she smiled at Libby and was about to say that everything was OK then hesitated, realising that she should at least be sharing the full details with her friend.

'No one seems to have been near the house but it looks as though someone has been walking about in the long grass near the side fence, close to that furthest shed. There's a side entrance into the grounds there from what looks like a rough track running up the edge there from the main road. You can see it better from the back of the house. And whoever it is has done some gardening too, weeding a small patch to give a group of seedlings room to grow, and watering them, would you believe?'

'Done some gardening? That's the last thing I'd expect an intruder to do. Tell me again exactly what you saw?'

'It looked as if seedlings had been freed from taller weeds near the hut. They're still quite small and look like rough rows of self-sets from last year, not tidy rows planted this year. If we want to keep them, they'll definitely need watering daily unless it rains.'

'We should go and check that part of the grounds properly, then, and do it before we even attempt to unlock the front door.'

'There was no sign that an intruder was still hanging around, really there wasn't, and no footprints or flattened grass on the land between it and the house.'

Libby shook her head. 'I know you're itching to go inside the house, love, but let's check anyway. With both of us, it won't take long.' She smiled and waggled one forefinger at her companion. 'Auntie knows best.'

'Neither of us seems to know anything for certain about

this place,' Miranda said quietly. And yet, for all the puzzling bits, she still thought it a lovely old house.

Libby put one arm round her shoulders. 'We really do need to be super-careful here, love. This house could easily have been broken into and if the person was skilful enough to pick one of the locks and put it back together again, we'd never even know. It's been left unoccupied for several weeks now, remember.'

She paused only for a moment then added, 'Come to think of it, there are several sheds to check as well if we're going to make a proper job of this. We should at least take a quick look inside each of them and check that there's no one lurking there. We'd notice a human being quite quickly if there were any.'

'Isn't that taking caution too far?'

'What price your safety, today and in the near future? I value that very highly indeed.'

There was no answer to that. It still made Miranda feel faintly surprised at having someone care so deeply about her and therefore about her safety after so many years of being totally on her own emotionally.

Chapter Fifteen

After a few days staying in the shed and amusing himself by doing a little gardening, Jim set out to buy some more food at the village shop. He was feeling cautiously optimistic about being able to stay here for a few days longer.

When he heard a car coming towards him, however, he slowed down to watch it as he moved slowly along, trying not to draw attention to himself. He kept a careful eye on what was going on around him these days, especially when he was coming out of a temporary hidey-hole only to buy food. He'd never even dreamt of studying passers-by this suspiciously when Gracie was alive.

By the time the car had passed him, he was nearly at the village shop, but he stopped in the shade of a big roadside tree, not even trying to go inside to make his purchases. Not yet. He hoped neither of the two women in the car had noticed him stop to watch them.

No vehicle only passing through the village would be

turning off to the big house, so he had to know for sure whether it was going to stay there. He hoped not, so that he could spend another night or two in that lovely cosy shed without worrying.

He felt uneasy. In the few days he'd spent here so far, he hadn't seen many people driving about in the village at this time of day. The main reasons for cars moving through it seemed to be for people to travel to work elsewhere in the early mornings or to come back home again at the end of the day. One young guy always came back around six o'clock. He had a trailer behind him with what looked like tools in it and *Mack's Electrics* written in bright red on the sides. It always had music thumping out of it. That'd not be good for his long-term hearing but at least he was definitely a local, living in one of the cottages and not going anywhere near the big house.

Who were these strangers currently driving through the village? The only other reason cars came here at this time of day was to go to the shop, which was well patronised by locals. But this vehicle had come from outside the village and driven straight past the shop. Why?

The main street didn't seem to lead anywhere except to a T-junction at the far end from the shop, where you could turn one way and rejoin the main road or turn the other along lanes that led to a few scattered farms. He'd walked partway along it on his second day to find out where they led, planning to pretend he was a hiker if he met anyone. Only, he hadn't run into anyone. This seemed to be a very quiet part of the country.

He knew some of the locals were aware of his presence on the block of land but they hadn't made any effort to get him to move on. A guy had come out of the top cottage at the side of the grounds early on as well to stare at him and scowl, then gone back inside.

Jim hadn't tried to chat to whichever of the pair of shopkeepers was serving him, just bought what he needed quickly and got out again, in case either of them suggested that he should leave the district.

An older woman had stopped him as he came out of the shop the previous day and thrust a package into his hand, muttering, 'This may help,' then she'd hurried away looking rather embarrassed and gone into a nearby cottage.

The plastic bag had contained some slices of stale bread in its original wrapper, plus a couple of slices of ham, two apples and a jar half-full of apricot jam. The latter had improved the taste of the bread considerably. He managed to light a small fire and toast it – well, more or less toast it. One piece fell off the stick he was using as a toasting fork and part of it got covered in ash and dirt, so he shared that with the birds.

The kindness of the woman's act had made him feel good, however, and it had saved him the trouble of going to the village shop that day.

She hadn't stopped to chat to him, though. People rarely did chat to strangers these days, he'd found. He remembered when he was a lad, his grandfather passing the time of day with strangers on the tramp or people who were just walking down a street towards him, as well as with the neighbours and friends he knew well.

Where were those women in the car going? he wondered now. Had they turned into the village in error or were they passing through on their way to a farm? He stayed where he was, mostly hidden by the tree trunk, keeping a careful eye on the car. He didn't want anyone to take him by surprise in his temporary lodgings in case they accused him of trespassing and called the police.

He was only staying in and near the shed furthest from the house and hadn't been near the latter because he didn't want to leave footprints and risk being accused of planning to break in or worse. He wasn't quite sure what the law was these days about vagrants but he didn't intend to find that out the hard way.

He wasn't ready yet to try to build a new life. Not quite yet, but he was getting there.

He had slept a lot of the time in the past few days because once he'd stopped, he'd been utterly desperate for a respite from trudging on and on. It was lovely and quiet on that piece of land, with a few mature trees in full leaf now and some birds nesting and feeding their tiny, clearly newly hatched offspring.

He'd have liked to stay there and work in the garden properly, extending it and turning it into a place of beauty not just picking out a few weeds. Even thinking about it made his hands twitch to pull up more of them.

Oh, no! He watched in dismay as the car slowed down well before it got to the T-junction and turned into the drive leading only to the big house. He waited, praying the turn was a mistake, as had happened once before, but this car didn't come back out again.

He was fairly sure the two women inside the vehicle wouldn't have paid much attention to him as they drove past. He'd be just another scruffy old tramp. But they'd have asked what he was doing there if they'd found him in the grounds of their house, he was sure.

Who were they? Were they coming to stay here? Was his wonderful new resting place to be taken from him after a mere few days of staying here peacefully? He'd even given in to the temptation to do a bit of gardening. It had felt wonderful to get his hands in the soil again and tidy up the area behind his shed. He'd be so sad to leave it all behind.

How would he bear it if he had to go on the tramp again? That thought made him realise how much he wanted to find a new home. He could feel deep-down weariness in every part of his body now and it was so bad today that he couldn't think straight. It felt as if the world around him was as blurred as his thoughts and he still didn't feel well enough to walk far, couldn't seem to shake off the cold or virus or whatever it was that he'd picked up a week or so ago.

Oh dear! He remembered overhearing various fragments of conversation in the village shop and suddenly they all clicked together like the pieces of a jigsaw puzzle to give him a deeply worrying whole. Apparently the former owner of this big house with its lovely grounds had been taken ill a few weeks ago and someone had recently got word that she'd died. She'd only been in her mid-sixties, too.

Now, it seemed, everyone in the neighbourhood was expecting the heir to come and take possession of the big house and its grounds. Well, everyone except him. Until now, he'd been too far out of touch with the people around him, had had to rely on snatches of information from conversations that he'd overheard fragments of. The new owner was another woman, they seemed to think.

Could one of the women in the car which had just turned into the grounds be the new owner? If so, she'd have a lot on her plate sorting out the old place. He'd spent time studying the exterior, for lack of anything better to do, and it was in a very run-down condition. He could list all the places that needed urgent attention and do some of the smaller outside jobs himself, too. He doubted that the place would be any better cared for inside.

As for the gardens, they must have been shamefully neglected for a long time to get into the state they were in now. His fingers itched to start setting things to rights every time he studied another part of them. There were some lovely plants fading away for lack of attention and some that desperately needed fertilising at this time of year. It'd be relatively easy to sort most of them out, would just take some ongoing efforts for a year or two. If only . . .

It would also take time. Plants need to grow again the way nature prefers them to, slowly and steadily. But he could have helped nature to get the necessary changes started and would have enjoyed doing it properly and carefully, too.

He sighed. He'd even found an old bag with some fertiliser left in the bottom and had been enjoying using a few little sprinkles here and there to bring one small corner of the vegetable plot back into order. Just a handful or two scattered judiciously could work wonders. Plants could be so wonderfully grateful for a little attention, especially from someone with an understanding of their needs.

Sadly, he'd been having to move about more slowly than usual because he still wasn't feeling very well. This cold or virus or whatever it was had made him feel rather weak and 'wambly', to use one of his late wife's pet words for a person being a bit under the weather.

He changed his mind about going into the shop. If he had to leave suddenly, he wouldn't be able to carry the tins of food he'd been planning to buy today. Pity. Tins of ready-cooked food made it much easier to feed yourself properly – well, more or less properly, now that he didn't have any cooking facilities. He had no way of cooking fresh vegetables and really missed them, with butter dobbed on top and melting slowly. He sighed and licked his lips at the memory of how good that could taste.

It would probably be wise to go back to the shed via the side entrance because if he crouched a little as he walked up the track he could stay more or less out of sight but still see what the two women were doing. He'd have to leave if they were settling in to stay there permanently, but it'd make sense to check first whether they were indeed doing that or just checking it out.

They had a house to sleep in, the lucky things, but if it was in a really bad condition inside, they might go and stay at a hotel or B&B for a few days while they hired people to sort out the interior. That would at least give him time to work out what to do next, and he could rest a day or two longer perhaps if he hid in the bushes beside the rough path at the side during the daylight hours. He was so very tired still.

Only – if they decided to stay here from now on, he'd have to leave today and where could he go so late in the day? He'd not have time to walk very far before it grew dark and he wasn't sure he could manage to tramp far yet anyway. You could only push a tired old body so much then it fell to pieces. No, his best plan might be to hide in that group of leafy bushes during the daytime, and stay a little longer. He could lie very still, cover himself with a few small branches and doze. He kept falling asleep anyway, whether he intended to or not, felt really dopey at the moment.

A tear trickled down his cheek. He couldn't help it. He

was a long way from his former home now, knew no one round here who would take him in till he recovered, and anyway, did he want to let his former friends know that he'd been living like a tramp? No, of course he didn't. And there were no B&Bs nearby, not that he'd seen on the way here anyway.

Oh, hell! What was he going to do? This settled one thing. It was time to stop wandering round like a lost soul. Gracie would be upset with him for giving in to losing her like a useless fool.

In the end he admitted to himself that he'd have to risk staying here tonight because he simply couldn't walk very far. But if he waited until it grew light before he left, hopefully after a decent night's sleep, perhaps he'd manage to find somewhere quite near to stop at a B&B. He couldn't walk far, he knew that.

Or he could go and find a park or public open space to spend the day in, then come back here after dark.

Yes, he might have to do that if there was somewhere in the village. He felt so weak.

He'd pack his things in one of the sacks and make it look like the other sacks full of rags, then leave it on the top shelf of the racks in the shed. Hopefully no one would realise it belonged to a temporary visitor.

No, not a visitor, just a very weary old tramp at the moment.

Chapter Sixteen

As he no longer needed to work all the hours he could stay awake to build up his finances for what he thought of as his 'great escape', Ryan decided to sit outside on the tiny front porch of his new home for a while. He'd enjoy the fine summery weather while watching people walk by, and he'd watch the small animals and birds too.

Before he'd moved there he'd stood in the back garden, looking along the fence line of the big house to the scruffy little cottage hugging one kink in the fence at the back of the same edge of it, just as his own cottage did nearer the front. He'd guess that the two pieces of land had been selected for the cottages, perhaps to house servants and their families, by the owner of the big house many years ago.

The guy who sometimes lived in the other cottage didn't seem to be in residence at the moment. Strange how he'd taken a dislike to that chap whom he'd only seen at a distance. They'd never even exchanged greetings let alone had a proper conversation, though that wasn't his fault.

At first when he'd passed the guy in the village, Ryan had nodded to him as you usually did to your neighbours, and he'd seen other people do the same to their neighbours.

The fellow hadn't nodded back once, let alone smiled, either at him or the others who lived nearby. After getting such an utter lack of response a few times, Ryan had stopped bothering, though he did nod to the rest of the locals – and they nodded back!

Living so close to the cottage, however, he couldn't help noticing what this fellow did when he was in residence. Not much, was a good summary of what went on at the other cottage. Its tenant polished the shiny red convertible regularly, though, heaven knew why because he didn't often go out in it and it wasn't usually dirty as he'd built a small roofed shelter for it at one side of his cottage. He sat in it sometimes, simply sat there like a fool staring into space.

His other main activity seemed to be spying on the big house or watching the people who lived near it. He tried to stay out of Ryan's sight when he was at home and did his spying from an upstairs bedroom. Only he often used binoculars and didn't seem to notice how they caught the sun and reflected its light at people.

Well, he was welcome to keep an eye on Ryan and good luck to him with that because there was nothing to be gained from what he saw. Ryan sat outside when the weather was good, painting, or he tended his garden. What he had of most value was inside his head, not external physical wealth-making systems.

He often sat in his small sunroom at the side of his cottage where it was presumably easy for him to be seen, because the walls were made mainly of glass panels. *You won't see me doing anything visually interesting or out of the ordinary, you idiot,* he thought sometimes. All he did was use his desktop computer for the small IT jobs which were all he took on these days or else he worked at his easel, painting the pictures of small birds and other creatures that were starting to sell occasionally. That was a far more enjoyable way of earning a living than working on a computer.

Why did that fellow want to see what his neighbours were doing when he didn't even know them by name? As Ryan's Lancashire grandmother would have said, 'There's nowt so queer as folk.' Only she'd always pronounced the last word of the old saying 'fowk' to rhyme roughly with 'nowt'. But she'd been right: there was nothing as strange as people and this guy was right up there among the leaders of the stranger inhabitants of the human world.

The people in the village knew when Westerby was in residence, of course they did, and Ryan had first learnt his neighbour's name by overhearing in the shop some of their adverse remarks about him and his unfriendliness.

He also noticed that they made no attempt whatsoever to chat to the fellow, simply walked past him as if he wasn't there. They were starting to chat to Ryan, though, and that pleased him. One or two of the oldies had dropped hints about which plants did well round here and when he listened to them carefully and did as they'd suggested, they started to offer him cuttings and seedlings as well, which he'd accepted as gladly as their advice.

Today one or two of them waved to him as they walked past and noticed him sitting there. And of course he smiled and waved back. He felt delighted the first time this happened. He had no desire to live like a hermit but he hadn't wanted to push himself at them so had waited to let them make the first verbal overtures beyond a hello.

He'd chatted a few times with Greg and Ashley at the shop in their quieter moments, and had got as far as admitting that he was into painting. Ashley had asked if he ever sold paintings and when he admitted that he did, she'd said she'd like to see them. If she thought folk round here might like them, maybe they could try putting one or two up for sale in the shop. They might be just right to brighten up the café's inner corner.

'I'll come over and look at them this afternoon, if that's all right with you,' she'd said. 'It's usually our quietest time of day. If I can sell one or two, I'll have to charge a twenty per cent agent's fee, but we'll both benefit from any sales, eh?'

'Happy to have you visit any time. And if you can sell a few that'd be good.' He didn't need the money desperately but it'd be good to move in the direction of selling the occasional painting, because the buyers' remarks gave him pleasure. And it never hurt to bring in a little more money even when you didn't mind living frugally.

He'd settled into mainly painting flowers, both wildflowers and garden blooms, as well as the little animals and other creatures he saw scurrying about on the ground and among lower bits of foliage round here. And he must have got his market right because a few people had bought the smaller or cheaper paintings from the shop and others had commented on them approvingly even when they didn't buy.

It wasn't to everyone's taste to live with wildlife on the walls, but he loved watching the animals and insects bustling to and fro near his cottage, and often finding a place for themselves in his latest scene as a consequence, even when they weren't the main focus of that painting. He hadn't set out to have tiny creatures peeping out from behind his images of wildflowers or from among the foliage of low-growing shrubs, but somehow they often did. And people liked seeing them there.

He'd felt he'd earned some relaxation time today because he'd had a very late night dealing with an urgent IT problem for the owners of the village shop. He'd been there when things went wrong and of course he'd offered his help.

This had turned into a paying job that would bring him a nice little chunk of money to swell the modernisation fund for this cottage, not to mention creating plenty of gratitude and goodwill, which was important too when you intended to make a place your forever home. He charged them only a modest amount because he knew they'd get quotes from others and could guess fairly accurately how much they'd be told it'd cost. So of course he won the job easily. He still made a profit, which showed that prices were sometimes too high for the 'little folk' of the business world.

The job he'd just finished had been a bit fiddly but he'd managed to retrieve their customer records after a sudden glitch had thrown their whole system into chaos and left the information in danger of being wiped out permanently. Fortunately they'd had the sense to leave their problem alone and wait for professional help to solve it.

In fact, the shop's computer system had been rather badly set up by some inefficient amateur and Ryan had thought it best to gently explain to them the details of why it was never going to work in a secure way for them. He wanted to make sure they understood the situation clearly so that they wouldn't blame him if it still wasn't totally reliable in future.

Ashley looked at him anxiously. 'That sounds as if you expect it to go wrong again.'

'I'm afraid I do.'

'Could you fix it properly for us if we paid you some more?'

'Yes, but you'd need to upgrade the software, I'm afraid, and that'd add to the cost. It's not a gigantic job and not hugely expensive, and I don't mind if you offset part of the cost in free groceries from your shop over the next month or two.'

He saw her face brighten and knew he'd hit a mutually beneficial target there, so continued to explain. 'However, doing it properly will cost about three times as much as the adjustments I could make for you to keep things ticking along for a while.'

They both sucked in their breath, looking at one another in shock, then Ashley took over again. 'Is that your best price?' She was definitely the money person in their small business and Greg provided the brawn, charmed the customers, male and female, because he was such a nice guy, and supplied ready-cooked meals, both frozen and fresh, because he'd previously been a chef. Good value they were, too.

Ryan knocked fifty pounds off his charges and they hesitated.

'If you do that for us, will it be completely reliable?' she asked. 'Greg and I can't afford to lose vital information. We need to keep our customers, stock and purchasing information absolutely safe.'

'Yes, of course it will be reliable, very reliable in fact because I can guarantee that any system I put in will do what I promise and not let you down. I can't do anything about overall outages of electricity that switch things off temporarily at the server and hit all the local customers, though.'

'We'll do it with you, then.'

'You'll have to give me a couple of days to finish another job first, then I could start work on yours. If I do another late night on it as I get to the final major changeover, you and your customers won't be greatly inconvenienced.'

Ashley took a deep breath and nodded. 'We'd be really grateful if you'd do that for us, then. Would you be interested in a deal for us paying you half in cash and half in Greg's cooked meals? We'll give you a discount on the value of the latter.'

'Sounds great to me.' He held out his hand and she shook it, letting out an audible sigh of relief.

Three days later, after careful preparations, Ryan kept his promise and worked through the night for a second time. This earned Greg and Ashley's gratitude and, he hoped, cemented the good start he'd made to finding a new personal friendship as well.

As he'd hoped, he was now starting to pick up occasional clients from the other two villages nearby – though Fairford Magna, the biggest village by far, boasted its own resident IT person, a lively young woman with a small baby and no husband or partner to go with it. She seemed to be doing all right so he tried not to tread on her toes as a fellow professional, but she stopped him in the street one day to introduce herself and say there was more work around than she could cope with on her own and how did he feel about her passing some queries on to him. So he stopped worrying about her.

He reckoned that whatever big businesses in this area

offered, some people still preferred to find experts to work on their problems from as close to home as possible and to have people recommended by word of mouth.

Well, he was similarly inclined and much preferred to have the services of a person not only recommended by someone but to like or at least respect that person when he got to know them. It might seem old-fashioned to some of the younger folk, but he reckoned it was still a better way of finding regular and reliable long-term help than making guesses from online adverts, which might or might not be telling the truth.

He suddenly saw a car he didn't recognise slow down and turn off towards what locals still called 'the big house', so stayed on his front porch, wondering how long it would take these people to find that the track led nowhere.

Only they didn't come back to the main road again. Could this be the new owner everyone was speculating about? If so, it was about time the person opened up the house again. It was a shame to let beautiful old homes go to rack and ruin.

As the minutes continued to tick past with no sign of the car leaving again, he rolled his eyes at himself for being so stupid as to wait this long to decide that it must be the new owner. He hadn't seen anyone else turning off on the rough dirt track that led only to an unoccupied house recently, had he? Both he and the guy in the other cottage had their entrances the other side of the big house's grounds, via a meandering dirt track leading from a narrow road which wound along the rear of the village street and served several other cottages set back from the main road.

The small track that led to the big house didn't even have a signpost on the main road indicating where it led but these people had turned into it without hesitation and not come out again.

Maybe he should amble down to the end of his long, narrow vegetable garden at the rear and find out what they were doing. He'd have a clear view of the big house from there. Yes, why not? There was still an outside chance that they might be thieves, but he didn't think it likely, not when they'd come here so openly. And he wanted to see what they were like because they'd be his next-door neighbours, or as near as you could get to calling someone that in this village, which had big gardens or chunks of land separating locals, and a rather higgledy-piggledy layout.

He wanted to know who was living nearby, for security reasons – and also, he admitted to himself, out of curiosity. He was amused at himself for that. He hadn't been at all like that when he lived in London, because he hadn't cared about the busy district with its anonymous crowds. He also hadn't been planning to stay there for longer than necessary, so he'd worked every hour for which he could find the mental energy. Most people there seemed to have been the same, too busy to be neighbourly.

But this village was an attractive place and had felt like home right from the start. He'd do his bit to help keep it safe and attractive. So here, he wanted to meet some of the neighbours, perhaps even make a few friends. Settle down.

People were slowly making him feel he could become one of them and if you lived in such a small community, it wasn't every day you acquired a new neighbour, was it? Or even every year. So the heir's arrival was an event worth watching.

Aw, who was he kidding? He was being plain, old-fashioned nosey, had the time for it these days.

Was one of these two smiling women really the heir?

He couldn't help wondering which of them might be the new owner, the one with silvery streaks at the sides of her hair or the younger one with the gleaming dark brown hair who looked closer to his own age? They'd been driving slowly enough for him to take a good look at them as they passed his cottage.

Miss Westerby had apparently collapsed several weeks ago, just after Ryan came to live in the village and he'd never even seen her. Fortunately the housekeeper had not only called an ambulance but had gone to the hospital with her employer.

It had been like watching a TV show, he was told. The unconscious woman had been taken to hospital in an ambulance with its siren blasting as it left the village. But it had been hard for them to get updates on how Miss Westerby was doing after that because though her housekeeper lived in the village, she was a nasty, stuck-up snob from a local family that wasn't liked, and she didn't even try to associate with anyone.

Strange how some people were like that. Did they consciously decide that they were superior to other people? Or were they simply born unfriendly? Who knew? As a result the only information that was verified every now and then came from other stray sources and was that Miss Westerby was still in the nearest local hospital.

The housekeeper, Selma Parnham, had apparently come back from hospital the first time and found that a lawyer's clerk had already brought in a locksmith to close up the house and change all the external locks. And another outsider, this one a female, had come with him to clear out the perishable food from the kitchen, which Selma could have if she wanted, otherwise it'd be given to a local charity.

She'd also told Selma that her services as housekeeper would no longer be needed, since her former mistress wasn't expected to recover.

Well, Selma had worked that out already from what the doctors at the hospital had said, hadn't she? What she hadn't expected was that the woman had already invaded her rooms and packed up all her possessions without letting her back into the house to check.

She decided to go and live in the cottage her family had left to her and her brother, and hope that her mistress would beat the odds and recover.

However, a few weeks later she'd come home from the shops in Fairford Magna to find a clerk waiting to give her the information that the old lady was dead, out of sheer courtesy he said. She hadn't left Selma anything.

So she'd had no excuse for getting back into the house. She'd tried to explain to the lawyer about the box and asked to be allowed to collect it. She'd been refused permission, however, because her former mistress hadn't said anything about it in the Will.

'We'll mention it to the new owner and she can deal with it once probate has been granted,' was all they would say.

Various versions of this story were told to Ryan with relish and no sign of liking or sympathy was shown by anyone for the dead woman or her former housekeeper. Well, even in his short time here, he'd realised that though she came from a family long established in the area, Miss Westerby hadn't been either a good neighbour or a decent landlord, unlike previous generations of her family.

And the housekeeper seemed to be disliked even more

than her mistress. That was apparently partly because she came from a village family whose members were not noted for their honesty and were not averse to playing dirty tricks on anyone who crossed them. The Parnhams had been known to use violence like broken windows or slashed tyres to get back at people.

'Never trust either of those two,' he was warned by several people with much wagging of right forefingers. 'That brother of hers has only just been let out of jail for burglary and as for her, she might not have been caught out by the police for doing anything wrong but she's as devious as they come. If sly tricks were an event in the Olympics, she'd win a gold medal for it, that one would.'

Ryan wondered vaguely how old the heir would be, because if she was another elderly person, she'd have trouble looking after that big old house. Would she hire the Parnham woman as her housekeeper? And come to think of it, would she have enough money to hire the necessary domestic help to deal with a house that was quite big, going on for two hundred years old, he'd guess, from the style of architecture, and in obvious need of serious maintenance and repairs?

After a few weeks had passed without anyone in the village seeming to know what was going on at the big house, Ryan had asked a woman who lived a couple of doors away from him if anyone had heard what was going to happen now.

'No. But it shows that even she couldn't have her own way in everything, doesn't it? Members of her family usually live to a ripe old age, but she didn't. Well, we all have to die sometime, don't we and no one knows when it'll happen.'

He blinked at the tone of her voice.

'She'd left general instructions to keep her alive if it was at all possible and they did everything they could when she stopped breathing that final time. Money always talks, doesn't it? But for all their efforts, she didn't show any signs of responding from a stroke that bad, so in the end they gave up, pronounced her brain-dead and turned off the life support.'

He nodded, hoping she'd go on sharing information. 'I was surprised that no one from the village had offered to look after her house and garden while she was ill, as I heard that neighbours had done for another older woman who was taken suddenly ill. Was there some reason for that?'

His companion rolled her eyes at his question. 'Did Miss Westerby ever even nod good day to you?'

'Well, no.'

'She didn't nod to anyone in the village either, even those who rented houses from her. Not even to him, the one in the cottage just up the field from you, and he's a distant relative of hers. And yet, some folk have lived here for many years, just as she had.'

'I couldn't help noticing that no one had anything positive to say about her.'

'Well, you would. It stood out a mile that she considered herself superior to the other folk who lived nearby. After she inherited the house from her aunt, you'd think she was queen of the district.'

'I hope the new owner will make a more pleasant neighbour for us all.'

'Only time will tell. You've fitted in well, but no one knows anything about this new owner. If she's anything like her great-aunt, you'd better not hold your breath and wait for her to say hello.'

And now, it looked as if the heir had arrived. Neither of the women in the car had been old, though, so he probably wouldn't be left with a crumbling ruin next door. She'd do something about maintenance, surely? After sitting there for a few more minutes, he gave in to temptation and ambled to the far end of his long narrow back garden, trying to keep out of sight behind a massive rhubarb plant that seemed to love where his predecessor had planted it, while he watched what the two women were doing.

The first thing he saw was them checking all round the outside of the house, which showed they had some common sense. He'd have done that too if he'd been taking over a place that had been left standing empty and without a modern security system for weeks.

He also saw something they clearly couldn't. The old man who'd been sleeping rough in one of the sheds was standing behind some tall bushes in the overgrown track that ran along that side of the block of land watching them as well, looking anxious.

He was taking advantage of the abundant foliage to keep out of sight but still keep an eye on the new arrivals. So Ryan couldn't help watching him as well as them. Poor old chap, to be reduced to living and sleeping rough.

After a while, as they started going round the big garden to check the sheds, the old man walked slowly down to the main road, looking very droopy and despondent.

Ryan felt sorry for the old fellow, who didn't look at all well, though he wasn't sorry enough to take him in. There were too many people in trouble to help all the ones you encountered. He'd done his share, more than his fair share probably, and helped people every now and then, but at present he was desperate for some quiet time for himself to recover from working too hard for a long time. He'd run himself ragged putting together enough money to buy a house and land in the country.

Apart from anything else, he wasn't sure how well he was going to settle into a life that was this quiet after working so hard for years. It had surprised him how long the evenings could seem when you were on your own. He'd have to find something other than watching TV to fill them now he wasn't working such long hours, because the television companies were showing some right old rubbish at the moment.

Well, hopefully he'd gradually make a few friends round here and maybe go out occasionally for a drink at the village pub. And perhaps there were clubs he could join. And there was apparently a library in Fairford Magna. Who knew what else he'd find to do?

He hoped the heir would be a nicer person than the old woman who had died and they could have the occasional chat over by the back hedge.

His life here was just starting. He had no idea where it would lead him. And she must be in the same position.

Chapter Seventeen

The two women checked the sheds, ending up at the one near the edge of the grounds, but they didn't find any intruders or signs of them anywhere.

'I don't intend to waste my time checking what's inside all those old bags and bundles,' Miranda said firmly as they stood in the doorway of the final shed. 'Not yet, anyway. You couldn't fit any adult human being into a small sack and therefore these bundles and boxes are no danger to us.'

'I agree. Ugh, I wonder where all these rags have come from. Some of the ones in the previous shed were utterly filthy. These are cleaner but I do wonder why so many useless bits and pieces are being kept at all.'

'Some of the older generations were brought up to use and reuse everything, and that was better for the environment, surely?'

As she led the way out of the shed into the fresh air again, Miranda wrinkled her nose in disgust at the memory of that penultimate shed. Smells like that could linger mentally as well as physically. 'So, dare we go and look inside the house now, Auntie dear?'

'Definitely. You're not the only one who's dying to see what it's like inside.'

Arm in arm, they strolled back round to the front of the building, where Libby unlaced her arm from Miranda's, gave a sweeping gesture towards the double front doors and stepped back out of the way. 'It's your house so you should go into it first, but take it slowly and be on your guard, in case there are any problems.'

'I'll just open one of the doors.' She didn't really need reminding about that when it was something organised by her great-aunt Phyllis but she took a deep breath and told herself to stay particularly alert and braced for trouble, then inserted the key and turned it. The mechanism worked smoothly with only the faintest of clicks, then she used the old-fashioned handle to open the door. The other door had a bolt that tied it to the ground, so she left that one alone.

The air inside was markedly stale and musty after the fresh air outside, causing them both to grimace, but the sight that met them was pleasing enough. It was no surprise to find the spacious hall lit in part by multicoloured light streaming into it from the narrow, ceiling-high stained-glass window panels on either side of the front doors.

They felt immersed in bright colours and both stopped instinctively to stare round, smiling and enjoying it.

Libby still stayed slightly back from her young friend, enjoying watching her reactions as well as staring round the attractive hall and enjoying it too.

Inside the house there was silence but outside birds were singing, several different birds pouring out a delicate chorus of notes.

'That's our welcome choir,' Miranda said softly. 'Don't they sound lovely? I think I saw a bird table somewhere at the back. I'll put food out for them regularly.'

'Good idea.'

As she took a step forward and prepared to follow her inside, Libby said, 'Just a minute.' She stopped and reached out to remove the key from the outside of the door and hold it out to her friend. 'I think we should lock the front door behind us before we go any further.'

'I suppose you're right but it'll make this entrance area darker, won't it? And we did check that there was no one around.'

'We still ought to continue taking every precaution.'

Miranda held up the front door key. 'I'm sure I saw a couple of keys like this one in that bundle, so we'll find you one to keep for yourself, Libby.'

'Thank you.' She waited for Miranda to slip the door key into her pocket. Her friend was clearly more cautious in new situations than she would have been. Well, poor Miranda had told her about one or two nasty experiences she'd had in the past. That old aunt must have been a madwoman!

Miranda tugged her sleeve. 'Let's explore the rooms on the ground floor first.'

'Lead the way, dear. You don't have to say anything unless you want to, just enjoy exploring your new home. I'll follow your lead and I'm quite happy if you want to move slowly or even stop to look more carefully at something.'

She wasn't surprised when Miranda nodded and led the way in silence, moving slowly and pausing every few steps to stare into another room, or open a door in the hall to reveal a cupboard full of coats. You never knew what you'd find next in a house abandoned as suddenly as this sounded to have been. There seemed to be little order or sense internally about how the place had been built and extended, even though it'd looked good from outside. Various contents were stored or displayed equally haphazardly.

But it could become a pleasant home if Miranda wanted to take the time and trouble to set things to rights, she felt sure.

Libby would have done the same as Miranda was doing now if this house had been hers. She'd have moved round slowly, not wanting to chat so as not to miss a single detail. If you hadn't grown up in a place, you had to catch up with what it was like as quickly as you could in order to settle in. She'd found that even when moving house from one small flat to another.

It'd be lovely to live in such spacious rooms, but she wouldn't fancy being responsible for maintaining and cleaning a house as big as this, and it certainly hadn't been looked after recently. Most of it was dusty and the furniture left out was scattered around any old how, or if not left out, merely piled haphazardly under dust sheets, except in the rooms the owner had clearly occupied.

Downstairs there were two large rooms on either side of the hall, then another room and a kitchen further back at one side. The latter was old-fashioned but still an attractively large space to do your cooking in, with a big window looking out onto the back garden.

Beyond and slightly to one side of it was a separate scullery and sticking out even further back were the more recently built extensions they'd noticed as they walked round. These looked to have been used as a small flat, with a sitting room and bedroom, a cloakroom and a rather cramped shower room squeezed in behind the house.

'Servants' quarters?' Miranda guessed.

'Probably the housekeeper's.'

There was also a door leading outside but that was locked and there was no sign of a key, even though Libby, who was the taller, felt all along the top of lintel, a frequent hiding place for keys to outer doors in old houses.

'The key might be in that bundle of old keys I have, but it'll be a long job sorting them all out and finding which one fits each lock. Why on earth were the spares not labelled?'

'Who knows? I bet your great-aunt didn't want anyone except herself and that horrible housekeeper of hers to know where anything was.'

'You could be right. But this will probably give us a second bathroom. Toss you for it.'

'You seem very sure of that.'

'I've been round a lot of older houses. The main bathroom is very old-fashioned, as dated as the kitchen, but they're both clean at least, if dusty at the moment. I don't mind taking this one if there's a better main bathroom upstairs for you. You are, after all, the owner, ma'am.' She bobbed a mocking curtsey and they both chuckled.

'All right. Thanks, Libby.'

'And since there are only the two of us to cater for, we can eat simply and you can take your time modernising the kitchen and main living areas. We'll need to clean the bedrooms we're using first to give us a start. Let's go and choose them now.'

She waited till Miranda had started up the main staircase, smiling to see how slowly she was moving and how she was still stopping every few paces to look at something. She let her friend get nearly to the top before following her, then they walked along the landing in silence with Miranda opening the doors and staring into each room revealed, but not going inside any of them.

'You were right, Libby. There is a big old-fashioned bathroom. I'll miss having a shower, though.'

They came back to stand near the top of the stairs and discuss what they'd seen.

Libby grimaced. 'There might be six large bedrooms but only one of the beds has been used and the rooms are all horribly dusty.'

'But at least there are a couple of mattresses that look new and unused.'

'I shall examine them very carefully indeed before I sleep on either of them.'

'I wonder if the elderly water heater that's set over the upstairs bath works and if so, whether it's safe to use it. I think we'd better get it checked by a plumber before we even try to light the gas.' She looked round. 'There aren't nearly enough amenities here for a modern family, are there, even though there are a lot of rooms?'

'Not nearly enough bathrooms and dedicated storage areas. And the bedrooms may be large but most don't feel as if they've been used for many years.'

'Yes, they feel like that to me too. And before I can sleep comfortably in one of them, I shall need a bolt on the inside of the door to feel safe at night. I'll have to make do with a chair under the door handle at first. Let's take a proper look round the largest bedroom now, the one at the other end of the landing. That must surely have been the one Phyllis slept in and who knows what we'll find in there?'

Libby rolled her eyes in mock fear. 'A big bad wolf hiding in the wardrobe probably! Or the old lady's ghost.'

Miranda didn't bother to answer, just smiled and led the

way into it. The smile soon faded. Someone had stripped the bed and stuffed the dirty bedclothes into a laundry basket in one corner.

'No one has attempted to come up and collect the dirty bedlinen to wash it, not during all the weeks the main house has stood empty,' she said in disgust.

'Perhaps the housekeeper stripped the bed earlier but wasn't allowed back to finish clearing up and remaking it.'

Miranda scowled at the bare, stained mattress. 'Perhaps the police took on the job of locking the place up but the lawyer told me they'd changed all the locks straight away to make sure it would be secure, because they didn't know who had had copies of the old ones and felt responsible for security till the heir took over. They told me not to give a copy of any of the new keys to anyone unless I trusted them absolutely.' She immediately presented Libby with a key. 'Here you are, then. I definitely trust you.'

They smiled at one another and both raised one thumb in triumph, then they carried on looking round.

There was a pair of wardrobes – pieces of furniture, not built-ins. One stood at either side of the door in the big bedroom. These were huge, old-fashioned things. Like the rest of the interior, everything looked old and dusty. There was a tallboy to one side, the small cupboard at the top of which seemed to have been used as a medicine cabinet. It was full of half-used potions and lotions.

'I'm chucking every single item out.' Miranda said with a shudder and disapproving flick of the fingers in that direction.

Then she moved across to open the doors of the wardrobes, flinging them open and ducking well back to make sure nothing fell out or worse, shot out at her. 'I feel stupid looking round like a timid child,' she muttered.

'Don't feel like that. It's better to be too careful with that woman than not careful enough.'

Both wardrobes were huge with a tower of narrow drawers running up one side of each. These were absolutely crammed full with clothes, some of them in one wardrobe clearly from decades earlier and all of them women's clothing, no sign of a man ever living here.

'There will be a lot to throw out,' Miranda said quietly.

'Yes. But some of the clothes may be worth money as historical artefacts, they're so old. And they don't look badly worn, so they'll bring top prices. Don't throw anything away till I've checked its value online.'

Miranda looked at her friend in surprise. 'I never thought of that aspect, Libby.'

'I've bought old clothes from car boot sales sometimes when they were just being sold cheaply, and made a good profit on them. But then, I do know what to look for.'

Before Libby could say anything else, someone hammered on the front door downstairs and they both jumped in shock.

Miranda peeped out of the window. 'Darn. I can't see who it is properly, except that it's a woman. We'd better answer it.' She led the way quickly down, wincing as someone used the door knocker even more loudly before anyone was likely to have reached it in such a large house.

Libby decided to keep out of sight till they were sure who this was because for some reason she felt uneasy. Whoever it was certainly had very bad manners and she'd not be surprised if they were violent as well, hammering on the door like that.

Had this woman seen her and Miranda arrive and waited till they'd gone inside to knock or was it by sheer chance that this unknown visitor had found people in what had previously been a deserted house? Neither possibility seemed likely, somehow.

Whoever it was hammered again, really violently.

'It's downright rude to bang so hard on the door for a third time without giving people time to respond in a house as large as this one,' Libby said sharply. 'I don't like whoever it is already.'

'I'll open the door,' Miranda said.

She did that before Libby could stop her and found a gaunt, middle-aged woman standing outside. She scowled so fiercely at the sight of Miranda that Libby didn't move forward to stand next to her friend but stayed out of sight. She could see the woman quite well through the tall stained-glass panel next to the door and was close enough to come to her friend's aid if necessary.

What an ugly, vicious expression the stranger had! It was as if she hated the younger woman, but how could she when they'd never met before? Libby was quite sure of that from her friend's expression.

She didn't understand why but she wanted to watch the visitor carefully before she showed herself. The woman would probably reveal more about herself and her attitude to the house's new owner if Libby didn't attract attention to her own presence immediately.

She stood perfectly still, surprised at herself for feeling so instantly mistrustful of a complete stranger! Well, who wouldn't when faced with someone who had such a hostile expression on her ugly bony face as she glared at your best friend? The woman was certainly radiating what could only be described as fierce hatred. Why?

When the visitor didn't speak but continued to study the person who'd opened the door to her as if furiously annoyed by what she saw, Miranda asked in her usual quiet way, 'How can I help you?'

Chapter Eighteen

'Who are you?' the stranger asked in a harsh voice. 'What are you doing here at the big house?'

'I'm the new owner.'

'Oh, are you? Can you prove that?'

Miranda might be quiet and polite but she was no pushover, Libby knew; she simply chose to face the world politely. So she didn't intervene to help but waited quietly and watched her friend deal with the rude stranger.

'Why should I need to prove it to you? More to the point, who are you and what do you want here at my house?'

'I'm Selma Parnham.'

'I don't think we've met before?'

'I was Miss Westerby's housekeeper for three decades. Does that count for nothing? The lawyers must have told you about me.'

'They might have mentioned, but so much has happened in a short space of time, my head has been all over the place.'

Selma Parnham breathed deeply for a moment or two,

as if calming herself down, then continued speaking more normally. 'The most important thing is that I've come for the box. I'd have taken it away and dealt with it before, as your great-aunt asked me to do if she ever died suddenly, but those fools of lawyers hired someone to change all the locks without even consulting me and removed my possessions from the house. Then the woman they'd sent to do that added insult to injury by refusing to let me come inside to retrieve that box.'

She was speaking in an arrogant way now, slowly and extra loudly, as if she considered Miranda too stupid to understand what she said otherwise. This surprised and annoyed Libby. She nearly stepped forward to join them and was itching to say something sharp about bad manners, but forced herself to hold back and wait a little longer. She could see that Miranda was also annoyed by the woman's tone and would leave it to her to take the lead in this.

'Let me get past, then!' Selma ordered sharply, stretching out one hand as if about to shove the younger woman aside.

Libby had been standing to one side and realised she mustn't have been noticed by the woman so decided it was time to move forward now and show her that her friend wasn't here on her own. As Miranda pushed the woman's outstretched hand away, Libby stepped out into the doorway to stand next to her.

Selma jerked back and let out a cry of shock at the sight of Libby then glared at her and snapped, 'Who the hell are you?'

Libby smiled sweetly and didn't move at all. 'That's none of your business.'

The woman grunted and turned back to yell at Miranda, 'If you are the heir, you weren't supposed to bring anyone here with you! Miss Westerby told the lawyers that. Why did they not pass the information on to you? She wouldn't have approved of you bringing a stranger here.'

'The lawyers didn't say anything and even if they had, I prefer to make my own decisions about who I spend time with.'

'You're the senior female member of the family and you're expected to live here quietly on your own, looking after the family's long-time home and dealing with the finances of the trust, as she did. Eventually you should pass them both on to the next person in line. The family connections are listed in the trust records.'

'But—'

The stranger interrupted, yelling loudly now as she continued her tirade. 'That's what the Westerby heir always does – except for begetting another heir at some stage – and even someone as stupid as you ought to be able to manage that because at least you're not ugly.'

Both the women inside the house gasped in shock at this rudeness.

The visitor just waited, not taking even one step back. And when Miranda made no attempt to move out of her way, she yelled again. 'Stand aside. I need to—'

However, Miranda continued to bar her way and this time she didn't wait for the stranger to finish what she was saying but spoke loudly and slowly in her turn. 'How I live or who stays here with me is none of your business now and you are not coming into this house again, whoever you are. If the lawyers haven't given you access, then I won't do so either.'

She wasn't speaking in her usual quiet way now but in a sharper tone than usual, Libby noticed in approval, but as her friend was about to continue speaking, their visitor spoke even more loudly and rudely cut her off again.

'Of course it's my business. Your great-aunt knew her health was failing and her instructions were that if anything happened to her, I was to stay on here as housekeeper, keeping the place in order till you arrived so that I could show you how things need to be done. Those stupid lawyers dismissed me immediately, even before my mistress died, which they shouldn't have done, but I've come back to finish what needs doing.'

'Thank you but I shan't need a housekeeper and I'll do things here from now on as I see fit. My friend and I can look after ourselves and we're perfectly well aware of how to run a house.'

'Look, as I've just told you, Miss Westerby, as the heir, you are not supposed to bring anyone to live with you. And anyway, even if this woman moves in for a while, she won't stay here. Outsiders never do. They don't seem able to settle down in such a quiet place.'

'I think that's my business now, not yours. I was informed that my great-aunt's housekeeper had already been paid off and given what was owing to her when it was clear the old lady wasn't going to recover consciousness. I gather the lawyers have already told you your services would no longer be needed. I definitely don't need any other help, so you really will have to find yourself a different job, Ms Parnham.'

'I shan't need to do that. I have a house in the village. I can't stop you bringing her here but I know how things should be done, and it's still wrong to bring in a complete stranger to mess the place up. I'll be waiting to get my rightful place back when you need my help to sort out the mess you'll get into. However, in the meantime, I still need to fetch the box down and deal with it straight away, after which I'll stay in Fairford Magna.' She gave Miranda a sneering look. 'You'll definitely need me before you're through, mark my words. You can send for me when that happens and I'll sort out whatever it needs to set things to rights again. The house comes first before my pride and it won't welcome outsiders like her.'

Libby was furiously angry by now and intervened. 'Are you deaf? How many times do you have to be told that your services here have been terminated before it sinks in that there is no longer a job for you here? There hasn't been for several weeks and there won't be at any time in the future.'

Libby didn't need telling that Miranda had taken one of her rare dislikes to this female. She hadn't taken to her either. There was something inherently nasty in her facial expression and scorn rang in her tone of voice, even though she knew nothing about the new heir.

The woman let out an angry sniff. 'You mind your own business. You're only her servant.' She turned back to Miranda. 'As I just said, if that's what you're going to do, I'll take the box and deal with it now, which my poor mistress asked me to do if anything happened to her. Then I'll leave you to get on with messing things up. I'll be available later to sort things out, not for you but for her sake and for the family I've served all my working life.'

Miranda was puzzled as well as annoyed. 'What box would that be?'

'The one Miss Westerby wanted me to take away if she died suddenly. We'd been sorting out its contents, and as she said, they were private and nobody's business but hers so I was to destroy them for her. I'd have done it straight away, which was what she really intended to happen, because we'd nearly finished sorting the contents out anyway, but she collapsed suddenly and they took her away. When I realised she wasn't going to recover, I came back from the hospital and tried to do as she'd asked. But that nosey new lawyer had sent his wife into my room to pack my things without consulting me and dumped them outside. They wouldn't let me come into this house again, even to do as she'd asked, and they threatened to call the police in when I tried.'

Miranda took a deep breath and raised her voice more loudly than usual. 'And rightly so. I'll say it again: your job was terminated weeks ago, so you have no reason to come into the house again. I'm surprised that you're still trying to.'

'I knew my mistress would want me to deal with the box for her. That lawyer said I wasn't to go back inside the house – me who'd worked and lived here for over thirty years and they set the police to keep an eye on the place! The cheek of it!'

That surprised Miranda. 'Did you live here too for all that time?'

'Of course I did. I was her personal maid and housekeeper. Though after my brother and I inherited our own little house in the village, I stayed there occasionally to clean it thoroughly. But I was here most of the time. I kept to the housekeeper's quarters when I wasn't doing the housework because I knew my rightful place. You should make sure she does that too.'

Ms Parnham jabbed one finger in Libby's direction and added scornfully, 'She isn't a Westerby, and your great-aunt didn't encourage people other than family to stay in the main house, or even to visit it.'

The two women inside the house said nothing, only exchanged puzzled glances, not sure what to do about her.

Ms Parnham yelled suddenly, 'Haven't you been listening? How many times do I need to say it before I get through to you? I need to come in and get my mistress's box. This woman shouldn't come in at all unless she's doing the housework. Only, she's not needed for that even, not really. We always had a cleaner from the village who knows her way round and would happily come back to work here. This woman should be paid off.'

She glared at Libby then turned her attention back to Miranda and waited, arms folded, foot tapping impatiently as if expecting to be let into the house.

When no one spoke, she repeated her demand, speaking in an even louder voice than before and enunciating each word slowly and carefully as if the two of them were stupid. 'I need – to come inside – to get the box.'

'I don't understand which box you're talking about, let alone why anything belonging to my great-aunt should need dealing with by you now. It doesn't belong to you, after all, and you haven't worked here for several weeks.'

'I didn't say it belonged to me. It was Miss Westerby's box and it contains the last of her personal things, which she'd wanted to destroy before she died. She knew she hadn't long to live, poor lady.'

She suddenly tried again to push past them and when they wouldn't let her into the house she yelled, 'Miss Westerby has a right to have her last wish respected. Why are you stopping me? This has nothing to do with you.'

'Where is this box?' Miranda asked.

'It's in her bedroom, on the table next to the window.'

'I saw a box there but it was a valuable antique!' Libby exclaimed. 'Far too valuable to be burnt – or given away to a stranger.'

Miranda nodded agreement. The two of them didn't always need words to know what the other was thinking, had seemed to be on the same wavelength right from the start of their friendship, which was why they now considered themselves more like relatives.

She turned back to Ms Parnham and tried to speak politely, though she felt more like telling her to get the hell out and stay away from this house completely from now on. 'Thank you for your offer to help us clear out the house, Ms Parnham, but we'll deal with both the box and its contents when we clear that front bedroom out. The lawyer has made no mention of anyone taking things away, but I'll have to check with him to see if he knows anything at all about this.'

'But—'

It was Miranda's turn to raise her voice. 'There may be family things in that box that I'd prefer to keep.'

The woman shook her head, still scowling. 'No! You can't do that morally! They're personal to my late mistress, I promise you, and getting rid of them is the last thing I can do for her.'

Her voice broke on that word and she had to take another deep breath and mop her eyes before she could continue. 'Look, I gave her my word and if she hadn't collapsed we'd have disposed of her things by now or at least she'd have had time to put it in the Will that the box was to come to me. She wanted the contents of the box burnt. They're nothing to do with you.'

'We have only your word for that, however, and I'd rather check what's in the box myself before I do anything. I don't know as much about my family as I should so the information this box contains could mean a great deal to me. You can be sure that if it's only old papers that are of no value to anyone now my great-aunt is dead, I can dispose of them without your help.' Miranda reached for the door handle. 'I'll have to get on with my day now. I'm rather busy.'

She was shocked when a man stepped forward suddenly. He must have approached the house without them noticing him and been standing to one side to keep out of sight.

He raised one clenched fist raised in a threatening manner. 'Do as my sister says.'

He was about forty or so, of scrawny build and medium height only, but he had such a battered face that he must have been in a good few fights in his time. He definitely resembled Ms Parnham and the two women guessed who he must be even before he spoke.

The housekeeper said, 'My brother Griff has come to help me.' She gave Miranda a challenging look. 'Now, please let us in. I know my way round this house so I can get the box very quickly. There is absolutely no need to trouble you with fetching it. I shan't feel comfortable unless I keep my promise to my late mistress.'

She seemed to be holding her brother back with one hand as she spoke and he was definitely looking furiously angry.

When she took a step forward as if to come into the house, he moved to stand close behind her, scowling at them and said in a harsh voice, 'I think you should let Selma do as Miss Westerby wanted, lady.'

Miranda didn't attempt to move out of their way. 'And as I just told you, the lawyers have said nothing to me about you or anyone else taking things from this house.'

He made a growling sound in his throat and suddenly shoved her out of the way, calling, 'Go and get that box, Selma. This female has no right to keep it.'

As he put out one hand to prevent Miranda from moving

back inside, his sister said in a flat, emotionless voice, 'Sorry, miss, but I always keep my promises, especially to someone who's passed on.'

While they'd been talking, however, Libby had surreptitiously picked up a heavy brass ornament from a hall table to one side of the entrance and she now stepped forward, surprising the male intruder with a sudden blow to the shoulder that made him stagger sideways, yelling in pain. Then she made sure he could see her holding the ornament in her hand as if about to hit him with it again and shouted, 'Don't you dare try to push your way in here or I'll crack you over the head with this next time!'

While her friend was speaking, Miranda quickly grabbed Selma's arm, taking her by surprise and shoving her backwards out of the doorway so that she had to clutch her brother to prevent herself falling.

As the two women struggled against the would-be intruders, Selma lost her temper completely and began screeching at them at the top of a very shrill voice, 'Get out of our way! Move away!'

For a moment all hung in the balance, then an even louder man's voice made itself heard from nearby. 'Stop that at once, Selma Parnham!'

All four of them stopped struggling and turned to stare in surprise at the newcomer.

Griff Parnham clearly knew who this man was because he jerked backwards, glaring at him but stopping his attack. He opened his mouth as if to yell back then snapped it shut again and breathed deeply, tugging his sister away from the door.

Miranda sighed in relief because the chap who'd yelled and was just moving forward to join them was wearing a police sergeant's uniform. Another tall man, not in uniform, was standing to one side, watching them with an air of faintly amused interest. He nodded to her and took a step closer, looking ready to join in and help if necessary.

'You can either leave this minute, go right away from this house and stay away or I can arrest you and take you even further away,' the sergeant told Griff Parnham sharply. 'You do remember the conditions applied to your being released from prison early, don't you? You'll be on probation for six months – unless you break the rules in any way, minor or major. In which case you'll go back inside quick smart.'

All hung in the balance for a moment, then Griff grabbed his sister's arm and pulled her even further away from the doorway.

Miranda was close enough to hear what he muttered.

'Give it up, Selma. For now, at least. Them papers aren't worth me getting into trouble with the law again for.'

Her hearing being excellent, Miranda was close enough to hear his sister's reply as well.

'But I promised Miss Westerby, Griff. I promised her faithfully and I've never let her down about anything before.'

He put his arm round her shoulders and carried on moving away. 'You did your best, love. You aren't letting her down on purpose. Them women have got the police on their side, damn them. If you're still set on getting hold of the box, you'll have to find a lawyer and make a legal claim to it.'

When she didn't move willingly, he gave her a jerk and repeated in a low voice, 'It's not worth me getting in trouble again with the law over a box of scruffy old papers that you were only going to burn.'

She was still hesitating and glaring at Miranda, then he tugged her arm again and this time she sighed and started to walk away with him. Just before they got into their car, however, she turned to scowl at them, the sort of look that said she wasn't going to give up.

The other man, who hadn't spoken yet, was now standing closer to the front door than his companion. He and the police officer hadn't spoken but were clearly together. He gave the women a nod and quick half-smile, staying where he was.

They all watched the police officer follow the Parnhams along the drive towards where a shabby van was parked under one of the big trees, where it was barely visible from the house.

He stood near the vehicle, arms folded, watching them, clearly waiting for them to drive off.

'I doubt those two would have made such a fuss if that box of old papers really was worthless,' Miranda murmured.

Libby and the stranger both nodded at that.

'I agree with you,' he said. 'I'm Ryan Sinclair, by the way, your new next-door neighbour. You can see my cottage across your grounds.' He pointed. 'That's my cottage, the one closest to the village. And my back garden runs along your fence for about twenty metres.'

'We're both grateful for your help.' Miranda rubbed her right leg below the knee. 'That woman gave me a nasty kick and looked ready to do it again.'

'I was glad to be of use. The police sergeant is my friend Col Barker, who is the law's main representative in this district. He'll no doubt join us again in a minute once he's seen them leave.'

'Pleased to meet you, Ryan. I'm Miranda Westerby and this is my dear friend Libby Tebbish.'

'Ah. You're the person who's just inherited this house, Miranda.'

'Yes, I am.'

'Welcome to the village. Look, I know this sounds cheeky but once Col has seen those two nuisances off, if he and I can come inside for a few minutes, we can share some information about the general situation here. It may help you to ease into this village and the nearby district with fewer hassles. Only if you want us to, of course.'

'What a kind offer! I'm sure it'll be useful for us to find out as much as we can about the situation we've walked into.'

'It could be, yes. Fairford Parva is an unusual little village, old-fashioned in some ways, and your family has probably lived here for longer than any other. And in this same house too.' He looked along the front façade admiringly.

'I'd be grateful for any information. Were you born here too?'

He shook his head and pointed to the cottage. 'No. I bought that recently, which is how I came to notice the arrival of the Parnhams on your property. I knew their reputation as troublemakers and I'd seen my friend Col following them on the main road so I called him to suggest he come and investigate what they were doing.'

'I'm glad he did.'

'Yes. Good guy, Col. As I have a long, narrow back garden which borders one end of your land as far as that gooseberry bush, I'm your closest neighbour. I probably see more of what's going on near the big house than certain local people realise. Those two had been keeping an eye on the entrance to your drive for a while from the main road and Col and I were keeping an eye on them, wondering why.'

'Oh. Right.' She was about to tell him about the box, but he looked as if he wanted to continue speaking and she decided that she'd wait till the sergeant returned and tell them both about it at the same time.

He gave her another of those lovely warm smiles. 'I'm not usually a nosey parker but I confess that I've been keeping an eye on what's been happening here because I've seen the Parnhams' van parked on the verge of the main road nearly opposite your entrance and close to my front garden several times lately and for a surprisingly long time, up to two or three hours. I came to the conclusion that they were watching who went in and out of your drive, because yours is the only house there, and I couldn't help wondering why.'

'I'm glad you noticed and came to check.'

'Col had popped in for a chat today and after you arrived we saw them drive partway up the side lane and leave their car then walk across to your house. We wondered why, since he'd already warned them to stay away from it. So we decided to come across and check that you were all right and they hadn't been annoying you.'

He frowned and shook his head as if puzzled by the situation. 'Previously they'd always driven away if anyone else actually stopped near them, so their recent behaviour seemed distinctly suspicious to us both.'

By this time the Parnhams had driven off and the sergeant was standing on a convenient chunk of rock watching their car vanish down the main road while speaking on his phone. After the call ended, he jumped lightly down and walked back towards the others. 'All right if I join you?'

Miranda nodded. 'Of course. Come in and I'll see if I can find the makings for a cup of tea or coffee while we chat – that's if you'd like one.'

Both men grinned and nodded vigorously, making approving sounds.

She cast a puzzled glance at the way they'd come, wondering if there was some gap in her fences. 'How did you get here so quickly?'

'We nipped across from my back veggie garden up the rough path at the side of your land.'

'I didn't know there was another path. It doesn't show from the house.' She stared across to the side, puzzled.

'It's hidden behind those bushes. I'll walk down it with you as we leave, if you like. It was probably how the gardener brought his stuff in and out in the old days, and it's still a useful shortcut if you want to walk into the village.'

'Thanks. I'd appreciate that.'

It didn't take them long to walk down the side of the grounds. The track was hardly visible, so it couldn't get much use, she thought as they stood at the bottom and stared along towards the village.

'It'll make a pleasant little stroll,' she said at last.

As they walked back up to the house, Col said, 'You'll hear the Parnhams' car if they come back anywhere near here again in the daytime. I could have warned them about their faulty silencer but I thought it was more important today to get rid of them and anyway, the sound of it will let you know they're around.

'I hope you'll enjoy living here,' he continued. 'Most local folk are very friendly, given half a chance, with one or two exceptions.' His glance strayed towards the cottage at the rear of the block as he said that, but he offered no further personal information about whoever lived there.

'Any advice on settling in will be welcome,' Libby said.

In the meantime, she liked the looks of both these men and hoped they'd get to know one another better. They had fresh, open faces and looked you straight in the eye.

Chapter Nineteen

'Do come inside and we'll chat in comfort over a cup of tea. I'm really grateful for your help in getting rid of those nuisances today.' Miranda led the way into the house, going straight across to the rear of the hall, which she now knew was one of two routes that led through to the kitchen and then to a large old-fashioned laundry at the rear.

As she was about to turn out of the hall she glanced back, intending to ask Ryan, the last to come in, if he'd lock the front door. To her relief, he was just turning the big key in the lock without being asked.

She nodded approval because she didn't intend to let those Parnhams find any weaknesses and sneak into her house again. Then she wondered if this door-locking was automatic for him, which it wasn't usually for people who lived out in the country, from what she'd heard.

Or was there a special reason for these men being doubly careful when coming to look round inside this house? Had her great-aunt upset people? Who knew? She had so much to learn about her new home and the people who lived nearby. She did hope they'd be generally friendly and that she'd make one or two personal friends from among them.

Thank goodness she hadn't come here on her own! She'd hate to be facing everything alone, though she'd have coped. She always did, whatever she had to face, she prided herself on that, but it didn't mean she liked having to struggle alone at times. Libby had made a huge and very positive difference to her life. She really did feel like they were family now, with a friendship both of them valued highly.

She waved one hand towards the big scrubbed wooden table. 'Do please sit down, gentlemen, while I check that the gas is still switched on. I've still got all sorts of details like that to check.' She turned a tap on the ancient gas cooker and heard a hissing noise so turned it off hastily and looked round for something to light it with.

The two men settled at the table and Libby began to fill the kettle then studied the old-fashioned gas cooker. 'Anyone got something to light this with?'

'We're neither of us smokers.' Col stood up and began to open and shut drawers. 'People usually keep matches nearby. Aha! Here we go.' He handed her a part-used box of matches. 'I think you'd better keep these next to the cooker. You can buy gadgets to light these old-fashioned burners with.'

Miranda looked across at the elderly cooker and grimaced. 'Or I can buy a modern cooker and get it installed as quickly as possible! I reckon this one is an antique.'

Libby lit a front burner and nodded in satisfaction as the flame burnt strongly and steadily, then she put the kettle on it. 'I'll boil this water then pour it away to clean the kettle, before I use any for making tea with.'

'Good idea,' Ryan said.

Miranda had been opening and shutting the wall cupboard doors. 'We're assuming there will be some tea-making supplies around still, because the lawyers didn't allow anything to be cleared out of the house even by their own clerk except for the perishable foods.'

'They sent a clerk and his wife across to lock the house up almost immediately. He took his wife with him to pack up the housekeeper's possessions because the hospital doctor had informed them almost immediately that Miss Westerby was brain-dead and not going to recover. They removed the housekeeper's clothing and possessions then paid to have the locks changed and the house secured.'

'Would you mind if I just check the rest of the ground floor before I join you?' The sergeant made a sweeping gesture with one hand as if to encompass the whole area.

'Be my guest.'

Col stood up and began opening and closing the doors leading out of the kitchen into the adjoining rooms. He vanished from sight for long enough to make them realise that he was going round the whole of the ground floor and they heard him opening and closing doors elsewhere.

Miranda was pleased about that because it made her feel more secure, though, as she admitted to herself, not completely secure. She was still wary of there being unpleasant surprises left by her great-aunt.

He came back a short time later, nodding as if to assure them that everything was all right, then rejoining his friend at the table. 'Dust everywhere, but no sign that anyone has been walking around disturbing most of it. The dust on the stairs had two sets of women's footprints showing. I'm guessing they're yours and Libby's.'

'Yes. There were no others before we went up.'

He sat down and began studying the roomy kitchen and the dining area at the side where they were sitting, as well as keeping an eye on Libby and Miranda as they continued to investigate the contents of the kitchen cupboards and pull one or two items out of them.

Miranda kept just as careful an eye on him, surprised at how intently he was studying everything and how alert he looked. He was very impressive, actually, and she'd like him to investigate the whole house. Would he do that for her? Did she dare ask him to? Was it even necessary when there had been no other footprints on the dusty stairs except for hers and Libby's?

Oh, what did she know?

She turned back to continue looking at the contents of the last pair of wall cupboards on her side of the kitchen and waved a packet of chocolate biscuits at her companions. 'These are past their expiry date but they're all we've got so we may as well give them a try.'

'The brew will still be nice and hot,' Ryan said with a smile. 'And I've probably drunk far worse.'

'Aha!' Libby took a packet of brown sugar and a carton of long-life milk out of the last cupboard at her side and brandished them happily.

'I'll let you make your cuppas to your own taste because there's plenty of sugar here, even if it is brown, as well as several cartons of this packet milk. Oh, and there's instant coffee as well, also past its use-by date, though it's not mouldy or anything like that.'

They all opted for tea and Miranda poured the just-boiled second kettleful into the pot and then put the chocolate biscuits on a plate.

Libby snipped one of the corners off a carton of milk and set it down next to the packet of brown sugar. Then she grimaced at a miscellaneous assortment of rather grubby-looking, tea-stained mugs and insisted on giving four of them a thorough scrubbing out under the tap before even trying to use them. Ryan came over and dried them, setting them out next to the kettle.

It was . . . cosy, Miranda thought. Almost as if they were long-time friends. And there had been no awkward silences either.

She gestured towards the teapot. 'We'll let it brew for a minute or two then you can help yourselves. Sorry about these mugs being rather chipped but the only other drinking vessels I've found are some small wine glasses and a set of tiny china cups which would hold only a couple of thimblefuls of fluid each.'

'I prefer mugs any day.' Ryan wiped the last one and put it with the others, looked round to see if anything else needed doing, found nothing to help with and sat down again.

What a nice man he was, Miranda thought, and rather attractive, too.

Libby gave her friend a quick nudge. 'You sit down as well, love, and chat to your first set of guests in your new home. I can finish making the tea on my own.'

Miranda joined the two men at the table. They didn't do anything very special, just made cups of tea and passed things to one another, yet somehow that broke the ice and she felt comfortable with them, as if they had somehow become friends. It had happened as quickly as that when she first met Libby, so she hoped this was a good sign.

'Did you know Miss Westerby well?' Col asked Miranda.

'No, not at all. I only ever met my great-aunt in person

when I was a small child, and once when I was fourteen, but she was my guardian for a few years when I was a teenager.' She grimaced involuntarily at the thought of how badly that woman had fulfilled her role as guardian.

'From your expression you didn't get on with her.'

'No, not at all. She usually communicated with me through her lawyers and dumped me in a boarding school for kids whose parents were working overseas during the school holidays and left me there. I always felt that she disliked me intensely, though I could never understand why. And I certainly disliked her from the start. I couldn't figure out why, but she always felt like an enemy.'

Both men looked at her in puzzlement and Ryan asked, 'Why would she leave this house and her portfolio of shares to you, then?'

'I don't think she had much choice with this house. It's owned by the Westerby Family Trust and I inherited it because I was the family member most closely related to her. It's only mine for my lifetime and then it has to go to my closest relative. If necessary the lawyers will search for other branches of the family to find that person.'

'There don't sound to be many other Westerbys left.'

'No. Apparently not. I'm the last in this branch and it must have galled her that she had no choice about who inherited the house. I don't actually know the details of the family tree, but she let me know when I was a teenager and she became my guardian that she'd not be leaving the family home to me if there had been any legal alternative.'

'How old were you when you lost your mother?'

She looked at him and suddenly her expression was deeply sad. 'Fourteen. She was knocked down and killed by a drunk driver.'

Ryan stared at her in surprise. 'What a nasty woman your great-aunt must have been to treat a grieving child so badly!'

'I've always thought so, looking back on that time from being an adult. But I coped.' They should write that on her gravestone, she thought, not for the first time: *I coped.*

'So you were expecting to inherit this house, then?'

'Yes. I don't know the full rules of how it has to be managed, though. They were set a long time ago.'

'No one's tried to revise the trust and make it more suited to the modern world, then?'

'My great-aunt certainly didn't try to change anything in her cosy little world and I've only just inherited the house. I've not even had time to walk round the whole of it yet.'

She couldn't stop herself frowning at the mere thought of that horrible woman.

'What brought that frown?' Ryan asked.

She hesitated, then told him. Why not? She wasn't a secretive type like her great-aunt. 'I suspect there are going to be some unpleasant surprises in store for me. There usually have been when dealing with any of the things that woman organised or administered. I'm sure she'll make me pay for it in some nasty way.'

'Well, if you need further help, don't hesitate to ask me. I'm only just across your field. I'll give you my phone number.' He got his phone out so she did the same and put his number on hers. Giving her number to him felt strange. She didn't often do that with anyone, let alone a near stranger. But she trusted this man absolutely, for some weird reason, him and Col both.

'Thank you. That's very kind of you, Ryan. I hope I shan't need to trouble you, though.'

He smiled. 'Independent type, eh? I'd be truly happy to offer help if you ever need it. Some things are better done with others helping. There will be less risk of your great-aunt's unpleasant surprises that way.'

Once again, she returned his smile instinctively.

There was silence for a moment or two, then Miranda looked away and noticed Col sitting watching them but not trying to join in the conversation. He seemed a quiet sort of man, a bit older than her and Ryan, and he too had a really kind smile. In fact, she'd met more nice people, the sort you'd want to make close friends with, in the last day or two than she had for years, since she left university in fact.

When they were all supplied with mugs of tea and chocolate biscuits, Libby sat down with them and Ryan looked across at the two women. 'What do you want me to start telling you about first?'

Miranda shrugged. 'How about starting with the local people, such as those two who tried to push their way in today?'

'The Parnhams?'

'Yes. I'm presuming you know something about them from the tone of your voice as you say their name? Why on earth did they try to do that? Surely that woman didn't think I'd just give her an antique box, considering that the house and its contents have been left to me?'

'I've picked up a few things about them from overhearing people whispering to one another in the village shop,' Ryan said. 'No one dares talk openly about either of them because the houses of one or two who did were vandalised soon afterwards, while they were out. The man is Griff Parnham and his sister is Selma. She's the older of the two by several years, I'm not sure how many.'

'Her eyes look old,' Libby said thoughtfully. 'Old and spiteful.'

Ryan nodded. 'I agree. Some people are like that and you wonder why. I've not been living here for long enough to understand all the background implications of the local situation.'

Col took over the tale. 'The man I took over from as sergeant here gave me some information about the Parnhams. Years ago, Selma and her brother inherited a scruffy little cottage in the largest of the three villages, from an aunt I gather. But Selma was already the housekeeper here at Fairfield House so she kept most of the furnishings and left some of her personal possessions there locked in the attic, but stayed on in her job. Her brother went away to work, took to crime and was caught committing a burglary. He had a record for violence, and attacked and wounded the officer who caught him, so was given a prison sentence.'

'Nice neighbour to have!' Ryan said.

'Selma then let the main part of the cottage to local people, always leaving the attic room containing her own and her brother's things locked up.' Col sighed. 'Unfortunately, Griff has recently been released from prison so I'm keeping my eye on him. He seems determined to stay out of trouble this time so I haven't caught him doing anything against the law, or heard any rumours of him causing trouble either. However, I suspect he's gone back to extorting money out of weaker folk with secrets to hide. He and his sister seem to have been doing that for years, or so I was told by my predecessor. Some of them are so terrified of him they pay him a regular amount to leave them alone. I can't get anyone to reveal the details of what's going on to me officially, though.'

'That's disgusting!' Libby exclaimed.

Col shrugged. 'My main advice is not to trust Griff or his sister, whatever they say or do.'

'Has Selma ever been in trouble with the police?'

'No, never. She and your great-aunt seem to have got on very well, were more like friends than mistress and housekeeper. People said that was probably because they were both nasty types. I kept an eye on what was going on after your aunt collapsed. She was taken to hospital but didn't die straight away, even though the doctors had said she couldn't recover, and judged her to be brain-dead.'

He frowned. 'So I felt I'd better take charge until an heir could be found. I got that new lawyer of hers to give Selma notice and he paid off all her accrued entitlements. I'd hoped that she would find herself another job away from here then, but she didn't even try to. I wouldn't let her go back into the big house, though.'

Col allowed himself a tight little grin. 'I give the lawyer his due. He acted quickly, not only taking over the legal side of things that your great-aunt had mainly been managing herself, but following up on my suggestion to lock Selma out of the house. He got his wife to pack her clothes and the other personal items from her quarters. She caught a glimpse of Selma's bank book while she was doing that and reckoned the woman must have been milking the housekeeping money for years to put so much money away. She told me about it. Unfortunately the woman had never been caught out doing anything illegal, so we couldn't pursue matters.'

Miranda frowned. 'If she'd already taken her own possessions away, why did she keep insisting there was some box she had promised to destroy for her late mistress?

When I refused to let her in to get it, she and her brother tried to push me out of the way. They'd have succeeded as well if you two hadn't come to my aid. As heir, I intend to find the box to see what it was they wanted to destroy.'

She stared into space and added, 'I don't intend to let her into my house ever again, though, whatever she says or does. She makes me feel uncomfortable, I can't work out why, but it feels as if I'm touching something dirty when I'm with her. I'm glad you two were around today, because she and her brother took me by surprise.'

Col frowned. 'I wonder what's in the box. Selma seemed desperate to get hold of it. I bet she'd have taken it without saying a word if that lawyer hadn't had the locks on all the external doors changed so quickly.'

'I'd not have handed it over meekly on her say-so, believe me,' Miranda said. 'I'd have checked it with the lawyer first. This house is my inheritance via a family trust and that box is surely part of its contents, don't you think? That gives even less reason for it to be any concern of Selma Parnham's.'

The two men both nodded, then Col said slowly, as if thinking aloud, 'She and Miss Westerby were apparently very close. And your great-aunt was known for treating her tenants badly, the ones in houses owned by your family trust.'

Miranda stared at him, even more worried now about what nasty surprises her great-aunt might have left for her. She hated the thought of being related to a woman as vicious as that and was worried about why she'd been left those extra bequests.

The two men waited patiently for her to pull her thoughts together and she was grateful to them for that. There was a lot to get her head around.

Chapter Twenty

In the end, Miranda asked quietly, 'Why would my great-aunt need to bully or blackmail local people?'

'The most common reason there is, I should think: money. I gather that rents were put up from time to time on some of the cottages Miss Westerby owned or so-called fines were imposed for alleged damage to the buildings. She and Selma were very clever at doing that only to people who were desperate to stay in this village and could squeeze out a little more rent money to pay her for the privilege of renting one of her houses.'

'Surely my great-aunt didn't need to extort money from people?'

Col shrugged. 'The older people from the village tell me that she inherited young and there wasn't a lot of money that came with the property. There was a need for it then. As the years passed, she wasn't slow to kick out the folk who didn't do as she wanted and then she gradually re-rented their homes to other meeker folk at higher rates. It's always been known that she was money-hungry and could never have enough of it.'

'I'm not like that.'

'No, you don't seem at all that sort of person. But I'm intending to keep a closer watch on the Parnhams from now on.' Col hesitated as if unsure whether to continue.

Miranda said it for him, and spoke more sharply than her usual tone. 'Well, you won't find me continuing to charge ridiculously high rents. I'm going to review them all and reduce any I consider unfair.'

'I didn't think you'd be the sort to take unfair amounts of money from people. You'll excuse me saying so but one has only to look at your face to realise you're a wizzywig sort of person.'

She looked at him in surprise. 'What does that mean?'

He grinned. 'It's short for "what you see is what you get".'

'Oh, that. I never tied the two concepts together. How can you be sure of that where I'm concerned? You've only just met me.'

Even Libby was smiling now.

Ryan spoke more gently. 'You have one of those utterly honest and transparent faces, Miranda. I bet you find it hard to tell lies at all.'

She went a bit pink and admitted, 'Well, yes. I do hate telling lies. People have done that to me, twisted the truth around and it can hurt, but I try not to do it to others.'

Libby put an arm round her shoulders and gave her a quick hug. 'Don't be embarrassed. It's an excellent character trait.'

'Well, after what you've said, I intend to conduct a review of the rents as soon as it can be arranged and if those on any of my houses are thought to be unfairly high, I shall reduce them immediately.'

'Good for you. There are laws about what you can and can't do as a landlord nowadays but they haven't always kept Selma Parnham toeing the line. She was apparently good at finding ways round rules and regulations. So well done you if you can manage to do that. And if you don't mind, I'll let it be known casually that I've met you and trust you. That should make things a little easier for you with the locals to start off with but they'll watch and pass judgement on you themselves as well. There are some canny folk living round here.'

'Thanks. I'd be grateful for any help in settling in.' She stared into space for a moment or two, then added, almost as if talking to herself, 'I've had experience of being bullied and been helpless to do anything about it, and it was usually done by my great-aunt or on her orders. I'd never, ever do that sort of thing to anyone else, believe me.'

Her three companions all nodded and looked at her sympathetically.

After a few moments, Col broke the silence. 'Well, I'm responsible for law and order in the area including all the Fairford villages and nearby farms, so I'll be available if you need help with the Parnhams or anyone else.'

'I'll remember that. Although I must admit that I'm still finding these villages rather confusing.'

Ryan smiled at her sympathetically. 'I'd have had trouble working it all out at first if it hadn't been spelt out for me by one of my customers. Let me do the same for you. Fairford Magna is the largest by far, Lesser Fairford is the next in size, but a lot smaller, and your own Fairford Parva is the smallest by a long way with just an uneven scattering of houses in the village, the big house that you own and a few small farms nearby. And yet, they all stay stubbornly together as a group from other local government areas, which can cause some confusion at times.'

'I see.'

Col gave her a wry glance. 'The chap who dealt with this area retired from the police force recently and doesn't seem to have put as much effort into keeping as careful an eye on people like the Parnhams during the last few years as he maybe should have done, which is probably why Selma and her mistress got away with some rather nasty ways of treating people.'

He hesitated, then added, 'By the way, if you get any more would-be intruders, I can get here in just under ten minutes from my base in Fairford Magna. And if you do ever need urgent help, Ms Westerby, make a 999 call rather than an ordinary phone call, and ask for me personally. Then don't open your door to anyone until I get here, especially a stranger.'

'You can call me as well and I can get to you far more quickly,' Ryan said. 'Actually, I think I'm your closest neighbour and I can run across your grounds in a couple of minutes at most if I'm at home.'

She was startled, looking from one to the other in shock, and Libby looked to be feeling similarly surprised.

'But there are two of us here and surely this was an isolated incident? That woman knows now that I shan't hand over the box, so we aren't likely to need help again that badly, surely?' Miranda asked. 'I mean, what is there in it that can possibly attract anyone else to try to steal it?'

Col took over again. 'I don't know but it's always useful to be prepared for the worst, don't you think? What if either of you are home alone and working outside at the other end of the garden? How will you get help then?'

She gaped at him, astonished at the way he wasn't letting this drop.

'You should perhaps carry a mobile phone with you at all times when you leave the house, even if you're still on your own land.'

'Really?'

'Yes, really. This house is very isolated, which is the main reason I'm bothering to go on emphasising your need to keep safety in mind at all times. If the Parnhams decide to hang around this area and continue trying to get hold of this box, you could be in trouble. They'd probably find it easy to get away afterwards too because they know the area well and you don't know it at all yet.'

'I will remember that,' she said quietly. Where her great-aunt was concerned, she was definitely wary about traps having been laid for her, only she didn't feel she knew these men well enough to confide in them about some of her past interactions with the old woman. It occurred to her now that her great-aunt might have set up the Parnhams to cause ongoing problems for her – especially if it benefitted Phyllis's dear friend Selma. Her great-aunt and her so-called housekeeper sounded to have got on so well that it was more as if they were the ones who were related.

Miranda realised both men were waiting for her to speak, as if needing to make sure she had taken their advice and comments to heart. 'I'll definitely heed your warnings and take great care how I do things.'

'So will I,' Libby said. 'There are two of us here, don't forget.'

Both men nodded and then Ryan changed the subject.

'Just for your general information about shopping and so on, Fairford Magna is still classified as a village but it's big enough to have its own supermarket and a few other shops of various types. Lesser Fairford is so close to it that it only has a market but that's well patronised. It's been taking place on Friday mornings for several hundred years. Fairford Parva is further away from the others and has only a single village shop. The owners are well liked locally and they're extremely obliging about getting things in that their customers purchase regularly, so they're keeping their heads above water financially.'

'Good. I like village shops,' Libby said.

Miranda nodded agreement. 'This sounds like an interesting group of villages, much nicer to live in than a big city.'

'It's interesting in several ways,' Col said. 'There are a few listed historical buildings round here and some parts of other buildings. Your cellars are among those listed. The western end of them is several hundred years old, possibly Elizabethan, it's thought, though it's been closed off for safety reasons for as long as most people remember. There are other parts of the cellars that are quite old and interesting, but not as unusual as the oldest cellars, apparently.'

She looked at him in surprise. 'Why did no one mention that to me?'

Ryan took over. 'Miss Westerby disliked strangers coming into her cellars at all apparently, let alone tramping about taking photos, so she refused to allow anyone to enter them unless she invited them. Which she didn't. But you may wish to change that once you've settled in. The local historical society would love to check the oldest cellars out for you, find out whether they're safe and what has been hidden away from the public. They'd also make sure for you that she hasn't damaged anything in them.'

'Would she have done that, damaged a piece of history?'

'I've heard people say they wouldn't have put anything past her, including murder, not when it was concerned with her family and her inheritance at any rate. And she sounds to have been obsessed with making money.' He smiled. 'Don't look so anxious. I don't think she was bad enough to commit murder.'

'Well, once I'm settled in here, people will be welcome to visit the cellars if they're interested in how people lived in the past,' Miranda said, 'and I hope somebody from the historical society will be able to show me what's important about those cellars first. Personally, I think historical sites are well worth preserving and their attractions should be shared with others. I like the idea of owning an old building or two.'

Col beamed at her. 'I've just joined the historical society. You don't mind if I pass that information on to the president about people soon being able to visit the cellars again? She'll be thrilled. Joyce knows this area far better than I do because she's lived here all her life.'

'I don't mind at all. And I shall look forward to meeting her too and picking her brain, historically speaking.'

'She'll be happy to share her knowledge.' He went on explaining the general situation as it had recently been explained to him. 'Selma Parnham isn't liked in any of the villages so I doubt she'd be able to get lodgings or rent a house near here but unfortunately, or so most people think, she and her brother inherited a run-down little cottage on the far side of Fairford Magna from an elderly cousin years ago so we've never been able to stop them living in the district. At least their cottage isn't here in Fairford Parva.'

Miranda studied the two men, liking them both. Well, what woman wouldn't? Each was quite tall, not good looking but clean-cut and healthy, and they had charming smiles. She was a sucker for smiles, felt they said more than anything about people's nature, especially when you first met them. She realised they were both staring at her and waiting so she said what she was thinking. 'I can't thank you two enough for your help today and I'm sure Libby feels the same.'

Her friend nodded vigorously.

'You're welcome.'

She looked from one man to the other and asked abruptly, 'What on earth have I walked into here?'

'Who knows?' Ryan asked. 'We could look at what's in that box of papers, if you like. Perhaps they'll tell you more about the background to Miss Westerby and her housekeeper's efforts. That woman was very keen to get hold of the box, after all.'

'I'm sorry I can't tell you much more,' Col said. 'I usually get to know the people in my area of responsibility, but I'm afraid I've not been posted here for long enough to be aware of all the subtleties of what's going on behind the scenes as well as I'd like, so looking at the papers may show us all more about the situation.'

'And I've only lived here for a few weeks,' Ryan added. 'But both you ladies can be sure that either of us will do whatever we can to help you at any time and if ever you feel threatened in future, you should contact us immediately.'

'Thanks. We shan't hesitate to ask if we need your help.'

Chapter Twenty-One

After they'd finished their refreshments, which included the men accepting the offer of the rest of the biscuits remaining on the plate and eating them with relish, Libby cleared the tea things away.

She was about to rejoin the others at the table, when Miranda stood up and announced, 'I can't put this off any longer, much as I'm dreading it. Let's all of us investigate what's in the box now. If that woman was so keen to take it away, it must be important and I'd value other opinions on what we find.'

'How about we take it into the dining room and spread the contents out on the big table there?' Libby suggested.

'Good idea. Ryan and I will fetch it down for you.' Col said.

They brought it and set it on the table. 'It's a rather nice box and when you study it more closely, it looks to be a lot older than I'd thought,' Col said.

They all took a closer look.

'Strange that we didn't notice that before,' Libby said. 'It can't have been handled much to stay so clean. There's only some surface dust on it. But you're right to be careful, Col. We don't want the box to slip and send its contents scattering everywhere. I'll help you carry it.'

'No. I've got it.' Ryan went to the other end and the two men nodded at one another and picked the box up at the same time then followed the women slowly towards the dining room.

Libby had stopped just inside the doorway to stare round and was now making some soft tutting noises. 'It's a long time since I've seen such a dusty set of furniture. Don't put that box of papers on the table yet, guys, or they'll get dirty when we pull them out. Can you hold it for a little longer and I'll go and find a duster or something I can use as one.' When they nodded, she hurried past them back into the kitchen.

When she didn't return as quickly as they'd expected, Ryan said, 'Let's put the box down on that occasional table in the bay window. It's surprisingly heavy.'

'We should stand near it and stay there out of her way,' Miranda suggested. 'It won't take her long, I'm sure. I've never seen anyone who can restore order to a place as rapidly as Libby.'

Her friend returned brandishing what looked like a small tablecloth. 'I couldn't find any cleaning materials. They're not stored anywhere obvious, that's for sure. But this was in a kitchen drawer and should do the job adequately. It's a well-worn piece so I doubt it'll matter to the new owner if we damage it.' She flourished it at Miranda.

'It wouldn't matter to me even if it were brand new, it's

so ugly.' She scowled at the garish pattern round the edges of the cheap material.

'I knew you'd love it as much as I did.' Libby grinned as she whisked round the table and dining chairs with her improvised duster. Then she rolled it up and dumped in on a hard chair in one corner before gesturing. 'Go ahead and set the box down. The table and chairs should be all right now, clean enough not to mess the papers up when we spread them out, which is the main thing. I'll wash that old tablecloth another time, or just tear it up for rags as is.'

'Rags!' said Miranda firmly. 'I couldn't live with those ugly so-called flowers round the edges. They don't look like any blossoms that I've ever seen.'

Everyone chuckled at her vehemence and the men put the box at one end of the big table, after which Ryan waved one hand at the two women to signal that they should take charge of it.

Libby lifted off the lid, doing it carefully because it had very pretty patterns inlaid in it. She held it out to admire it for a moment and show it to the others, then stood it on end against the wall and sat down again waiting for her friend to deal with her new possession.

Miranda peered at the contents then lifted the edges of a few of the tightly packed papers it contained, first ones near the top then selecting others at intervals lower down to get some idea of how its crowded contents had been arranged and how old they were. Mostly they seemed to go by date, but occasionally someone seemed to have been careless, or had they been hiding some information? It was hard to tell.

Near the top she found used envelopes stapled to papers she presumed were the letters they'd contained, some just scribbled on, others typed neatly. She read a couple but they were simply arrangements to meet at times long gone. There were also occasional slender folders of various thicknesses and who knew what else these contained?

She didn't stop to find out at the moment but looked round at the others. 'This box seems to be full to bursting and with a mixture of what looks like business paperwork. Someone must have been stuffing stray documents, old letters and who knows what into it any old how for decades. They can't have been pulling most of them out again, either, so they're more or less in date order still.'

'You may as well start at the top, then,' Libby suggested.

'I just want to see what's at the bottom first.' Miranda grasped a handful from near the bottom and lifted one edge, staring down at what was near the bottom in surprise. 'Good heavens! Some of these papers lower down are from decades ago, well before I was born! They just seem to have been dumped in the box and left there ever since, then others dumped on top of them. See, they're not crumpled and most look brand new, though the paper is slightly yellowed with age, perhaps.'

Libby frowned down at the ones she'd pulled out then at the box still crammed with papers. 'How should we organise ourselves to sort it all out accurately? We don't want to just pile these in random heaps, surely?'

'How about we first decide on the best way to sort out the papers roughly,' Col suggested. 'And after that's done, we should look at how to group them further. It should be how you want to make a more specific investigation from then on, Miranda, because these belong to you now and possibly refer to your ancestors. I doubt we'll be able sort many of the piles out properly today, whatever method we use. There are a lot and they look to be in a right old mess at the moment.'

Libby waited a moment or two and when neither her friend nor anyone else volunteered any other suggestion, she glanced at Miranda, who nodded at her slightly, so she took charge and began organising them with her usual efficiency, passing each person a pile of papers, but keeping the individual piles together and going round from one person to another and checking, then warning everyone not to mix up their piles since the papers were already more or less in date order.

'Now, let's each make an initial check of our own pile. We can flick through them then share our findings. I don't think doing this by dates alone will be much use as we get further into things.'

There were more nods and murmurs but they were all looking at her for more specific guidance, she could tell. People at work often did ask her help about arranging and organising things once they got to know her and admire her skill at that.

'Once the box is empty, we can each go through our pile quickly, trying to get some idea of what it contains: envelopes, letters, other papers, miscellaneous scraps, whatever we find.'

She waited and when they nodded, she handed fistfuls out. 'Here you are. Just look through your own fistful.'

They began to do this and found it fairly effective, but as they were getting near to emptying the box and about to start flicking through their own piles, Libby sat staring at the things in front of her. 'These papers at the bottom of the box looked different, so I kept them together.'

She used both hands to lift out two faded, scruffy folders

from the box. Each folder looked to be chock full of loose papers and letters.

She took a quick look at a few, then said, 'I think someone has sorted these out already. They're very fragile so I'll have to go slowly.' She had to hold each one with both hands and move it carefully to stop the contents sliding out. Then she set them down one on top of the other in front of herself. 'I'll just take a quick look at this one.'

But when she opened the top folder and began to go through the top papers she gasped, looking shocked. She checked a few more pages, not saying a word, only holding up one hand to stop them interrupting her concentration.

She was looking more and more upset and the others stared in surprise, exchanged glances and waited quietly for an explanation.

Instead, Libby closed that folder then passed it with the other one from the bottom of the box to Miranda. 'Take a quick look at the top papers.'

While her friend was doing that, Libby turned to the men and said, 'I think it may be better if Miranda and I sort these out initially on our own and then go through them with you later, since we both have some idea of the Westerby family background and the – the implications of these.'

'Does that mean you already have some idea about what the contents are dealing with?' Col asked.

Libby hesitated, then said, 'I don't exactly understand all the details, but they seem to contain some rather private information that Miranda should see first and think about, before even I look at the rest of them.'

They looked at her in surprise, especially as she shot them a quick, pleading glance and put her forefinger to her lips in a gesture to keep silent and then set an example by waiting, motionless. But she was unable to hide how really worried she was about something she'd found.

It was Ryan who caught on to her unspoken plea first. 'Why don't you two go into the next room then and take a preliminary look in peace? You can spread these papers out on the table there, the one near the bookshelves. Col and I can keep watch on the approach to this house from here as well as continuing to go through some of the other piles of papers and making sure those papers are in the right sets, give or take. Or we can just leave them and wait for further instructions.'

'I think we should wait. But it could be even more important now to keep watch.' Libby picked up her own folder and beckoned to her friend. 'Come on, love. We'll go and spread these out next door.'

But the minute the two of them were alone, Miranda asked, 'What were all those meaningful glances about? You've looked at more of these papers than I have. I'm a bit puzzled by what I've seen so far and it just doesn't make sense. Is this something else my great-aunt has done that needs to be broken to me tactfully?'

Libby hesitated, then nodded and gestured to the folders. 'It looks like it, I'm afraid. I only know because I got this pile first. If what I'm guessing is correct, these are definitely the papers your great-aunt would have been eager to destroy. She must have asked that horrible Selma creature to do it if she died before she had sorted out the information she wanted to keep from you permanently. Why don't you have a quick glance through them and I'll wait for you to tell me what you think before I have another look or do anything else.'

Miranda shot her an anguished glance, then reluctantly

picked up the top folder of the two and removed its contents.

'Take all the time you need, love. Even a quick glance told me that they're going to be extremely important for you.'

She gave Libby a little nod, took a deep breath as if bracing herself and began to study the papers from the top folder as her friend set them aside, drawing in sharp breaths of shock several times before they'd got even a quarter of the way through the contents.

After a while, both women finished reading the first group of papers in the folder and looked at one another. Miranda said in a choked-sounding voice, 'These aren't forgeries, are they?' It was a statement as much as a question.

'I don't think they are. In fact, I now think the others you were given must have been the forgeries, made to look as if they were the family papers. These that we've now found seem to me to be the genuine ones. Both sets look old, but these seem old in more subtle ways, now that I can compare them. Some have slight wrinkles and faint marks here and there as if they've been handled and looked at dozens of times.'

Miranda looked more closely and nodded. 'Yes. I agree.'

Libby took over again. 'And my other big reason is that some of these have a smell I recognise from regularly visiting research libraries during my university years and working as a weekend volunteer in a small private reference library for a few years at one stage. I think of it as the smell of truly old papers and books. You can't mistake it and I don't think you can fake it.'

'I could smell that too and I agree with you about it.

Why would anyone have falsified the first set of documents, though?'

She stared blindly down at the piles of papers, then answered her own question before Libby could say anything else. 'The forged ones must have been to keep the genuine information about my family away from me. I don't know why she even kept the latter, though. To gloat, perhaps, or to check information she wanted to add to it.'

She fell silent for a moment or two then her pain burst out. 'Was there nothing that horrible woman wouldn't do to spoil my life? Even after she's dead she seems to be reaching out to hurt me.'

After a moment she tapped the pile of papers with her right forefinger as she worked out the answer to her own question. 'She wanted to make sure I couldn't find out who I was genuinely related to.' In spite of her efforts to stay calm, a sob escaped her and she pressed a hand to her mouth. 'Cutting an orphaned child completely off from her remaining family was vile. Why would anyone do that?'

'I can't think why she did it but it shows she was utterly wicked and selfish beyond reason.'

'Or vengeful about something!'

'Yes. The latter I'd guess. You've always said you could tell she hated you but you didn't understand why.' Libby frowned and stared at the papers again. 'You know, these could have far wider ramifications than only affecting you. She must have known about your real family connections for years, perhaps even kept an eye on where some of these other people were living. They'll surely want to know about your existence too. How would you feel about that?'

'About having genuine relatives? I'd be over the moon.' Miranda's voice broke.

Libby didn't say anything, only gave her friend a hug. She knew how it had always upset Miranda not to have any relatives at all apart from that horrible Phyllis and one distant cousin whom she'd never even met.

Miranda asked hesitantly, 'Do you think we should keep this information to ourselves at first? Not because I don't trust Ryan and Col, but because the fewer people who know, the safer the information will be.'

'Hmm. I'm not sure I agree about that. Apart from any other considerations, as a police officer Col might have access to some helpful sets of data that aren't available to us. Or know people who could help you.'

'I never thought of that. And he may be able to help us to keep those papers safe from that Parnham creature. But there are quite a lot of them to hide easily. I don't want to lodge them in a bank because I want to carry on going through them. Give me time to think about it.'

'All right.' Libby shrugged. 'So we'll just keep them either with us or somewhere safe in the house. The information they contain is going to impact on other people's lives as well as yours in the future.'

'Who knows what other branches of my family will be revealed and how that could affect their future children, not just as an inheritance but if they need financial help from the Trust.'

Libby nodded. 'It's there for members of the family who have emergencies, after all, isn't it, not just for the heir?'

'Yes. Ah, who can be sure of anything at this stage?' Miranda ran one hand through her hair, not seeming to realise how wild and untidy she was making it.

Her friend continued to study the papers. 'We'll have to tread very carefully indeed till we're one hundred per cent certain we understand the whole situation.'

There was dead silence for a few moments, then Miranda wiped away some more tears that had escaped her control, whispering, 'Fancy trying to take all my family connections away from me and leave me alone for the rest of my life! What could have made her hate me so viciously?'

Libby gave her a quick hug and said in a whisper, 'Perhaps we should leave worrying about that for the moment and concentrate on getting settled in here. And I don't think we should reveal anything about it to other people until we've gathered a lot more information, which includes that distant cousin of yours, the one your great-aunt left tenancy of the cottage to. Whatever you decide to do, you know I'll help you in any way I can.'

Miranda gave her a wobbly smile. 'I'd rather taken your willingness to do that for granted because you feel so much like a close relative. Are you sure you want to help me sort things out? I feel guilty asking you when it's not your family and blood relatives involved.'

'Didn't you mean it when you adopted me as your aunt?'

She stared at Libby in surprise. 'Yes, of course I did. But I didn't think it'd bring you such troubles and difficulties to face, ones as nasty as these may turn out to be, since we're dealing with my great-aunt and the Parnhams.'

'Well, too bad. You've got me by your side now, through thick and thin. You feel like family and I no longer have any close relatives left in England, so I need you as well as genuinely caring about you.'

After another pause, she added in a low voice, 'The enormity of what your great-aunt did, her horrible unkindness and deliberate neglect of you, all the lies she told – well, it sickens me as well as you. Two heads are usually better than one in solving problems, as the saying goes, especially when dealing with such a puzzling situation.'

Miranda nodded. 'I agree. So I think our first step has got to be to rough out what we can of the genuine family tree, then hide the originals we've found somewhere safe. In this era at least we can photocopy them and store them digitally as well as finding a physical hiding place for the originals. Phyllis never came to terms with doing things online, so didn't really understand what can be done or found digitally, or what can be hidden there, so that's a weakness in her planning that may be to our advantage long-term.'

'And I wonder whether the Parnhams are any better at managing things digitally.'

'It'd help if they weren't but you can't guarantee anything.'

'Well, we'll keep our eyes open and hunt for the truth, whatever it may turn out to be. Thank you for trusting me to help you.' Libby patted her arm. 'I'm sure that other people will benefit as well as you if we can sort out the nasty mess that woman left.'

'Didn't just leave – created. Of course I trust you. And I promise you that whatever we find out, you will never stop being the family of my heart, even if you and I are not blood relatives and even if we find others to whom I am related by birth.'

The two women hugged one another again quickly, both blinking more sentimental tears away, then Libby said slowly and thoughtfully, 'I'll do what you want about it but I still think it'd be better to tell the guys what we've found out. Col will have a lot of contacts from his years in the police force and he may also be able to point out different avenues of enquiry to pursue. And Ryan is a really decent and intelligent person. Who knows what he'll be able to contribute? I can't help liking him, can you?'

Miranda's face softened into a smile. 'No, I can't. And he also lives nearby in case we're attacked in some way. I just wish that guy didn't have the right to live in that nearby cottage. What was my great-aunt plotting when she left him that?'

'Who knows? He may be much stronger than either of us so could be physically dangerous. I wonder if we could set up some sort of loud electric alarm, one where we can press a button and let Ryan know we have a problem. I trust him implicitly, don't you?'

'Yes, I do. What is there about some faces that makes you feel sure they're owned by good people?' Her expression softened again as she said this, then she frowned and went across to look out of the window.

Miranda sighed. 'I can't help wishing I didn't feel so threatened still, but I do. I feel the need to check everything around me.' She shivered. 'There's something going on and if she planned it, you can be sure it won't be good for me.'

'We have enough on our plate at the moment sorting out these papers that your great-aunt arranged to have destroyed.'

'This all sounds so horribly melodramatic, doesn't it? I'd just like to settle down to a normal home life here and make a few friends. Maybe even find a family by marriage.' It was what she'd longed for most of all since her mother died when she was a teenager.

Libby gave her shoulder a quick squeeze. 'We'll cope, love. And I'm sure we shall gradually make new friends in the village.'

'I know we'll cope and work things out in the long run, but what we've found out so far isn't just melodramatic; it's a true horror tale as far as I'm concerned,' Miranda said bitterly.

After a pause she added, 'I still find it hard to believe what my great-aunt has done to me, how she separated me from my real family from when my father died. I was only a small child than. She must have started making plans and fooling my mother straight away. And I fell into her hands like a ripe fruit waiting to be stamped on when it dropped off the branch after Mum died. There have been so many lonely years and I had to learn the harsh lessons of facing the world alone.'

'Well, you coped. You're a strong woman now. And you'll never be so alone again. The past is fixed, but the future can still be changed into a better focus.'

'Yes. And perhaps you're right. If the guys are settled round here, we should include them and tell them what's going on.'

Libby stood up. 'I'll go and ask them to join us, then, and outline briefly what we've found. All right? I'll not bring them back quickly. You've had a horrible shock, Miranda. Take a few minutes to calm down.'

'Thanks. A little quiet time does sound rather good.'

Libby went into the next room and outlined the situation succinctly to the two men, who stared at her in shock when she finished explaining what had happened to her friend over the years.

After a moment or two's thought, Col asked a few questions, shaking his head sadly at the answers. 'What that old woman did was criminal as far as I'm concerned, but it's too late to call her to account for it now. Pity. But we can try to make sure her housekeeper doesn't carry out any of her late mistress's wishes.'

'We'll do more than try; we'll succeed. I'm determined on that,' Libby said.

'Good.'

'We'll give Miranda a few more minutes to pull herself together, shall we?' Col suggested.

'Yes. And then we'll see if we can find some practical ways to help her to deal with the whole situation. In the meantime, you two can show me what you've sorted out from the rest of the papers.'

'Not much of interest, I'm afraid. It was those two folders which revealed most, showing exactly what that harridan had been up to and that has given us a lead to the true extent of the situation.'

'There is one paper which might lead to another family connection,' Ryan said. 'Not as close a relationship as Miranda's but still this guy is somehow connected to her and her family. Let me find it. It must have slipped off.' He fiddled about and came up with a scruffy-looking piece of paper and held it out to Libby.

She glanced at it and nodded. 'Yes. But I think it's the start of another trail, so put it away carefully and we'll look at it in more detail later. We can't solve every problem at once.'

Chapter Twenty-Two

About ten minutes later, Miranda, who had been staring blindly into space, heard footsteps. She looked across the room to see Ryan and Col follow Libby in to join her and smiled at them all. She might not have family but she did have good friends now.

She was feeling calmer. Well, sort of calmer. Behind that self-control, she was still shocked by these revelations, not only shocked but angry and even more deeply hurt than usual by her old witch of a great-aunt.

This wasn't the first time she had found out that something she thought had happened by sheer hard luck had instead been set up deliberately by Phyllis to upset her!

There was no reason that she could figure out for depriving her of knowledge about the real facts of this family situation, only there had to be more to it than simply hurting her out of sheer spite, surely? Even with her great-aunt. Why go to such lengths? She had never found out the reason for Phyllis's hatred, though she'd felt its impact enough times to be utterly certain that it existed.

But though she'd been helpless to do anything about it before, she wasn't as helpless now. Money could achieve a lot, money and kind people like Libby. The two men seemed kind as well and she hoped to get to know them a lot better.

Perhaps, with the others' help, Miranda would at least be able to find out some of the details of what had been done to her and her family in the past and she might even manage to set some of the records straight. That would make her feel a lot better, she felt sure.

They moved most of the miscellaneous papers to one of the smaller tables stationed here and there round the edges of the room, their only function seeming for each to hold one of her great-aunt's ornaments standing in the exact centre on a neat lace mat. They stood the china crinoline ladies and their mats on a windowsill for the time being but if Miranda had her way, they were not coming back into her home or life.

After that she and Libby settled down at the much larger table in the centre of the room and began doggedly sorting through the items from the two oldest folders while the men each put one of the bundles of documents on a smaller table ready to begin sorting through them.

'How about we take it in turns to patrol the interior of the house, Ryan?' Col suggested as the men were settling down. 'You can see a lot of what's going on outside from the various windows.'

'Good idea. And I'll enjoy stretching my legs at the same time. I could never do an office job again.' He shuddered at the thought.

Their alertness made Miranda feel a lot safer. She hadn't

had other people to rely on before and had never trusted anyone as she did the three other people in this group.

The key to this puzzle was here, she felt sure. It had to be. But there seemed to be so many papers and some were quite crumpled from being crammed into smaller folders for years or possibly even decades. She and Libby sorted out some loose birth certificates into groups, dated by decade and then found some others here and there, which seemed to have been stuffed into folded pieces of paper rather haphazardly.

As Miranda opened one of the folded pieces, its contents slipped out and revealed some crumpled papers. When she smoothed these open and started to read them, she said, 'I'll have to check these carefully, but I can't do everything at once.'

Some were for the decade of her mother's birth, others for the next decade and then a couple were dated closer to the present, for Miranda's own birth decade. Only, she'd never heard of these people, either children or parents.

Libby looked at her sympathetically. 'It has to be your great-aunt's doing.'

'Who else could it be?'

'It must have taken a lot of effort for Phyllis to keep you almost completely in the dark about your family background. Why go to such lengths? It's all bizarre. That's the only word for it.'

'This is like a jigsaw puzzle with some of the pieces still missing.'

As one thing sank in, she looked at Libby and couldn't prevent tears from welling up in her eyes and overflowing.

'What is it?' her friend asked gently.

'I do recognise a couple of surnames from my childhood,

and these individuals must be fairly close relatives. Phyllis had convinced me I had faulty memories because of being so young but I didn't have, did I? I remembered correctly and she persuaded me otherwise. Why?'

'Because she was a wicked woman.'

Miranda continued to frown. 'But she must have had a reason, mustn't she? I don't understand what that could be.'

It was left to Libby to say the unpalatable truth aloud. 'Because she hated you.'

There was dead silence, then Col asked, 'Do you think it was why she was trying to keep control of you?'

'She found out I wouldn't do as she wanted after I grew up and was able to earn a living.'

'All right, then. What's puzzling you most? Let's start with that and not try to solve all those other mysteries at once.' He waved one hand dismissively towards the papers on the other table and then looked questioningly at her.

'There could also be a positive side to this,' Col added quietly.

She splayed one hand across her chest above her heart and nodded, saying in a husky whisper, almost as if speaking to herself, 'I know. I'm trying to think about that. Surely some of them are correct and they mean that I'm not alone in the world, as I'd always believed.'

'You're not alone in the world anyway, now. You have some good friends.' Ryan laid his hand briefly on hers and squeezed it gently. 'You must adopt us. It'll make me very happy for one.'

The smile he gave her was so warm and caring it made her feel better straight away and she was talking to him mainly when she replied. 'I now also wonder if I do have some other blood kin, kinder people than my great-aunt. That could be very comforting. I've always refused to count my great-aunt as a genuine relative because I'd rather not have any at all than just her. And anyway she's always behaved more like an enemy than a friend.'

A hand clasped hers briefly and Ryan said, 'She was a wicked woman and not just when dealing with you. Most people in the village disliked her intensely.'

'She must have set this up on purpose to cut me off from my family, but why? I always come back to that: why would anyone do such a cruel thing to a girl who'd lost her mother and had no relatives other than her in the world?'

'Criminals can do the most inexplicable things at times, and I consider your great-aunt to have been one, not just for the way she treated you, but for the way she treated her tenants,' Col said quietly. 'I'm finding a lot out about her, and little of it good. But one thing that comes to my mind is that money is often at the heart of all sorts of crimes, so let's look at that first as possibly the main reason for this.'

'Yes, but most people are fond of their relatives, or at least loyal to them,' she said bitterly. 'They don't put money ahead of them.'

'She doesn't sound to have cared about anyone from what people say about her. Except perhaps Selma Parnham.'

Ryan looked across at Miranda. 'How old was Miss Westerby exactly when she died?'

'Just turned sixty-five.'

'That's considered young these days, too young for dementia in most cases and she wouldn't have expected to die for another decade or more, would she? These days, lots of people live till around eighty at least. Well, all the people I know do.' Col gave them a wry smile. 'Not that

I'm in that age bracket yet, but I certainly do have certain long-term aspirations about how long I'll live because my family has already spawned three centenarians during the past century and a half, and I'd love to follow their example.'

'I hope you do make a hundred,' Miranda said warmly. 'Or a hundred plus, even. What do they call that? A super-centenarian?'

'No, that's people over a hundred and ten.'

'Well, the world needs more decent people like you so I hope you make it. You should certainly ensure that you have several children to carry on your genes. And perhaps offer to donate some to a sperm bank as well.'

Col went a little pink at that forthright set of advice and Ryan took pity on his friend and diverted the conversation away from him by tapping the nearest few papers. 'At least your great-aunt couldn't have had all these people killed. Some will have died of natural old age, given their dates of birth, but some of them should still be alive and if we trace any of them that would give you a chance to start pulling your family together again.'

She nodded, her eyes suddenly bright with hope – and tears. 'Yes. And I'll have the money to do it now. I never knew how wealthy the Westerbys were. It's going to be a difficult puzzle to solve but you're right. I'll be able to afford to do it now because I don't want to hoard money but use it wisely to make people happier. And perhaps also to start to pull my family together.'

'Sounds like a good idea. You go for it,' Ryan said.

They exchanged smiles, then she said, 'It won't be unrealistic to hope that I can find some genuine relatives, will it, even if I have to hire a detective to help me?'

She'd do whatever she could, she decided there and then, search for the scattered family members by any means she could think of and surely she'd find some relatives!

Col's voice was as gentle as ever. 'I'm sure you'll succeed in finding several of them. You'll have enough money to hire an investigative genealogist to help you, for a start. They can work wonders.'

'Oh, yes. I'd forgotten there were people who specialised in that sort of detecting. I haven't got used to the idea that I'll not have to do everything myself from now on. I'm not used to having enough money to hire the necessary expert help. That still hasn't really sunk in. And I think you were right about the main thing that drove her to do this, Col: money. And perhaps that was because of her inability to create her own children.'

The others were all looking at her with kind, patient expressions, giving her time to pull the facts together into patterns that made sense.

'It was money and the power that gave her, wasn't it?' she said quietly. 'The two often go together. My great-aunt wanted to retain total control of the family money, which means the trust. To do that she'd have had to stop others from inheriting and keep a child as the heir. That would leave her in charge for several years to prepare for the next stage.'

Col nodded. 'I'm sure an adult would have become much more aware of what she was doing than you could have been.'

'But how could she have been sure of keeping that child under her control?' Ryan frowned.

'She was either very lucky or even more of a criminal than we thought.'

There was another silence as the horrendous implications of that sank in.

'Would it be unrealistic, Col, to think she'd not have balked at murdering one or both of my parents?'

'Not totally, but we'll never really know, will we? The time for pursuing that possibility is long past. Don't waste your life obsessing and trying to find out, Miranda. Move on. She's dead. However wicked they have been, criminals can't be brought back to life and punished.'

Her voice was spiky with anguish. 'I suppose you're right. My great-aunt managed to retain control of the trust for decades by using me.'

'If she was breaking other legal rules, the family lawyers ought to have been aware of it,' Col said. 'But they didn't seem to be. So she must have been very convincing.'

'Until this new lawyer took over the management. He's very shrewd and has been asking questions. The one he replaced just fiddled with papers on the few occasions I met him, looking bored.'

'Your great-aunt managed to twist the rules over the decades. From what I've found out, no one else has ever been in charge of it all for as long as her but the lawyers dealing with her probably changed every few years, so they must have let her guide them as to how things were done.'

Miranda's voice was bitter. 'I understood from an early age that she was dangerous and was frightened of her, so I tried to stay out of her way.'

'Probably you did just what she wanted you to, so she didn't feel the need to get rid of you.'

'But her own body let her down in the end, didn't it? She didn't live nearly as long as she always told me the Westerbys do.' She sighed. 'I wish I weren't part of a family that breeds women like her. I wish . . . that I came from a gentle, loving, normal family.'

Ryan looked at her sadly, starting to understand more of what she must have gone through during the years of being without any real family. He couldn't even imagine how he'd have coped with that, because he'd always had family to turn to, always known he was loved, always had what this lovely woman seemed to have longed for in vain.

Miranda stared into space then sighed. 'I'm only just beginning to understand how deep her obsession about money went and I'm amazed she got on so well with Selma Parnham.'

'Perhaps her housekeeper was also fond of money, as well as being a useful tool for many years.'

'Who knows?'

'Well, we can speculate all we like about her motives but we'll never really know for certain,' Col said quietly. 'Don't waste your life on angsting about it, Miranda. Some famous criminals in the past have acted in a similar way. They were talented people, who could have done positive things for humanity but instead turned to darker deeds because all they cared about was money or property or some other obsession.'

He paused then looked across at Miranda with an expression that was both gentle and kind. 'I hope you'll let me help you try to sort out your present situation. As a police officer, I have access to databases which most of the public don't even know about. Some of them may come in useful to you and to us as your fellow searchers for the truth.'

'I'd welcome any help you can give me and I know you'll

keep all this to yourself, Col. Indeed, I trust you two guys absolutely.'

She looked across at Ryan, feeling a little sad. She had been hoping that the spark she felt whenever she looked at him would flare into something brighter and more lasting. But now, she felt that it couldn't do that at a time when her whole life was being turned upside down, and when she was trying to right old wrongs.

For years she'd recognised her own intense need for some genuine biological connection to others. It was a need lodged deep in her soul after all the years of feeling so utterly alone. She was sure knowing more about her family background would make for a happier life one day both for her and any man she cared about.

As Col turned to say something to Ryan, Libby touched her friend's arm to get her attention and murmured in a low voice, 'You won't go without an extended family of some sort whatever comes of this, Miranda dear. There are other people in the world who will love you over the years as much as I do now. I'm quite sure of that, because it stands out a mile to me and to all normal people that you're innately decent and lovable.'

Miranda blinked her eyes furiously. 'That's a . . . a wonderful thing to say.'

'I meant it. And hopefully one day the guy you love will become more than a friend, and you'll be able to create a brand-new family together, a family that no one can take away from you.'

Libby hesitated then added, 'A happy marriage was something I always wished I could find for myself but it never happened, and I saw enough unhappy marriages to know I would never want to take second best.'

'Perhaps it's not too late for you.'

Libby's expression was suddenly bleak. 'It's too late for me to have children.'

It was Miranda's turn to give her friend a comforting hug.

After that, Libby couldn't help shooting a quick glance at Ryan and hoping he would stay around long enough to get to know her adopted niece much better. He was obviously attracted to Miranda but she guessed he was sensitive enough to hold back to allow her the freedom to sort out the other aspects of her life first. Only a truly good man could or would do that. Unless she'd read the situation wrongly, of course. Or they encountered other problems.

In the meantime, Miranda was deeply upset by what they'd found out and needed loving support. Who wouldn't be upset when they found out they'd been the victim of such vicious manipulations for most of their life? People needed relatives and close friends who cared about them, not ones who tried to destroy their hopes.

It was a good thing for Miranda that the horrible old great-aunt had died. Libby couldn't even have imagined being glad that someone had died until now, but that old woman seemed to have caused nothing but misery and often by villainous actions.

She was going to keep her eyes open for the Parnhams from now on. Selma seemed so attached to the memory of her former employer with whom she had clearly shared a close bond, and Libby worried that she would still be hoping to carry out Phyllis's final wishes and ruin Miranda's future if she could.

But no one was going to hurt Miranda from now on if Libby could help it, whatever it took to prevent trouble.

Chapter Twenty-Three

Jim felt worse and worse, dizzy when he stood up and though he rubbed his forehead it did nothing to help rid him of a thumping headache. But he knew he had to get out of the shed for the day, just had to, or the owners might find out he'd been trespassing on their property and report it to the police.

He was terrified of being shut away, had always suffered from claustrophobia, and even in winter he hadn't been able to sleep without an open window nearby bringing in fresh air.

He knew logically that he could breathe even with the window shut, but couldn't carry that through into how his mind and body reacted to the lack of fresh air. Gracie had understood and held his hand for comfort in difficult situations. Not many other people had even made an attempt to understand his problem and some of them had been scornful and told him to snap out of it or get help, so he'd hidden it as much as possible – till his world had been torn apart.

He stopped first to take a long drink of the lovely clear water from the stream that trickled down from a spring at the higher end of the land along the hedge. Water like this always seemed so much nicer than the chemically doctored stuff that came out of taps.

He staggered away step by feeble step, using a fallen branch he'd found as an awkwardly held extra walking stick as well as his actual stick, the one Gracie had given him. As he began moving down the rough track, he felt so weak and dizzy he had to stop and lean on both his supports a couple of times, before managing to continue slowly down near the hedge.

After only a short distance, however, he felt too weak to continue even with the help of the sticks, just couldn't do it and fell to his knees. So he crawled under some convenient bushes, whose lush foliage would ensure that he'd be mostly out of sight if anyone walked casually past as he rested. Thank goodness he was wearing dark clothing, which wouldn't stand out against the shadows the bushes cast.

He didn't remember much after that and must have fallen asleep, because he suddenly sneezed and jerked awake. It took him a moment or two to remember where he was then he clapped one hand to his mouth, terrified of sneezing again as he looked round and listened intently. Had anyone been close enough to hear his sneeze and come to investigate?

But there were no sounds, either of footsteps or voices, and no one pulled aside the leafy branches of the shrubs to look for what had caused the noise. He closed his eyes again with a long, trailing sigh of relief.

One good thing about feeling unwell was that you didn't

get hungry, so he had no need to go into the nearby village to buy food. And anyway, there was an old saying: feed a cold and starve a chill, and this felt to be far worse than an ordinary cold. It must be a chill, surely? So that meant he was doing the right thing to help his body get better.

He dozed intermittently, shivering and huddling down, using the spare clothes he had with him as extra coverings in a vain attempt to get warm. The rest of his spare clothes were in the bag of oddments which he'd stupidly left in the shed. It was another fine summer's day and he shouldn't have felt cold but he did.

As the day waned and the sun sank lower in the sky, he realised it was teatime and he hadn't eaten anything all day, or drunk much either, not for several hours. He forced himself to eat the last of his biscuits, a few broken pieces in a crumpled plastic bag, even though his mouth was dry and it was slow going.

After that he moved along near the bushes, crawling to stay out of sight as he made his way to the little stream. He couldn't stand up and anyway he'd have to get down on his hands and knees again to reach the water, which wasn't far away, so why bother to try?

He drank as much as he could force down and then crawled back even more slowly, feeling utterly weary. Well, he had nothing to hurry for, did he, and this was as good a hiding place as any. He'd move on and get further away from those two women in an hour or so, after another nice little rest.

He didn't wake until the middle of the night, judging by the position of the half moon in the sky. He didn't have the strength to sit up, so lay there feeling shocked that he was still in more or less the same place he'd been the previous morning. He'd meant to continue his journey and get right away from here to somewhere near shops to buy food and aspirin, and perhaps even to stay in a cheap bed and breakfast for a night or two till he was feeling better.

He wasn't short of money, had set off walking because he wanted to avoid people who knew him and because he wanted to find somewhere new to settle. He tried to sit up but was shocked that he still felt too weak to manage that.

He could quite easily have gone back to sleep but forced himself to crawl back to the stream and take a few more big mouthfuls. He knew better than to go without drinking, even if he didn't feel particularly thirsty.

When he looked down at his wrist and then the scrawny ankle that was showing under one rucked-up trouser leg, he was shocked. He'd started this long journey sturdily built but must have gradually lost weight. He'd told himself at first that it'd be good for him to do that at his age, but he hadn't been feeling well lately and had lost even more weight, enough to worry him now.

His mouth felt a bit better now he'd had a drink, so he looked across to the shed he'd slept in last night and where he'd left his bundle of spare clothing and the oddments in the plastic bin liner, which included some scraps of food. He couldn't resist going across to it again because it was a far better place to sleep than the damp ground. With more covers he'd surely get warmer and that'd make him start feeling better. Yes, that was the way to go.

He managed to pull himself up after a while with the help of a bent, twisty little tree, but staggered and nearly fell as he began to move along. Thank goodness for the sticks. He didn't dare try to go faster and had to hope no one would be out for a walk and spot him before he could hide again. He knew he couldn't manage to run away, not till he was feeling a lot less dizzy. He was too old to risk a bad fall.

He let out a little groan of relief when he got to the shed. Its door was closed but not locked. And thank goodness his bag was still where he'd left it, so those women couldn't have noticed it. He looked round carefully and there was enough moonlight shining through the doorway for him to see a warm, fluffy though rather ragged old blanket folded up neatly at the far end of the top shelf.

He hesitated, tempted to borrow it. The blanket didn't look grubby, just rather worn. He could lie on that far more comfortably. He pulled it down and put it round his shoulders and oh, how wonderful it felt! There was another blanket crumpled at the back of the shelf behind it, more ragged but still fairly fluffy. He could lie on half and cover himself with the other half then perhaps he wouldn't shiver as much. This was a bad dose of the flu, the worst he could ever remember having.

It wasn't till he woke up again that he realised he'd left his knapsack under the bushes. Tears came into his eyes. How stupid could you get? He'd better go and retrieve it before someone came along and took it away.

Only then did he notice something else rather important: it was fully daylight now. He didn't even dare leave the shed so couldn't retrieve the knapsack, because he didn't want to be seen by those women. They might think he was a peeping Tom creeping around to spy on them. And what if they called the police? He shuddered at the mere thought.

In the end, after letting himself lie down 'just for a minute or two' to gather his strength, he fell asleep again without intending to and it was a while before he woke again, or half-woke. He couldn't remember ever feeling so weak and unwell. He'd have to give himself a few more minutes before trying to move on again.

After sorting out the various documents and letters for what suddenly seemed to have been a long time, Miranda stepped away from the table, stretching and moving her body about. 'My back's getting a crick from bending over looking at these papers and other parts of my body are sending out warning signals and threatening to sue me for abuse.'

The others chuckled and straightened up too.

'I think I'll find something else to do for a while to give my poor body a bit of a change,' she went on, 'something that involves movement, preferably. And you guys ought to do the same, engrossing as these are.' She gestured to the documents.

'You're right.' Ryan stepped away as well and started waving his arms about and rolling his shoulders in a similar way.

Miranda stopped wriggling. 'That's better. Um, I've been wondering about something. Do you think there's anything interesting hidden in the attic? We only gave it a cursory glance when we first went for a look round the house, because we were mainly checking for people hiding there. There were no people-sized surprises, but I've been wondering whether there's anything else of interest.'

'It wouldn't hurt to go and have a more thorough look at what's stored there, would it? That'd also get us moving around for a while,' Ryan said.

They nodded.

'I don't suppose there's anything valuable left after all

these years of the house being occupied by that old woman and her housekeeper, though if I remember correctly, we had to edge round piles of stuff and it looked as if people had simply thrown things down anywhere there happened to be a space or else piled them on top of similar items and been doing that for a good many years.'

Ryan looked thoughtful. 'We can also check what can be seen from the dormer windows while we're up there. We can put CCTV cameras up there to keep watch for anyone approaching or hovering nearby.'

Col nodded. 'Ryan's right. You're so isolated here, it would definitely be worth sorting out a proper security system. You should also have a camera and mic just outside the front door so that you can see who it is before you open it.'

That suggestion was greeted with more nods of approval from the others but although Miranda agreed with Ryan, it also made her feel a bit under siege to think of doing that. Did owning property always bring you a series of worries, or was this a deliberate part of her great-aunt's legacy?

'I could nip into the nearest town or wherever there's a big hardware store selling security equipment and buy a whole system then install it for you when you're ready for that. I'm pretty good with setting up protective systems, if I say so myself,' Ryan offered.

She pulled herself together. 'Good idea. As long as you let me pay you for doing it. It's a big house and I'm not short of money now.'

They stared at one another as if each was trying to outstare the other, then he shrugged. 'There really isn't a need. I probably don't have as much money as you now do, but I've been rather successful with one or two apps a friend and I worked on, so I'm not short of it either. What matters to me most is to get you and your house properly protected. I don't want you to get hurt.'

He stared at her and added in a low voice, 'I'd like to get to know you better once we've sorted this mess out.'

'Oh.' Then she told herself not to act like a coward and said quietly, 'I'd like that too.'

'Good.' He turned to the others, waiting to see if someone else had anything to contribute and Col said, 'Well, if you've got experience in setting up security systems, Ryan, I'll stay down here and keep an eye on the front while you three go and check round more thoroughly upstairs and start working out roughly how many devices and sensors will be needed.'

'Right. Yell if someone turns up and I'll come down to join you.'

'I will. But just to put in my twopence worth, I reckon the first thing that should be installed is a camera to give the person answering the front door a clear view of anyone outside it before they even think of letting a stranger in. And it should make a recording of the incident, too. You don't want anyone sneaking up on you, not now or in the future, do you? This is quite a big house. The situation won't always be so chancy but at the moment, with the Parnhams still nearby, you should be super-careful.'

'That sounds good advice,' Libby said at once.

Miranda shuddered. 'I think so too. I definitely don't want intruders pushing their way in. That horrible Selma creature and her brother would have managed it if I'd been on my own. It's going to be difficult keeping a good watch on the house in the early days of settling in, because it's big and we don't know it or the surrounding grounds very well yet, either. I won't feel safe till there's a proper security system installed, so I'll be really grateful for your help, Ryan.'

Libby nodded vigorously. 'Also, until we've been here for a while and we're used to what are normal and what are unusual sounds, we'll be unsure whether some noises indicate intruders, won't we? Especially at night, when we won't be able to see what's going on.'

'You're right to be wary.' Col hesitated then asked, 'Look, how about Ryan and I stay here at night for the time being? You'll be rather vulnerable here at the moment. When you have a system installed, you can re-evaluate how you feel. I really don't like the thought of you two being here on your own in such a big house after dark with no neighbours near enough to call on for help.'

Miranda stared at him, relief running through her. 'Are you sure about that? Ryan's got his own cottage to look after.'

He took over, smiling at her. 'I don't have anything valuable to tempt burglars, especially in the bedrooms, and I already have a system fitted in the living area which would make a lot of noise and take photos of intruders, storing them online.'

'You were quick off the mark with that.'

'I already had an old system I could adapt.'

'You're sure you wouldn't mind staying here?'

'Certain.'

As she still hesitated, Col said, 'Think about it: even though Ryan might live nearby, he's not really within shouting distance once he's back in his own home, is he? And it'll take time for him to get across to you physically, even if you do have some way of calling him for help.'

'I'd been thinking the same thing,' she admitted, 'and

wondering whether it would be cowardly or sensible to accept your help.'

Ryan glanced from one woman to the other. 'Please don't turn the offers down. We all need help sometimes and taking sensible precautions in an unusual situation could save you a lot of bother in the long run.'

Miranda smiled at him. 'OK. You've made your case and I won't turn your kind offer down. This situation had taken me by surprise, even though I was half-prepared for my great-aunt setting up something unpleasant to greet me. And I confess that I'd started to wonder whether you two might agree to spend the next few nights here if you're going to be staying in the area. Only I was going to wait a little longer to ask you till I felt sure it was the right thing to do.'

'It is. I'm glad you're showing some good sense about the situation.'

'I'm a liberated modern woman mentally, I hope, but I don't think I'm a fool. I know my own physical limitations and when it comes to emergencies like fighting off one attacker let alone two, as I've nearly had to do already, there are limits to how much is possible for a smaller woman not used to fighting of any sort. So thank you very much and we both accept your offer of help with gratitude.'

She looked at her friend, who nodded vigorously in agreement.

Miranda was relieved that they were going to help. And she'd known Libby would agree with what she was doing. Her friend was only a bit taller than her and their two male companions both looked fit and strong.

Chapter Twenty-Four

Libby took over and began organising them all, as usual. 'If you two men will choose which rooms you want to sleep in, we'll make beds up for you. And we'll provide you with a hearty cooked breakfast too, if you're into that sort of thing. Not everyone eats large breakfasts, but just let me know and I'll get the frying pan out.' She waited for an answer.

'Yes, please,' both men said at once.

She'd guessed right, she thought smugly. 'Good thing I brought a packet of bacon I had left over in case we needed food, eh?'

'Very good idea.'

'We'll have a think about where to sleep as we go round and get to know the house, then discuss the situation further,' Ryan said. 'You two would be safer sharing a bedroom, Miranda, then you can help one another, if there's any trouble.'

Col took over. 'You and I should perhaps be located on

the ground floor, Ryan. One of us could be near the front door and we could take it in turns to patrol the two main corridors for a couple of hours or so, keeping an eye on the outside, then wake the other.'

As they nodded at one another, Libby and Miranda also exchanged glances, but theirs were of frustration at their own physical limitations.

'That's settled, then,' Col said. 'Now, I'll keep watch near the front door and you three can continue getting to know the upstairs of the house better. I'll go round it again on my own later.'

Libby looked at him with a wry smile. 'After which I bet you'll know the layout by heart.'

'I'm pretty good that way. It helps to have a good memory for the layout of interiors in my job.'

This time the three of them went round the linked open spaces of the attic very slowly, studying the piles of miscellaneous objects, which looked to be mainly junk and were lying around in haphazard heaps on the bare floorboards. They stopped at each of the four windows to get an idea of what they could see from there.

It was Miranda who noticed that the door of the shed furthest away from the house, which was the nearest to the fence line, was partly open. She tugged Ryan back to keep him with her. 'Is it my imagination or is the door of that shed partly open now and moving to and fro in the breeze?'

He stared out again and nodded slowly. 'Yes, it is. Perhaps the catch has come loose.'

'I don't think so. Why would it have just come loose? I always check external doors very carefully indeed when I leave somewhere to make sure they're properly closed. It's a long time habit of mine on account of having to rely on myself to stay safe. You might not have noticed me doing it but as we looked round the sheds, I made sure every single external door was properly closed and firmly latched behind us.'

'Are you sure you were that meticulous?'

'Absolutely certain. I learnt to do that when dealing with my great-aunt, as well as having extra locks fitted to which she didn't have keys put on the external doors of wherever I was living. If I didn't take care, my possessions would mysteriously vanish.'

He stared at her for a moment, wondering what other sorts of nasty tricks her great-aunt had played to make her this careful. She must have had an even more difficult upbringing than he'd realised. 'We'd better go across and have another look inside that shed, then.'

They called Libby away from sorting through a pile of decades-old clothing that had simply been tossed into one corner. She'd pounced on it in delight, saying some of the pieces would be quite valuable in antique shops if freshened up a bit because they weren't nearly worn out.

When she came to look out of the window at the shed, however, she forgot the clothes and confirmed that Miranda had indeed shut that door properly and was always careful about doing that.

'I'd better go and check that shed door again then,' Ryan said. 'If the catch is loose, it'll have to be repaired, which probably won't take much doing. But if someone's been following us round, we have to find out who it is and where they've been hiding, also who is likely to be paying them to do it.'

'I agree. We can't be too careful.'

'Let's go down and tell Col, then he and I can nip across and check it.'

'No. You and I will check it together, Ryan. I'm good with details and anyway, this is my house now.'

When Miranda stared at him challengingly, he stared back for a moment then shrugged. 'OK. But I will suggest you go downstairs and send Col up to the attic first so that he can have a look too. I'll study the grounds more carefully from here while you're doing that. I'd like to get a better idea of the area round that particular shed, for example whether the grass has been flattened by someone walking across to it.'

'I'd never have thought of doing that,' Miranda admitted.

She was sometimes such a townie, he thought, smiling and mentally adding, but a very pretty townie.

The two women kept watch near the front door while Col went up to join Ryan in the attic and study the area near that particular shed.

'There's a lot of trampled grass nearby and trails of flattened vegetation here and there as if someone's been walking to and fro across the part of the garden beyond that shed for a day or two,' Ryan said thoughtfully. 'Could someone have been staying there?'

'Or even still be hanging around?'

When the two men came down again, Col said, 'I think us guys had better go and check that shed. It might simply have a loose catch but it looks to me as if someone has been nosing round nearby, possibly even staying there at night.' He saw Miranda open her mouth to protest and held up one hand. 'We might need physical force to deal with them. In which case the strongest people should be the ones to confront them.'

Miranda scowled at him and he guessed why so added gently, 'It's not sexist to say that. It's the simple truth. Us two guys are definitely bigger and stronger than you two women. Not all guys would be and some women are stronger than some men, but I doubt you two are.'

She hated to admit it to herself, but he was right, only she couldn't hold back a little growl of irritation. 'I suppose so. I can't help feeling rather proprietary about this place. I could carry something to bash an attacker with, you know, and probably would do that efficiently enough. I went to a series of classes once to learn how best to defend myself when I'm out and about. And I've had to actually use those tactics once in real life and threaten to use them a couple of times. I came out of those encounters safe and sound, so I wouldn't be totally helpless.'

He stared at her thoughtfully, then grinned. 'Well, all right, you can go across to the shed instead of me. You looked nice and fierce as you said that. You go with her, Ryan, and I'll stand at the front door with Libby. I'll come running if either of you call for help and Libby can hold a big stick and defend the house if necessary.'

Ryan didn't look best pleased with this, but Col said firmly, 'I'm approving of that, Miranda, because if there are any decisions to be taken quickly when you first get to the shed, you as owner will be on the spot to take them.'

She nodded. 'That'll work for me.'

The two of them walked outside and Ryan took her hand. When she looked at him in surprise, he grinned and blew her a kiss with his other hand. 'Just trying to look like a pair of lovers out for a casual walk.'

But there was a gleam in his eye and a tingle in her hand, and she was only too aware that they had both stood staring at one another for longer than they needed to before they set off.

They tried not to be too conspicuous as they strolled up the slightly sloping piece of land, moving towards the shed in a roundabout way, pausing under some trees at one stage but not lingering there for long.

'Can't see any signs of other people hanging around in this part of the gardens,' he murmured at one stage.

'No. Let's go and check that shed with the swinging door.'

She led the way to the shed door and stepped to one side, flourishing one hand to signal to him to go inside first.

He pushed the door fully open and immediately called out, 'Oh, hell! Come in here quickly, Miranda!' He moved to the side a little and as she stepped forward he gestured. 'This old guy doesn't look at all well, does he?'

She stared in shock at an old man, who was lying on the ground looking feverish and distinctly unwell. He wasn't unconscious but he didn't seem fully aware of what was going on around him either and he was making no effort to stand up or even speak to them. 'You don't need a thermometer to see that he has a high fever.'

Then the man seemed to realise suddenly that someone had come into the shed, opened his eyes and blinked at them as if surprised.

Ryan tugged Miranda back a little way, just in case the fellow got aggressive.

He showed no sign of it and tried to sit up, but was unable to do so.

'Are you any good at first aid?' he asked.

'Well, I've done a first aid course. Let me have a better look at him. I'm clearly in no danger. He's too weak to hurt anyone and he doesn't look at all aggressive anyway.'

Ryan gestured to her to edge past him and she bent down towards the intruder, not feeling at all concerned about her own safety because he had such a gentle expression. 'My name's Miranda. I own this place. Will you let me check your temperature and pulse?'

'Sorry to trespass,' he said in a thread of a voice. 'I've had the flu. Can't seem to shake it off. Just as bad today as yesterday.'

It was only too obvious that he wasn't lying to them and was no threat.

'We'd better call an ambulance,' Ryan said.

The old man clutched her arm. 'I'm sorry to be a nuisance, but I'm not bad enough for a hospital. If you'll just let me stay here for a day or two, I'm sure I'll be well enough to move on. I haven't damaged anything and I won't leave a mess.'

'But you need help.'

'I just need to rest. Look, I can give you some gardening advice to pay for my stay if that helps. I'm a trained gardener and you have some plants that desperately need attention.'

She looked down, touched by the way he was still clutching her hand as if desperate for human contact more than help, but he clearly hadn't realised that he was doing it. 'Why don't you want an ambulance called?' she asked gently.

'They'll shut me up inside a building and I can't bear being shut up. I suffer from a sort of claustrophobia and I need to be in the fresh air, among the plants and trees, always have done. I've worked as a gardener all my life.'

'I don't like being shut up, either.'

'Then you'll understand how I feel.'

She patted his hand. 'I do indeed. What's your name?'

'Jim Tucker. And you said you're Miranda. Lovely name, that.'

She wondered why he'd hesitated to say his surname but didn't ask. 'Thank you. Did you weed round those little plants?'

A faint smile passed across his face. 'Yes. They were being smothered, poor things. I knew how they felt. I don't like to see plants die from neglect or from too much attention, either.'

He began to cough and very politely tried to aim it away from her. She moved back a little, out of the way, fumbling in her pocket and thrusting a couple of crumpled tissues into his hand. 'Here. Use these.'

'Thanks. I've run out of clean ones.'

She turned to Ryan. 'I think he's right and it's the remains of the flu. What he needs to recover completely is probably only a few days' rest and some good food.'

'Shall you let him stay here in your shed, then?'

'No, of course not. He needs to be somewhere more comfortable than this, as well as having nutritious food to build up his strength again. He'll have to come to the house. There's plenty of space.'

'You're kind but please don't shut me up inside,' the man pleaded.

'Well, we can't leave you lying out here on the ground.' She frowned then snapped her fingers at a sudden idea. 'There's a conservatory at one side of the house, though. How would you be in that, Jim? It's all glass and sunshine during the day, moonshine at night, no doubt.'

He gave her a faint smile. 'Are there plants in it?'

'Yes, but they need attention. You can help me care for them as soon as you're able, if you like. I have no expertise. There's plenty of room for you in there as well as them.'

'I'd love to help with your plants as I – get better and—' He broke off to cough and splutter again.

'We'll take you there,' she said when he'd stopped coughing.

Ryan tugged her aside. 'Are you sure about that? You don't know him from Adam.'

'Yes, of course, I'm sure. You can see at a glance that he's no threat to anyone and anyway, he looks just as I've always imagined a kind grandfather would.'

Ryan stared at her, a smile replacing the anxiety. 'You're a real softie. And that's incredibly kind of you.'

It occurred to him at that exact moment that he'd fallen in love with her, deeply in love. He hoped she'd come to feel the same way about him, even if it took longer for her to realise it than he had. She was special, so very special and beautiful too in a soft, feminine way. But her kindness was far more attractive to him than mere good looks.

She gave him another of her beautiful gentle smiles. 'I've been treated unkindly in the past, Ryan, so I try to help people whenever I can.'

'You're a wonderful woman.'

She flushed and gave him a shy smile, then turned back to the man. 'My full name is Miranda Westerby and I own this house. So, Jim, will you come and stay in my conservatory till you're better, and by then we'll perhaps have found you something more permanent to do with your future?'

'Westerby,' he murmured in a low voice, then stared at her again, looking a bit shocked.

Before she could ask him why he said that as if he knew the name, he stared at her again. 'I can't believe you mean that.'

'I've needed help at low times in my life so when I can be there for other people, I try to do whatever I can to help them. I've just inherited this house and there are several bedrooms. I can offer you somewhere to sleep till you're better.'

He stared at her as if reading her soul in her eyes, then said simply, 'My late wife would have liked you, Miranda. She died recently and I haven't been able to settle since then. But I'd love to stay with you. Thank you.'

'You must miss her.'

'Yes. Very much. She was – wonderful.'

'Have you come far?'

'I feel as if I've come a long way. I seem to have been wandering round like a lost soul the weeks since Gracie died, trying to find somewhere to settle. I lost her seventy-two days ago. I've marked them off on my walking stick.'

'Why did you leave your home?'

'We were in a house tied to my job as gardener and the family who owned the big house and its grounds had just sold it for building blocks, so my job was terminated and the owners wanted all the houses back as quickly as possible. They gave me notice to leave and wouldn't let me buy it, so I just walked away one day and went on the tramp, vaguely hoping I might find somewhere to live without her, but not doing much real looking. I couldn't seem to think straight for a while.'

'It must have been hard getting used to life without your wife.'

'Yes. Gracie wouldn't have liked me to live like this,

though, and I'm ashamed of how I've behaved.'

She took his hand again and patted it. 'Well, we'll set that straight later. I think what you need most at the moment, Jim, is a good rest, so why don't you come and stay in my new home and finish getting better there. It has a lovely conservatory with walls of windows warmed by the sun and surrounded by flowers and shrubs. I don't think you'll feel too shut in there, especially if we leave the doors open. The conservatory is very run down and needs the right plants putting into it. Perhaps you can help me do that once you're better?'

He looked astonished at her offer. 'Are you sure of that, lass? I don't want to be a burden.'

'Yes. And I doubt you will be because you'll probably sleep a lot and you won't need physically caring for, just feeding and a comfortable bed. We'll bring one down to the conservatory for you. That room hasn't got any curtains but I doubt you'll care about that as there are no neighbours near enough to intrude on your peace.'

Tears filled his eyes and he let out a long, tired sigh, reaching out to take hold of her hand again, this time in both of his. 'I'll happily accept your wonderful offer, Miranda, and after I'm better, I'll help you find the best selection of plants to finish off your conservatory, if you like. That'll be – worth doing. It's a lovely place. And I'm a good gardener.'

'That'll be a big help. I grew up in towns and have a lot to learn about plants and the countryside generally. Now, let me introduce you to my friend and neighbour, Ryan.'

They all smiled at one another, then Jim said again, 'I can't tell you how grateful I am.'

She saw more tears well in his eyes. 'We'll talk again

later, Jim, and you can tell me more about your wife as well as starting to teach me about plants. For the moment, let us help you to stand up then we can help you back through the house and out to the conservatory.'

'I can't stand up. I'm too dizzy. The whole place starts spinning round me if I move my head.'

'Oh dear. Well, I suppose Ryan and I can try to carry you.'

Jim frowned, then said, 'No need. I noticed a wheelbarrow behind this shed. It'll be easier to wheel me across to the house in that, if you don't mind doing it. I'm sorry but as well as the dizziness, I haven't been eating much, wasn't hungry at all, so I'm weak as a child.'

He closed his eyes for a moment, then said quietly, 'I don't feel strong enough even to crawl, especially not over such rough ground.'

He looked so sad and helpless she had to give him a quick hug. He clutched her for a moment. 'I'm sorry. I've never been this weak before. I don't want to be a nuisance but I don't know what to do.'

It upset her to see such an old man looking distressed and she turned to Ryan. 'Would you see if the wheelbarrow is big enough to hold him? And strong enough. If it is, that will probably be the easiest way to get him round to the conservatory the outside way.'

Ryan nodded and slipped out of the shed.

She patted the old man's hand instinctively in an unspoken offer of comfort.

He smiled up at her, a very soft, gentle smile that surprised her by making her feel as if he'd given her a warm hug.

'I think you must be the kindest person I've met since

my wife died, lass. Eh, Gracie and I would have loved a granddaughter like you.'

She didn't have to think about it. The response was so obvious given her reckless mood about people and families lately. 'I'd have loved a grandfather like you. How about we adopt one another from now on?'

His mouth literally dropped open in surprise then tears welled in his eyes. 'Do you mean that? No, you wouldn't be mocking me, not with that kind face.'

'I'd never mock you, Jim.' *Or anyone*, she added mentally. She been the butt of a certain person's mocking herself and it could hurt a lot, whether you let the person see that or not.

'That's a truly wonderful way to face the world.'

'I haven't got any real family, so when I meet someone I like I've started trying to find a way to stay connected. That's how it's been with Libby. I adopted her as my aunt and I feel as if she really is a relative now.'

'I'd love to be adopted like that. I don't have any close family left and I never did have many.'

He was such a lovely, kind-looking old man, something inside her felt happier for his agreement. 'Stay here with me and we'll both give our relationship a try, eh? And I'd really welcome your help in the garden.'

'I'll stay happily but if you change your mind, you have only to say and I'll move on. I don't want to impose on anyone. And I'll try not to be too much trouble.'

'I'm sure you won't be.'

He nodded, still smiling. 'I can help you with the garden once I'm better. I'm really good with plants after working with them all my life.'

'It's a bargain, then.'

She held out her hand and he took it, then his eyes closed and he let out a long slow sigh. He didn't let go of her hand and he had a faint smile on his face now, not that deep, gut-wrenching look of sorrow that had made her want to hug him.

And actually she liked the feel of his hand in hers, it was so warm and firm. He was like everybody's image of a kindly grandfather. She didn't at all regret making the offer to let him stay.

It was her life that she was reshaping now that she was free, and it felt so good to create a new family for herself. So very good.

Chapter Twenty-Five

The path led them to one side of the house. Miranda stopped at the front door. 'I'll go through the house and unlock the double doors at the side of the conservatory. If you wheel him round the outside of the house, Ryan, you'll see that it'll be easy to get him into it that way.'

'Are you sure about this?' he asked in a low voice.

'Yes. He'll love being in the conservatory, I'm sure. It's a bright room and we can open some of the windows.'

The two women went through the house, locking the front door carefully behind them. The men were waiting for them outside the conservatory with the wheelbarrow and its occupant.

Miranda went across to unlock the outer doors of the big, sunlight-filled room and flung them open, gesturing to the garden sofa at one side of the big, hexagonal space. 'I think that's big enough to use as a bed for the time being, and if there's a narrow single mattress in any of the bedrooms, we might be able to lay that on top of it. If not, we can put the cushions from the seats of the other chairs on top of it.'

'I'll go and see what bedding I can find.' Libby hurried out.

The men waited to move Jim inside the conservatory until Libby called from upstairs for someone to help her with a mattress and Col went to do that.

They laid it on the sofa and it only overhung the edge a little.

'Wait a minute.' Libby ran back upstairs and came down again clutching a bundle of bedding. She quickly made up the sofa as a bed and only then did they lift Jim out of the large wheelbarrow and lay him on it.

He lay staring round the sunlight filled room with a smile. 'This is a beautiful conservatory. It's quite an early one, almost feels as if I'm outside in the fresh air.'

'Know about the history of conservatories, do you?' Ryan asked.

'A little. I used to be head gardener at a big country residence.' He broke off abruptly, looking sad.

'You'll have to tell us more about this one when you're feeling better,' Miranda said. 'I've only just inherited the house and have never lived in the country before.'

'I'll be happy to do that. Oh, I shall so much enjoy staying in here. It's much nicer than an upstairs bedroom.'

Libby said in a low voice, 'I'll go and get some clothing for him. Your ancestors must have been real hoarders. There's a huge linen cupboard full of stuff.' She hurried out again.

Jim didn't make any comment about the house and she guessed he wasn't a local, but as he looked round, she could see deep sadness in his face.

'I really can help you sort out some plants for this place when I get better. I'm an experienced gardener and it'll help repay you for coming to my aid today.'

'That'd be a big help. I grew up in towns so don't know much at all about gardening.'

'So could I . . . stay for a few days, do you think? Till I feel truly better?'

'You're very welcome to stay as long as you like.' She hesitated then added, 'Permanently if you want a job – and a new family. Or have you changed your mind about letting me adopt you as a grandfather?'

He stared at her, happiness gradually replacing the sadness on his face. 'I haven't changed my mind at all. You really mean that, don't you?'

'Of course I do. I'd not say so otherwise.'

'You're such a kind lass, the very best.'

'I'm a lass without any family and you're the second person I've adopted, so be warned: it won't only be me you'll have to put up with. There's Libby too, and who knows what other folk I'll find to join my family.'

Her friend returned just then and Miranda gestured to her. 'This is my adopted aunt, Libby, and this is Jim Tucker, who is now my adopted grandfather. What does that make him for you? Some sort of an uncle?'

The other woman gave him a very searching stare as if trying to spot whether he was taking an unfair advantage of Miranda. But her expression gradually softened as if she was satisfied with what she saw. 'Welcome to the family, Uncle Jim.'

And when he instinctively held out one hand to seal that bargain, she took it and held on to it, so that he had two women holding his hands now. That felt so good. He realised at that moment that Gracie would have approved and wanted him to go on with a new life and that he'd found a place where he felt able to do that. And more than that, if this lass was a Westerby, Gracie would have wanted him to tell these two women about his secret. And he would do later.

His wandering hadn't been in vain after his wife died. He'd rather have had Gracie still with him, of course he would, but there you were. Life simply carried you onwards and sometimes if you were lucky in a new direction. Or as was happening now, back into an old one. Hmm. He'd have to think about how to deal with that once his mind was clearer.

When Libby let go, she sorted out the bundle she'd been carrying and fumbled through an amazing assortment of stray items of men's clothing. She pulled out a pair of faded pyjamas, some old trousers and a shirt or two. 'There are all sorts of oddments in the linen cupboard, some of it decades old, as well as household items. I won't be long.'

She saw Jim's eyes flicker closed for a minute, then he jerked awake again, so she looked across at Ryan. 'Could you guys help him put on these pyjamas and get into bed?'

'Yes, of course.'

'And maybe you can help him wash his hands and face while you're at it. I think that'll make him feel more comfortable. I'll leave a bowl of water and a facecloth for that on the little table in the hall. Oh, and if you give me the clothes you take off him, I'll wash them for him. I've found a washing machine. It's a bit old fashioned but it seems to be still working and we're going to put a few of our own things on to wash.'

Ryan glanced sideways. 'I'll be happy to help him but then I think we should leave him to sleep.' He made a shooing motion with his hands. 'Now, go away. I think he'll be more comfortable about undressing if we don't start doing that till you ladies leave us.'

She chuckled. 'Yes, of course.'

They left the men to help their unexpected visitor but on the way out Libby picked up his backpack and the bin liner he'd been carrying. 'I'm not only washing those clothes he's wearing as soon as he's settled, I'm also washing anything else that needs it.'

'You can't just fumble through his possessions!' Miranda exclaimed.

'Just watch me. Its contents don't smell all that wonderful, do they?'

'Well, at least ask him.'

'If he stays awake long enough.'

By the time the men had sorted Jim out and got him comfortable in the bed, Miranda had found a medicine cupboard in the kitchen where there was half a packet of rather elderly aspirin tablets. Libby began to prepare warm drinks for everyone.

While she waited for the kettle to boil, she took a glass of water into the conservatory and Jim drank it all, seeming very thirsty. He was now rosy and clean but seemed very sleepy. She went back to find a carafe, so they could leave him some water and an empty glass next to the bed.

'I was just about to put some washing on,' she told him, trying to sound casual. 'Shall I throw your things into the washing machine with ours?'

He looked at her and let out a sniff of wry laughter. 'Very tactfully said. Yes, please, Libby. I'm not usually lacking a change of clean clothes.' His cheeks turned a bit pink as he said that.

'I'm happy to help you.'

'I do appreciate that. I've not been coping well on my own and I've absolutely hated being so dirty. My Gracie would have gone mad at me.'

'Well, we'll sort your clothes out, don't worry.'

Miranda joined them. 'And then see if we can help you make some future plans once you're well again. But I really do need a gardener if you want a job.'

He gave her a considering look. 'Did you say your name was Westerby?'

'Yes.'

He was about to speak when he was overtaken by a huge yawn. 'I'm too tired to say anything carefully, so can we talk about that tomorrow?'

'Yes, of course.' Miranda helped him settle more comfortably and sat beside him while he took a few sips of the weak tea Libby had made.

As he smiled at her, he reminded her suddenly of her mother, both of them dark-haired, with widow's peaks in the hair of their foreheads and lovely kind expressions. Strange, that.

When she pushed a box of tissues closer to him, he nodded a thank you, but couldn't keep his eyes open any longer.

She watched him for a few moments but he didn't stir and he looked peaceful now. Clearly, what he needed most of all at the moment was sleep.

She left him to 'knit up the ravelled sleeve of care'. There she went, she thought with a smile, quoting Shakespeare to herself again. That brilliant writer seemed to have had such clever and memorable ways of describing just about any occasion or emotion in life.

* * *

'I wonder what he was doing in the shed,' Ryan said when the four of them had gathered round the kitchen table with fresh mugs of tea.

Libby shook her head. 'Who knows? I think he'd just sought shelter there and was resting. Judging by the state of his clothes, he's been on the tramp for a while.'

After a pause, Miranda said, 'He can stay here till we help him sort out some more permanent way of life. I really am going to need a gardener, though, aren't I?'

'You should let me check his background first,' Col warned her. 'And he's a bit old for heavy physical work, surely?'

She shrugged. 'I don't think it's necessary to run police checks on him. You only have to look at the gentle expression on his face to know he's not dangerous.'

'You can't always tell.'

'I usually can,' she insisted.

Ryan joined in. 'He mustn't have any family to turn to and that's rare. So you do need to be careful about checking before you offer him a job.'

'It's not that rare,' she said, unable to prevent her bitterness about that showing. 'I didn't have any either until my great-aunt left me the family house, and her housekeeper failed to destroy the information the old witch had been keeping from me for most of my life. I know exactly what it's like to have no family to turn to.'

'You have people who care for you now,' Libby said quietly, reaching out to give her hand a quick squeeze.

'And this man needs help too, so if I can I'll make sure he gets it here. We can always spare a little kindness for a fellow human being, can't we?'

The others nodded.

'I'll still check that there's no one with his name missing,' Col said. 'I think we all admire how you're planning to use some of your inheritance, but I'm making sure you take care how you do it.'

'Thank you. It's good to have friends.'

Ryan gave her a quick hug. 'You definitely won't lack them.'

She gave in to temptation and leant against him for a few moments, loving the feeling of quiet strength that he seemed to exude – yes, and the way he was starting to show that he cared for her. She didn't think she was fooling herself about that and couldn't help starting to care about him too.

'I'll ask him more about himself when he wakes up,' she promised herself. But she didn't think that would reveal any problems.

An hour later, Jim stirred and Miranda put the kettle on, then went to sit next to him. When he opened his eyes she smiled at him. 'Tea or coffee?'

'Either would be wonderful.'

'Do you have any connection with this area? Or did you just come here by accident?'

He looked round, smiling slightly. 'By a happy accident. There was a connection to the Westerby family. We stayed away to avoid a certain lady's attention, the one you've had trouble with, but I suppose that now she's dead, I can use my real surname, the one I dropped when I married Gracie and adopted hers.'

'Which is?'

He glanced at her. 'Westerby.'

There was dead silence and the others, who could hear

what they were saying from the table at one side of the kitchen, didn't try to hide their shock.

Miranda stared at him. 'Westerby? Are you – a relative of mine?'

'I think so. But long ago that woman, your so-called great-aunt, had made it hard to trace the connections. Her housekeeper told me when I asked that they'd destroyed all the old birth and death certificates and threatened that her brother would come after me if I caused trouble, so I left the area and changed my name.'

'They tried to destroy the records again recently, but with Libby's help, I managed to prevent that.'

'You did?' He beamed at her. 'Well, if we can look at the relevant paperwork, I can show you something that I very much hope is true: that I think I'm some sort of relative of yours.'

He smiled at her and held out his hand. 'I hope I'm right.'

She smiled back and took his hand. It felt very right somehow. 'What sort of relative might you be?'

He took a deep breath and put his other hand on hers as he said, 'I think I'm your grandfather.'

Libby looked across at her. 'Col and I can check that for you, if you like.'

'Please do.'

The minutes ticked past as they went through one set of documents. Then suddenly Libby let out an exclamation and pulled a paper out of a pile they'd found in one of the two older folders at the bottom of the box. She passed it to Col, who studied it and nodded.

They both looked at her as Libby held it out, nodding and smiling.

Miranda took it from her, holding her breath as she stared

down at it and read what it said, then read it again before passing it to Jim.

He too nodded, then looked at Miranda. 'Would you like a genuine grandfather, lass?'

Tears began to roll down her cheeks as he held out his hand. 'I'd like that very much indeed. I wish my mother had been alive to see this day.'

'So do I. But I had to flee for my life. If I hadn't, I was quite sure your great-aunt would have had me killed.'

'I believe that now. She was proved to be truly wicked. That really is the word for her.'

'But your mother wasn't, just weak and not in the best of health. And you're a strong young woman. You've coped well with a hard life.'

'Why didn't she have me killed?'

'She needed you as a figurehead when you were a child, then must have had some small shred of humanity, because though she banished you, she didn't try to have you killed. I think she really did want to pass the big house to a Westerby born and bred, instead of to your distant cousin. Though I'm quite sure she didn't expect to die so young, and what you've told me only reinforces that.'

They were still holding hands and joy suddenly welled up in her in place of the sorrow. 'So I really do have a relative.'

'Yes. And we might even find others when we go through those papers.'

'You'll come and stay at the big house, won't you? You are a Westerby, after all.'

'I'll come and stay with you and take over your gardens if you'll let me. I'm not hungry for big houses or money.'

'I'm hungry for relatives,' she said simply.

'Then you can hire an expert to go through those papers and I'd guess you'll find others.'

'But you and Libby will still be the closest kin to me emotionally. Let's go and tell her.'

That evening they had an impromptu party, opening a bottle of champagne and toasting the future.

Miranda had said she'd look for her other relatives, but for the moment she was glowing with happiness and Jim sat beside her for much of the evening, holding her hand often.

The others let them deal mainly with one another, because after all this time they were clearly deeply joyful about finding some family. It was a wonderful sight.

ANNA JACOBS was born in Lancashire at the beginning of the Second World War. She has lived in different parts of England as well as Australia and has enjoyed setting her modern and historical novels in both countries. She is addicted to telling stories and recently celebrated the publication of her one hundredth novel, as well as sixty years of marriage. Anna has sold over five million copies of her books to date.

annajacobs.com